P9-CMT-851

DEATH IN ELYSIUM

DEATH IN ELYSIUM

A Jodie Welsh Mystery

Judith Cutler

This first world edition published 2014
in Great Britain and the USA by
SEVERN HOUSE PUBLISHERS LTD of
19 Cedar Road, Sutton, Surrey, England, SM2 5DA.

British Library Cataloguing in Publication Data

Cutler, Judith author.
  Death in Elysium.
  1. Murder–Investigation–Fiction. 2. Spouses of clergy–
  Fiction. 3. Country life–Fiction. 4. Detective and
  mystery stories.
  I. Title
  823.9'2-dc23

ISBN-13: 978-0-7278-8396-4 (cased)

All Severn House titles are printed on acid-free paper.

Severn House Publishers support the Forest Stewardship Council™ [FSC™],
the leading international forest certification organisation. All our titles that
are printed on FSC certified paper carry the FSC logo.

MIX
Paper from
responsible sources
FSC® C013056

Typeset by Palimpsest Book Production Ltd.,
Falkirk, Stirlingshire, Scotland.
Printed and bound in Great Britain by
TJ International, Padstow, Cornwall.

*To the huge army of unpaid, unsung churchwardens, upon whom depends the
smooth running of our churches, with extra thanks to Colin Rank, who knows more
than most about the latest in fashionable accommodation for cattle.*

ONE

I wasn't put on this earth to be a vicar's – even a rector's – wife. Nor, come to think of it, an amateur detective doing the police's work for them. I was put on this earth to be the consort of a multimillionaire, preferably one with his own yacht. But thanks to the curious love life of an old friend, Sarah, and her failed date with a man she'd met on the Internet, a rector's wife I am. And an amateur detective, of course.

In the absence of a suitable, indeed likeable, plutocrat, I'd made my own good luck. After gaining my doctorate at Imperial College, I thought I might be an academic, but spread my bets by studying for an MBA at Harvard – financed by a little IT company I set up. The little company grew bigger, and I allowed it to be taken over, trying not to roll my eyes at the number of digits on the cheque. Then I settled for a corporate career, swiftly moving into the very highest echelons of management as IT consultant or director – in blue-chip companies, you understand. By my fiftieth birthday I was heart-whole and solvent enough to celebrate by acquiring a better Porsche. My life couldn't have been better. Then, wouldn't you know it, I was invited to join the ranks of the newly-redundant unemployed. Don't shed any tears for me; save them for the people whose whole lives are torn to pieces when they lose their jobs. I might have had my pride dented, but at least I was very much more than solvent. My mortgage was paid off long ago. I'd made some extremely shrewd investments. And my golden handshake was nothing short of embarrassing. My financial adviser told me what I already knew: I need never work again – I could simply retire and indulge myself. But I couldn't imagine a life of leisure, and was delighted when many of my old contacts were willing to offer me contract work, pointing out that as a freelance I'd never have to get out of bed for less than twelve hundred pounds a day. I got out of bed most days – even some weekends.

But all that changed.

My life hadn't been entirely devoted to Mammon: throughout my adult years I'd enjoyed a series of fleeting but highly enjoyable flirtations, often with people in the arts, thanks to my position as trustee or board member of a number of musical organizations. But marriage had never really presented itself as an option: either I had been too busy testing each rung of the corporate ladder, or any putative partner had whizzed off to dance or play in New York or St Petersburg. With hindsight, and with that backward-looking morality that some people adopt, some of my liaisons might have been seen as inappropriate for a clergyman's wife, so I didn't mention much of my past when I moved to Lesser Hogben, where even the height of my heels seemed to shock villagers I passed in the street. This was compounded by the embarrassing time I walked up the aisle to take Communion and got firmly stuck in a heating grating. Eventually the Louboutin stayed where it was, and, like any true penitent, I had to make my way to the altar rail in my stocking feet.

Thanks to Sarah, however, I was now more concerned with my future than my past. Widowed after twenty-five years of happy marriage, Sarah had decided, after a decent interval, to get back on the dating scene. Safety first, I counselled, worried that she was vulnerable in so many ways. But she carefully sorted the sincere wheat from the kinky chaff. Just when she decided she was simply wasting time and money, not to mention emotional effort, she moved to a Christian introduction agency and struck gold: she connected with a widower of the right age, in his fifties. And a clergyman to boot. Theo Welsh. At least he wouldn't be a useless pervert, not if his drily funny emails were anything to go by. But like the sensible woman she was, when it came to meeting this guy in the flesh, she arranged to meet him in public and told me to phone her halfway through the evening to see if she needed rescuing. When I did, her coded reply told me that they had all the mutual attraction of sausage and custard. So as promised, I happened casually to drop by the wine bar to find them – as if by accident. My dear kind friend, her pretty mouth drooping with boredom, was sitting opposite six foot two of the most desirable man I'd seen in years. Why hadn't he been attracted by her beauty, her stunning figure? Why hadn't she been entranced by his startling blue eyes, his smile, his gorgeous laugh? Heaven knows. All I knew was that Sarah was soon sitting back and watching her date and her rescuer fall gobsmackingly in love. Just like that.

There was a happy ending for her, too, as it happens. A man at the next table, stood up by his date, registered all the drama and stepped over with his bottle of champagne. If Theo and I could hardly tear our eyes from each other, Sarah and Mr Fizz could scarcely keep their hands to themselves. In fact, they left first, wrapped round each other like cling film. It transpired they shared a mutual passion for tandem cycling too, so their future seemed – still seems – assured.

'Do you think things will be so easy for us?' Theo had asked as we polished off the champagne. 'Our backgrounds are chalk and cheese after all.'

They were. Who'd have imagined a country parson falling for a woman who had made her life in the city – and indeed the City?

'Who wants easy? I've always found overcoming difficulties the most exciting thing in life,' I declared.

'Your life could be about to get a whole lot more exciting, then.'

We shared a smile at the ambiguity.

'I certainly hope so,' I said, taking his hand

I can't deny that there were problems – his late wife hovered on the verge of becoming one. Perhaps for fear of hurting me, he was very reluctant to talk about their life together. He described her as a good woman, whom he'd married young. Merry – a pet variant of Marilyn – was a civil servant and he a teacher; he'd not become a clergyman till he was forty. He said, with something of a sigh, that she'd thrown herself into parish work, doing almost as much as he. It had been her idea to move to his present parish from Birmingham, which he claimed to have loved. One thing in its favour, I suppose, was that it was only just over an hour by train from London.

Now he lived geographically closer, but in attitude and even rail journey time it was much further away.

Kent.

Rural Kent.

A village. Lesser Hogben.

Not even Greater Hogben.

During the six months before we got married, Theo must have become sick of each station, each hole in the hedge, as we pursued in what more leisured days would have been called a courtship. Any other man and we'd have been at it like rabbits from day one – but Theo's religion was more than dog-collar deep, and don't forget I was committing to a great deal more than I could begin to understand at that point. Why, for instance, did he always come up to London to see me, and not the other way round? At first I was inclined to be a touch miffed: was he ashamed of me? And why could we never spend more than one day a week together? And why, most of all, even when our engagement was official and the banns read, was he still most insistent that I should keep the St John's Wood pad when I moved to the country? Such extravagance was most unlike him: he was embarrassed by my accumulated wealth to the point of being in denial about it.

If I didn't really understand all his churches' problems (he had seven or eight in his care), I soon understood, and shared, his need for a bolt-hole. Two months into our marriage, I understood a lot more about being a Kentish parson's wife. Life had become very interesting indeed. The honeymoon was over, in more than one sense – except on the one day a week we managed to shoot back to St John's Wood, where he shed ten years and remembered how to laugh.

As a matter of fact, on a day like today, I admitted to myself that Kent might not be too bad a place to live, though at first I'd hated its remoteness and the fact it wasn't London. That especially. It had been a long, hard winter, bad enough if you lived in a city, with a wind coming from Siberia without pausing for breath, drying everything in its path like a hairdryer set to icy. But now what seemed like permafrost had thawed, a random leaf or two was risking a quick look at the world, and I'd swear I heard a brave bird testing its vocal chords.

While Theo went about his parochial duties, I'd just run up the hill overlooking Lesser Hogben, at a second or two beyond my previous best. I could reward myself with a few minutes looking at the view if I kept running on the spot. Yes, from here it was truly idyllic: the landscape picturesquely spread before me, with miniature farms and Lego villages.

I looked harder. As if bored with Toy Town, someone was busy rearranging part of it between here and Greater Hogben – deep in a hollow, which you could only see from up here, men were busy with what looked like heavy diggers and JCBs. A spring ritual, no doubt – something to do with ploughing, perhaps, though they seemed to be dealing with some huge trees. And by *dealing with*, I mean cutting down. Then grubbing out the roots. You couldn't do that in cities without planning permission, but I supposed that a different set of controls regulated rural activities. Nothing to do with me, anyway.

Much closer, just a couple of miles away, was Lesser Hogben itself, with St Dunstan's at its heart. It stood with the solidity of a thousand years, surrounded by the yew trees that made the churchyard famous, looking benignly over the village green, which was large enough to host the local cricket team. A second side of the green was dominated by a handsome Regency house, The Old Rectory. The third was occupied by a duck pond, still not fenced in despite the loud insistence of the families who weekended here, fearful that their little angels might drown. A hit into the pond was counted as six and out. Overlooking the fourth side was what should have been a vibrant village pub, thatched roof and all: the Walnut Tree, known by the cricketers who adjourned there after their toils as the Pickled Walnut. Apart from them, there were very few drinkers.

But it was not cricketing weather yet; there was still a mean breeze, just enough to chill vulnerable muscles. I needed to start moving properly again, soon accelerating down the long, gentle slope towards home.

The activity in the churchyard announced itself way before I reached it: any venturesome birds were outsung by an even more premature strimmer, snarling and whining round the graves where Ted Vesey's sit-on mower wouldn't reach. He'd donated the mower to the church but kept it for his exclusive use, despite the fact that he never sullied his manicured hands in his own garden. Actually the mower wouldn't reach many of the rows at all: the headstones defied health and safety recommendations by leaning at all angles, and a dear old push-and-pull lawnmower, the sort that made stripes my father was always proud of, would have been far more effective.

Not as a status symbol, however.

If Ted was proud of his mower, it didn't take more than one precocious buttercup rearing its head to bring out George Cox's strimmer, but not the ear and eye protectors I'd have thought essential. He would take huge pleasure at being at work before Ted, whether the graveyard merited such attentions or not. Whatever their rivalry did to their souls – and that, since they were churchwardens, was Theo's business, not mine – flourishing the strimmer certainly wasn't good for George's body, or his heart at least. Where his cheeks weren't purple they were grey. At least my appearance gave him the excuse to switch off the machine and lean casually on it, obviously settling down for a restorative chat, in which I was supposed to talk while he caught his breath.

'Afternoon, Mrs Welsh,' George greeted me, still ignoring my constant pleas to be called simply Jodie. After all those years as a Ms or preferably a Dr, I couldn't get my head round Mrs. Not in connection with me, at any rate. The new surname itself had been a major shock. But Theo had broken it to me that the villagers wouldn't like it if I insisted on using the maiden name I'd legally retained, by accident, as it happens. I'd been so overwhelmed by the wedding ceremony I'd simply forgotten to sign my new name. Thank goodness we'd been married back in St John's Wood: I can't imagine the churchwardens here keeping that titbit under their hats. But then, despite their differences, both were men who preferred a funeral to a wedding.

This cold wind was bad for both of us. At least my running thermals would protect me when I really ought to be keeping the muscles going in a warm-down, but George was in his late seventies. Though he sported a woolly hat and hillwalking-quality fleece, he must have been vulnerable. So I manoeuvred him into a patch of sun, sheltered from the worst of the breeze by a grandiose Victorian tomb, complete with winged angels and some overweight cherubs apparently blowing raspberries at my quads and hamstrings. A knowing look in their eyes told me that all this mowing and cutting was none of my business, and that any offer to fund a maintenance contract before someone dropped dead on someone else's headstone would have to be carefully, perhaps anonymously, done. Theo and I had had some of our few awkward moments when I simply wanted to throw a fistful of cash at a problem, church or village, that bowed him down, but he had won hands down when he reminded me of the proverb: *Give a man a fish and you feed him for a day; teach him how to fish and you feed him for life.*

'Run far, have you?' George said.

'Just up to the ridge across the Downs and back again.'

'Just! You're planning on some marathon, are you?' He narrowed his eyes, as if appraising a willing pupil.

'I was. But I hurt my leg before the wedding, so I'm not going to be fit for London this year.'

His eyebrows shot up. 'The London Marathon! That's a shame. But it doesn't stop you running altogether.'

'I'd hate to give up,' I confided. Actually I rather suspected it was time to give up competing. But I'd not give up non-competitive running: it gave me far too much of a buzz, and my body complained if I dropped from my regular regime.

'And you kept it up through all that snow and wind?'

'At least the weather's looking up,' I said with a smile.

'Hm. But they say it won't last.' George sounded grimly satisfied at the thought of more cold greyness. Perhaps that was what years as a primary school head did to you.

'That's a shame – there's a wedding on Saturday, isn't there?' As if I didn't know each and every service Theo was scheduled to take: I'd done a spreadsheet for him, after all.

'Only rich Londoners wanting some arty photos. Not proper parishioners. Just people renting a place so they can claim the right to use the church.' I'd swear that if he hadn't been on hallowed ground he'd have spat. Actually no, not an ex-head, even one who with his gnarled hands and bent shoulders looked like a countryman straight out of Thomas Hardy. Of course he wouldn't. 'Let them go to a register office, that's what I say. Or one of those wedding venues. You know, a golf club or something.'

Theo hoped that the experience of a Christian ceremony might encourage the happy couple to explore more fully the religion they'd embraced for half an hour. *Maybe some of it will rub off* was his mantra. And each time he read the banns he made sure the congregation prayed for the unknown couple.

I murmured something to that effect to George, who responded with a face that wouldn't have disgraced a gargoyle. I could also have pointed out that St Dunstan's needed the money as much as any golf course, but the church's funds, or rather lack of them, was a contentious issue, dividing the Parochial Church Council and indeed the handful of parishioners who rarely – or do I mean barely? – filled the pews.

'They won't hear of the Flower Guild ladies doing their flowers – they've brought in some designer florist. And, mark my words, their guests will throw all that damned confetti,' George concluded, levering himself upright with the strimmer.

Rectors' wives were supposed to think of tactful responses. *Get over it* wouldn't quite do, would it? Since I'd spent all my working life overriding *Can't do* arguments and making sure those working under me understood that they could overcome any blip, temporary or otherwise, I found it very hard not to snarl at him. But he was a volunteer, for goodness' sake. Mowing grass wasn't part of a warden's job description and he was risking his health to boot, so a reassuring smile was in order. 'I'll get Theo to remind them to save it for the reception.'

'I'm afraid people just don't want to listen. Still, Theo does his best, which is all we can ask, I suppose,' George conceded, switching on the strimmer to prevent any further argument.

Perhaps I could find a leaf-blower cheap on eBay: that'd deal with any residual confetti *and* Theo's conscience.

With a smile and a wave, I went on my way, jogging now, rather than running, towards The Old Rectory – in which we did not live. It was no longer church property. It had been sold fifteen years ago, but had recently changed hands. Now it belonged to a guy who'd made even more money than I had in the City.

Dapper and upright, and always immaculately coiffed, manicured and dressed, Ted Vesey was just crossing the green. Perhaps five years younger than George, he was the vicar's warden to George Cox's people's warden, a distinction I still didn't understand, since they both seemed to do exactly the same in church. This afternoon his Barboured dignity was somewhat diminished by his yappy little dog and a full poo-bag. 'You've still got that young layabout from the sink estate working for you, I gather?' Vesey greeted me, taking in with one dismissive glance my running gear.

'Burble?' I wasn't criticizing Vesey's beautifully enunciated speech: Burble was an unemployed village lad whom I'd dragooned into doing some odd jobs around the garden.

'He must have a proper name! Why doesn't he use it? Have you counted your spoons recently? That sort'll take anything they can lay hands on. He's probably one of the gang stealing cycles from people's garages,' he declared, his voice carrying in an actorly way. No one knew exactly what he'd done before he retired, and he discouraged all speculation with a suave change of subject.

'He's clearing the brambles at the end of our garden,' I said mildly and truthfully. He was also doing it very slowly, but Mr Vesey didn't need to know that. Despite being randomly articulate and obviously bright, Burble had been – officially still was – a NEET: a young person not in education, employment or training. Now at least he was gaining a few skills and a few legitimate pounds. Not enough to affect his dole, though I would have paid him three times over just to get some pressure off Theo, whose little spare time could be more pleasurably spent than dealing with twenty years' worth of horticultural neglect. But breaking the law wasn't an option for the rector's wife, was it? Actually, just to set the matter straight, it had never been one of my options, even pre-Theo.

The dog, which, working at the very limit of its extendable lead, was checking for messages along the neighbours' hedges and fences, showed what he thought of Burble's activities by cocking its leg. Vesey looked over my shoulder at his own

home, Church Cottage, which was more or less the same period
as The Old Rectory, only more inclined to the Gothick in style.
I'd thought cottages were two-up, two down houses for the
rural poor; this was a four-bedroomed gentleman's dwelling
with stables and goodness knows what else to the rear – all
tastefully converted now to an exclusive holiday let. Just as
the Farrow and Ball colour-wash was perfect, so the garden
might have existed in a different microclimate from the rest
of the village – none of the bushes seemed wind-burned, as
ours did, and bulbs which had sensibly declined to emerge
from most flower beds nodded graciously in his. Vesey's slight
but audible sniff told me that had a bramble appeared in his
vegetable garden, it would have done so by appointment only,
producing the finest, most succulent blackberries.

'I'd have happily recommended the contractors who maintain my grounds,' Vesey said kindly.

'They do a really excellent job, don't they? But once Burble's
tamed our patch, I ought to look after it myself.' That was the
sort of thing rectors' wives were supposed to do, wasn't it?

He looked straight at me and blinked in what appeared to
be genuine surprise. 'You don't, I have to say, look much like
a gardener.' He gave a courtly little bow.

There wasn't much I could say to that, was there?

'In any case, you're too busy running, they say.' As I winced
at what was definitely a barb, he continued, now sounding
genuinely interested, 'Do you have a preferred route?'

'Up hill, down dale,' I said, gesturing vaguely at the
surrounding ring of hills. 'Forty miles a week on average.'

'How very energetic. Yet I hear you've turned down the
chance of joining the bell-ringing team,' he said, picking up
the dog and fussing it.

'Time,' I said vaguely, implying I didn't have much to spare.
He wasn't to know how heavily it sometimes weighed on my
hands when Theo was working one of his six fourteen-hour
days each week; I'd illicitly polished silver that the team of
cleaners had systematically missed for months, darned holey
kneelers for those still able and willing to use them, and sorted
the intact hymn and prayer books from those that fell apart if
you opened them. 'In any case, the team practises on Monday

nights, and that's Theo's only night off. And don't think I believe they should change the night to suit me, because I don't – I've never rung a bell in my life, and would probably make a complete hash of it.'

'And of course you and the rector always dash off somewhere on the said night off.' Even less approval, though it came with a charming smile.

Which I returned, wishing he was less opaque: was he simply an old gentleman with outdated notions of how to treat a woman? Or was there a lurking hostility? I replied as if I simply took his comment at face value: 'Yes. And we stay away all Tuesday.' We came back to the village on Wednesday morning well before nine, when Theo's working day officially began: one parishioner made a point of phoning, or even turning up at the front door, at eight fifty-five. One day, when there was a problem on the railway, we'd taken a taxi all the way home to make sure the wretched woman didn't report him for dereliction of duty. I added sunnily, 'It's the bishop's advice for priests working in busy benefices like this.'

Whatever his real attitude, he recognized a trump card when he heard it. 'So it is. And in any case, the bells may not be heard for much longer.' This time it wasn't hard to pick up the anger in his voice; the dog certainly did, producing an anxious growl.

'Has one of them cracked? They sounded beautiful when they rang last Sunday.'

'Beautiful! It's a good job someone thinks they're beautiful. Because someone else wants them silenced.'

'The bells? Silenced?' I repeated stupidly. So much for my incisive business brain.

'At the behest of a newcomer, one gathers,' he said, with a hard and suspicious stare at an undeniable newcomer, 'who alleges that they constitute noise pollution. An official complaint has been made to the council. Environmental health.'

Unfortunately at some point in my career I'd learned to swear, though not as prolifically as young Burble, and still hadn't got my head round rationing expletives to hammer and thumbnail moments when no one could hear. 'Bloody hell!' I exploded.

There was a genuinely shocked silence. He put the dog down; now it sniffed ominously at my feet.

'I'm sorry. But who on earth objects to church bells? Apart from the victim in *Nine Tailors*, of course.'

He didn't pick up my mild quip. 'Who indeed, when they or their predecessors have rung, at a conservative estimate, for a millennium? Apparently the bells for the morning services disturb the complainant's slumbers,' he snarled ironically. 'At nine in the morning, God bless us. It isn't as if we can find any ringers for the eight o'clock Communion.'

I didn't respond to the pettishness in Ted's last sentence, but asked a question I genuinely wanted an answer to: 'How can one complaint stop something that the whole village identifies with? Every time there's a christening—'

He gave a gentle smile, which felt as if it was designed to put me in my place, though he might simply have been trying to help me. 'I think you'll find it's more properly referred to as a baptism, Mrs Welsh.'

'Jodie. Baptism. And for every wedding. The organizers always ask for the bells.' The dog had started to tug my laces. The more I shuffled away, the harder it tugged. Dare I kick it? Absolutely not.

'This would be a time-related injunction, I should imagine. No bells before midday or something like that.'

'But most chr— most baptisms take place at a nine thirty service. So to silence the bells then would be to deny parents and godparents their wish. How are we going to fight this, Ted? Do you need legal support? Some of my legal friends might take on a cause like this *pro bono*.'

'I'm sure the Parochial Church Council will come up with a strategy,' he said tightly. 'It's within their remit, after all.'

I, however, was the one with experience of fights both clean and dirty. But it wasn't my job to yell at a man telling the truth outside his own house, though I did draw the line at his dog trying to hump my best running shoes. 'Good boy – why don't you go back to Daddy?' Turning back to Vesey, I continued without a break, 'I'm sure they will. But Ted, I also know some people in the media you might find useful. If you – if the PCC – want me to call in a favour, just let me know. Please.'

'I assure you that a church's representatives would never fight dirty.'

How did Theo manage to swallow down comments and smile? I'd better try myself. 'I suspect the only ones fighting dirty are the anti-bell lobby. Environmental health indeed! Actually, I'm wondering if ridicule might be your best weapon. Yours and the PCC's,' I amended quickly.

He looked at me with narrowed eyes; I swear I saw amused approval alongside comprehension. I hoped so. Theo's job was tough enough without me deliberately creating enemies for myself. I did it accidentally easily enough.

'Ridicule? Something along the lines of these people who a month ago swanned into an age-old village and then want to change the traditions of centuries?'

'Yes, something along those lines.'

There was a glimmer of a smile. 'I shall raise the idea with the PCC – we have to arrange an emergency meeting to discuss . . . one or two matters.' Which he did not propose to share with me. 'I take it Theo is expecting George Cox and me this evening?'

Shaking my head slowly, I said, 'I have an idea he's talking to some parents about their baby's chr— baptism.'

'Ah, he said he wouldn't be available till eight thirty. So we'll see him then.'

'It's awfully late to start a meeting,' I said, tactlessly but truthfully.

'We have something requiring immediate thought. Incidentally, Mrs Welsh, as Neighbourhood Watch representative, I have sent your husband an email about rural theft, but in case he's too busy to read it, I'll convey the message via your good self. It concerns cycles – which I mentioned earlier – and garden tools, some from garages and sheds which weren't even locked or padlocked. The sort of crime disaffected youngsters commit, Mrs Welsh. Beware. Keep a very close eye on that young protégé of yours. He'll bring, as my grandmother used to say, trouble to your door – you mark my words. Now, I'll bid you good day.'

I jogged back home to the dispiriting Fifties outskirts of the village and the shabby house that had replaced the Regency gem as accommodation for the rector. Although our neighbours might have envied its detached status among all the semis, it wasn't great to live in. For one thing it was badly insulated and needed a completely new heating system, but any improvement – as I'd found to my frustration – had to be sanctioned by what was quaintly called a faculty, granted by the bishop's office. So though I would have gladly paid three times over for a new energy-efficient boiler, an upgraded bathroom and a kitchen in which it was possible to cook, nothing could be done without permission. Of course, the house wasn't Theo's property but the diocese's. I knew there had to be a system in place to stop people making foolish or unsafe changes, but the delays were achingly long.

There was no sign of Theo apart from a hastily scribbled note comprising one big X, and Burble seemed to have called it a day. I willed myself not to go and see if the cycles were still in the garage.

With the house to myself, I could have a long, luxurious shower, singing at the top of my voice – though it had to be said it was one that failed to meet the church choir-mistress's standards. Unfortunately, one of Theo's little funniosities – one, believe me, I was working on – involved keeping both the central heating and the hot water on a very strict timer, and though pressing override was the first thing I did, I knew I was doomed to sweaty coldness for at least half an hour.

On my millionaire's yacht there'd have been a Jacuzzi and a plunge pool.

TWO

I was still huddling over a fan heater when I heard more activity in the garden. Burble had returned, and was wielding the long-handled loppers with something approaching enthusiasm. For a few moments. Soon he was puffing on a roll-up, hunching his thin shoulders, and bunching scuffed knuckles around the illegal cigarette. I could see why Ted Vesey was nervous of him; it didn't take the black eye he'd acquired from somewhere to make him vaguely menacing. His posture, knife and fork haircut, apparent reluctance to wash his person or his clothes, and a few random piercings did that.

Donning a duvet-thick jacket, I headed out with a couple of mugs of drinking chocolate, apparently his favourite non-alcoholic tipple, since for so far unexplained reasons he didn't touch caffeine in the form of tea, coffee or even Coke. We both pulled a face when I registered that the roll-up was in fact a spliff.

'Where do you get the stuff?' I asked, as if I might fancy some weed myself.

'This guy. Grows his own.'

'Even so, Burble – still illegal, still harmful. Theo could be arrested simply for letting you smoke it if one of our neighbours dobbed us in.'

He looked helplessly for somewhere to dispose of it.

My eyebrows shot up when his hand drifted towards the garden refuse bin. 'The local media would just love a Rector in Drugs Row story, wouldn't they?' I said, with a grin severe enough to brook no argument.

The spliff went back into his baccy tin.

'Got more than that to worry about, ask me,' he snarled, punctuating the utterance liberally with expletives, as he did everything he said. Many of the words began with F, since I had absolutely forbidden the C word here or anywhere else I might overhear it. Pausing, he drew on the hot chocolate as if it was nectar. It pretty well was. It might now live in an innocuous supermarket tin, but it certainly hadn't started out in it. If he'd known its price, Theo would have worried so much about the extravagance that he might even have given up drinking it. Since it was such a harmless indulgence, I thought the tiny deceit was justified.

'Such as what?' I prompted him.

'Fucking shop going and all. Shit, innit?'

'The shop?'

'Post office got to close,' he explained, less tersely than that. 'The Big Bosses say so. There's no way old Violet'll be able to keep the shop going without it.' He sucked on his teeth, and might have spat, but clearly even a punkish eighteen year old had reservations about doing it on rectory land, albeit somewhere as downmarket as this. He'd have quite understood George Cox's restraint, though George might have been surprised to see it in him.

'That's dreadful,' I said. And *dreadful* was a massive under-statement. If the shop went, I couldn't see the pub surviving – it was very much down on its uppers already. If the pub went there'd be nowhere for the village's old-stagers to nurse a pint, or the odd family to risk a cholesterol-filled but at least home-cooked meal at the weekend. There might be an impact on the playgroup, the primary school (at the age of eleven they left for schools in nearby towns) and – yes, the church. The place would in all likelihood degenerate into a mere dormitory village for Maidstone or even London.

Predictably he swore profusely but very unimaginatively. The gist of his utterance was that the village wasn't much cop now, and would be even worse with nowhere to buy stuff. By *stuff* he no doubt meant the tobacco and cheap booze that were the average village youngster's only means of entertainment, since the funding for a once-weekly youth club had been withdrawn.

'Will Violet retire, do you think?' I asked.

He looked taken aback to be asked for his opinion, but at last shook his head doubtfully. 'Won't want to, that's for sure. She'll keep going till she has to quit, knowing her. But no one's supposed to know, like. She's my gran's cousin.' Which was, I supposed, an explanation of how he knew. 'Total shit.' He sniffed.

I had a suspicion that promising to ask Theo to pray for Violet might not fill Burble with joyous optimism. 'We should do something,' I said, probably sounding vague but actually determined.

'Do you reckon you can?' I'd never heard him sound remotely eager before. Actually, on a scale of one to ten, this would just about creep up to one, but there was something else in his voice – something that sounded suspiciously like trust. 'Thanks,' he added, passing me the empty mug. 'Is it true, Jodie, you used to drive a Porsche? How did you manage that?'

I didn't want to sound as if I was preaching, but I told him straight: 'A lot of hard work to get my qualifications, and a lot of hard work once I got a job.'

'And a silver spoon to start with,' he jeered.

'Stamping books at a library? I don't think so.'

'Come on . . .'

'Do you really want to know what kick-started me, Burble? Because I'll tell you. In those days, if you were young your employers had to send you to get your qualifications by way of something called day-release at college. A bit like an apprenticeship. I was messing around in someone's class – poor cow, we were probably making her life a misery – and one of my fellow students said the teacher – only they called themselves lecturers – was wasting her time; we'd never get anywhere because we'd all had such unhappy childhoods, rotten parents, and so on. And for some reason the teacher broke this stick of chalk in two. She said she could either moan about not having a decent stick of chalk and throw the pieces away, or she could simply use what she'd got to write with. And while she wrote words like *analogy* and *metaphor* and *simile* on the board, I came to a big decision.'

'To use your half piece of chalk?'

'Exactly.' I could have hugged him. 'And I hope you'll use yours. Now, I don't reckon you got as much out of school as you could have done. So we need to start from there.'

'We?' He blinked.

'It's one thing filling refuse bins with brambles,' I said, 'but real gardening's another.'

But my mental quest for something to fire him with enthusiasm and a belief that he could not just actually earn enough money to come off the dole, but also have a realistic chance of getting a horticulture qualification, wasn't matched by any glimmer of a response. I could see that helping Burble was going to be like trimming those brambles – a long and not necessarily rewarding battle.

Since Theo hadn't heard even a whisper of Burble's news, we agreed over an early supper that neither of us should mention it to anyone else until it had become a decent-sized rumour. As I'd told Ted Vesey, Theo was going to see a couple of non-churchgoers about the baptism of their baby, to suggest there might be some significance to the ceremony apart from unseasonal strappy dresses, heels more vertiginous than mine and silly hats. And then of course was the late visit from the churchwardens. In the absence of anything more tempting, swathed in my quilted jacket, thermal gloves and a couple of scarves, I popped my running hat on and headed for the village hall, armed with enough pound coins for the electric slot meter to keep us at least tepid all evening.

Seven or eight WI members were abuzz with something that snapped their mouths tight shut when I pushed the door open. When a collective turn of heads established it was only me, however, I was loosely admitted to their circle, like a new satellite orbiting the accommodating earth. After all, I was now officially a member, and here for the business which the committee had unanimously decided should be dealt with before the talk; if it was left till later, to a woman everyone bolted. But whatever they'd been talking about must wait till they'd inspected and transferred from their plastic box to a china plate covered by a paper doily the cupcakes I'd brought along as my contribution to the refreshments. Imagine Jodie Harcourt – Jodie *Welsh* – with time to make cupcakes. Not very well decorated ones either, truth to tell, despite the Dr Oetker toppings. At least the bag of toiletries I'd brought for the evening's raffle was decidedly if discreetly upmarket.

The meeting, which simply involved reading minutes and correspondence, was swiftly over. Mrs Mountford, it was noted, had sent apologies.

These days, to boost numbers and add to their coffers, the branch welcomed visitors of both sexes. These now started to trickle in to hear tonight's talk, which was to be on the merits of wormeries. This was actually a subject in which I was interested, as much to my surprise as Theo's. It'd be nice to do something useful with all our weeds. Meanwhile, as we waited for the speaker, conversation sparked up again. About the post office, of course.

Their teeth might not have been biblically gnashed, but they were certainly sucked. How could old people survive in a village with no provision for pensions, food, or even – perhaps, in fact, most important – a public space for casual but life-enhancing conversation? And why should people with young families want to move in?

I could have pointed out that young people would be far less dependent on a single shop. They could do a supermarket run, or, more likely still, shop online. Instead I asked what I should have asked Burble: 'What will happen to the premises when the post office closes? Can Violet keep on the shop lease?'

Elaine Grant, a bright Scot hitherto by some twenty years the youngest of the group and thus pretty much my contemporary, shook her head, setting Pre-Raphaelite coppery tresses aswirl. 'That's the problem, actually. Not the post office people. They'd more or less tolerate it there, since it runs at a slight profit, but it's the shop itself that can't survive. Not the way that the rental's shot up. They say there's already been a change-of-use application. Another bijou commuter residence, I suppose. So I'm afraid it's—' She drew her hand across her throat.

How had Burble got it so wrong? All that pot in his brain, perhaps.

At this point our speaker arrived, needing help, he said,

with his equipment. At least the worms he'd brought weren't
about to be let out of a can.

The PowerPoint presentation over, it fell to me to make the
vote of thanks. Reminding him I was the rector's wife, I told
him how much I liked the idea of worms being at supper on
something other than the occupants of the graveyard. There
was a shocked silence; presumably no one picked up the allu-
sion to *Hamlet*. Raffle time: the speaker won the toiletries and
looked genuinely pleased. I won a bottle of wine I wouldn't
even cook with, but mustn't think of declining. Everyone laid
into the wonderful cakes, but it seemed to me that there were
just as many at the end as there had been to start with. Talk
about loaves and little fishes. There was a general allocation,
everyone, including the speaker, leaving with a portion of
leftovers.

'Heart attack on a plate,' Theo observed sadly, the biology
teacher he'd once been surfacing briefly. 'Refined flour, refined
sugar, cholesterol by the bucket.' With a grin, he added, 'Just
one slice!'

'Only if you join me for at least half a mile jog tomorrow,'
I said. 'Even if it means getting up half an hour earlier.'

He pulled a face, and poured another half glass of red wine.
'I'm protecting my heart with this,' he said. 'OK, I know
you're right. But I feel such a wimp, knackered after only a
few minutes. Even after that ligament problem you must be
covering five or six miles a day.'

'It's just a matter of practice,' I said briefly, dismissing all
the hard work, pain and boredom. 'How did it go tonight?'

He rolled his eyes. 'The wardens have called an emergency
parish church council meeting tomorrow at seven. And –
because it's choir practice night – it'll be here, I'm afraid, not
in the vestry. So you might need to commit yourself to another
run, because if you're in the house you'll find yourself acting
as usherette and tea lady and everything else you loathe rolled
into one. And if Mrs Baker's arthritic hand is still too bad for
her to hold a pen, we might even ask you to minute the
meeting.' He eyed me narrowly. 'Why don't I hear squeals of
protest?'

'Because I might – I just might have the glimmer of an idea.' Little wheels were turning briskly in my head.

He held up an authoritative hand in the sort of gesture he never made in London. I knew his schoolmaster voice would come next. 'It's a PCC meeting dealing with church business, Jodie.'

'Oh, so is my idea – if it ever grows into a fully-fledged one, that is. What I thought was—'

The phone rang. He spread his hands helplessly. 'I'd better take it.'

The phone conversation went on and on. I poured him another glass of wine, only to find myself absent-mindedly drinking it myself while I waited. When he returned, he was almost staggering with weariness, so I didn't mention my idea. In fact, I'd much rather say nothing even to him – perhaps especially to him – until I'd thought it through properly. Nothing was worse than a good plan spoilt by lack of preparation.

At last, as he was halfway up the stairs to bed, he said, 'You were talking about something earlier? A plan?'

'We'll talk before the meeting. Promise. Please don't look so worried – you know I'd not do anything deliberately to annoy the PCC.' Even Ted Vesey, I added under my breath.

The following morning, showered and perky after my favourite morning exercise with Theo, I was in church, armed with a tape-measure and a notepad. Since the church was always kept locked, I'd borrowed Theo's key: he was busy taking assembly at a local primary school in a nearby village. It might be that my theory wouldn't work in practice, and I wanted to be the first – and in that case, the only – person to know.

On my hands and knees, I was interrupted by the sound of voices outside. But your knees are not a bad place to be in a church, so I stayed put and waited to see who it was. The door opened slowly and with the sort of clichéd creak you'd expect in a bad movie. It turned out to be a party of walkers, all loudly apologizing for disturbing the quiet of the place when they saw me, but desperate to see the famous brasses. They were so keen they all slipped their boots off, leaving them neatly in the porch, as if entering a mosque.

I didn't quite gawp, but I did wonder what on earth they were talking about – and where the brasses might be. I'd never heard of them, even though I'd helped the team of cleaners a couple of times. Looking around, which didn't take all that long since apart from the cross-shaped body of the building, there were only two side chapels, a vestry and a square annexe leading to the bell tower at the rear, I realized the obvious place must be in the chancel floor. This was mostly covered by a piece of rather viciously-patterned Seventies carpet which was, come to think of it, quite out of keeping with the rest of the interior. While I thought about the wisdom of pulling it back in the manner of a hopeful magician – ta, da! – I directed them to the remains of medieval wall-paintings in the tiny Lady Chapel and the very handsome alabaster tombs in the choir. While their backs were turned I lifted the carpet. It was a good job I'd been circumspect: one end concealed a floor safe; the other revealed two beautiful delicate brasses, the sort that had been stolen from many churches like this. Perhaps – but only perhaps – that was why outsiders were locked out. But it seemed such a waste. Things so lovely should be seen by as many eyes as possible; it must be the brass-rubbing equivalent of having a couple of Fra Angelicos and keeping them under the carpet in your private office.

The walkers were thrilled by the sight. They respected my suggestion that since the brasses were so important (were they? I was only quoting what they'd said, after all), they should look but not touch, and take memories but not photographs. They offered generous donations but I couldn't locate a single Gift Aid envelope to put them in, cursing the loss of valuable potential income from the tax man. So several fivers and one tenner went naked into the collecting box, which I needed to remind someone to empty. The walkers, by now my new best friends, then wanted guidance to a good eatery: was there a pub in the village? Or at least somewhere they could buy snacks? I directed them to the post office, in the hope that Violet had something suitable in her chiller.

Slowly I picked up my measure and pad, said goodbye to God, and left, carefully – but very reluctantly – locking the door behind me. After all, thanks to the walkers, who should by rights have found themselves inhospitably locked out, there was now enough money in the rusty old wall collecting box for someone to risk taking a jemmy to it. And if anyone did, I knew who the blame would fall on: Burble and his mates.

And me, of course, for letting them do it.

Theo was spending the afternoon visiting the sick, so after a run I still had time on my hands. I spent it at the computer: it seemed my plans might have support in high places – and maybe even High Places.

THREE

Minuting meetings was usually my idea of hell on earth, especially when I had no idea of the import of what I was jotting – allusions to places, organizations, abbreviations and even people I'd never heard of. Worse, I hardly knew the PCC members themselves. However, this time Machiavelli would have been proud of the way I grasped at the chance with both hands. On the grounds that I couldn't both write and make tea and coffee, I provided wine, with savoury nibbles instead of the remains of the WI cake laid out on the teak Sixties sideboard in the dining room that we'd only ever used once for its proper purpose. I'd not had time to tell Theo my plans, because he'd spent most of the day at the hospice, arriving home with three minutes to spare. Grey with exhaustion, he collapsed on to a chair at the big dining table. All the same, he was alert enough to look at me quizzically. 'This plan of yours, darling?'

'It's controversial, I admit, but— Drat!' The front door bell was already ringing loud and long.

It was Ted Vesey, impeccably dressed as ever, who looked sideways at the glasses and the labels on the wine bottles – not my WI prize, let us say. It wasn't, of course, that I wanted any of them tiddly, but some decisions were better made when one was relaxed. Any committee members who were teetotal would get environmentally-friendly tap water – none of your bottled Fiji stuff – but at least it would come in a crystal jug and be poured into crystal glasses too, imported from my London home.

For once the wardens had put aside their mutual dislike and agreed that the news was doom-laden. Every five years each church's fabric has to be checked from tower-top to crypt. The latest quinquennial inspection of St Dunstan's had shown major problems which had to be addressed. The finances would hardly run to them. Bleakly, chaired by Ted Vesey, discussions ran to fundraising, from a book sale, vetoed on the grounds of e-book proliferation, to an egg and spoon race. Theo hardly spoke, which no one except me seemed to notice; I had a sense he was waiting for the storm to blow itself out. Or perhaps he was just too weary. When someone suggested a teddy-bear parachute jump from the tower, and the idea was taken seriously, I knew I had to offer my own plan. But first I got up to serve the wine or water, hoping to give the impression that I was not a secretary or even someone gatecrashing the PCC – just a parishioner with a suggestion.

I started by talking about the walkers I'd met in church.

'You? What on earth would you be doing there?' Mrs Mountford demanded. She was one PCC member I had encountered before, generally very early on Wednesday mornings. 'I suppose the devil makes work for idle hands,' she concluded.

It might have been what they'd all been wondering, possibly even thinking, but none had thought it tactful to ask aloud. Mrs Mountford, a lady of a certain age, whose spirit seemed the same colour as her iron-grey hair, was a former warden absolutely convinced that she'd done the job better than Ted or George could even dream of doing. She had eleven years' experience after all, when the maximum recommended was three. The bishop himself had tried to ease her out. However, impervious to his kind tact, she'd clung to office, much to the chagrin of Theo's predecessor.

Though Theo never admitted it, I was fairly sure part of his remit when he'd been appointed was to get rid of her. This saw the uneasy reign of Ted and George commence, though since former wardens were entitled to remain on the committee for a year, Mrs Mountford continued as an *ex officio* thorn in the PCC's side – and now in mine. I couldn't recall who her co-warden might have been. Perhaps he or she was one of those who had sent apologies. I was just thankful there wasn't one more strange face to deal with.

Knowing that Theo was perhaps literally praying that I would button my lip, I produced a serene smile. 'I was doing what people usually do in church, I should imagine,' I said.

'But how did you get in?' she continued. 'I hope no one was careless enough to leave it unlocked: there are valuable items in there. Silver! And with all these thefts around the village—'

'Quite,' I said mildly, determined not to let her throw accusations around about Burble. My former colleagues had always worried when I dropped my voice and smiled like that. 'It's a pity no one can be there to keep an eye on the place all day.'

'You want the church to pay for a security guard?' she exploded. 'G4S in our village church?'

'The idea's preposterous,' Ted Vesey declared. 'My dear Mrs Welsh, whatever are you thinking of?'

'After the Olympics fiasco? Not of G4S, I can assure you.' I picked up someone's sharp breath – Theo's, at a guess, though I was careful not to look at him. He still didn't know my plan to get the group to accept something he had been desperate to achieve as long as I'd known him: a church left open all day, not just for tourists, but also for parishioners. I just hoped he wouldn't rush his fences in his desire to support me. I passed round a placatory plate of smoked salmon on rye, waiting to be invited to continue. Or better still, for someone else to come up with the idea now fully formed in my head.

Elaine, the flame-haired WI member, was looking at me shrewdly. Although she said nothing, I sensed she'd back me.

'What the walkers wanted to see was the De Villiers brasses,' I said, still not resuming my place at the table. 'They wanted to take photos, which I didn't feel I should allow, not without your permission. All the same they wanted to leave donations. I did search for Gift Aid envelopes to increase their value – someone ought to empty the collecting box, by the way – but couldn't find any. And then they wanted refreshments.'

'So you want drink and confectionery machines in church!' By now Mrs Mountford had garnered several supporters, who chimed in with accusations. 'To turn the place into a haunt of Mammon!'

Elaine's eyes were very bright by now. 'Where did you send them, Jodie?'

'Now the Pickled Walnut's only opening in the evenings, I said there might be snacks in the chiller at the post office. But I felt very ashamed – for the village.'

Our dear ex-warden was on the attack again. 'Given your taste for consorting with low life like that so-called gardener who's almost certainly a cycle thief, I'm surprised you didn't shepherd the whole lot here. I'm sure they'd have loved smoked salmon!'

I couldn't resist a waspish reply: 'It's not my house to invite them into, is it, Mrs Mountford? At least, not at a time when Theo may be here counselling and praying with parishioners in need,' I added quickly, with a touch of pathos worthy of Dickens in Little Nell mode.

'I can't help thinking,' Elaine said slowly, 'of all the food we WI women prepare for every meeting. Nine-tenths of it goes to waste – or at least to each other.'

'Forgive me for saying so,' Ted Vesey quite properly interrupted her with a wave of a beautifully manicured hand, 'but that is a matter for you ladies. It is certainly not germane to the matter in hand, which is supposed to be saving the church by raising money. If you would be so good as to sit down, Mrs Welsh, and resume your secretarial duties, then we might make some progress. We had agreed to hold a sponsored parachute drop for soft toys. What other suggestions do we have?'

To my surprise George spoke up. Indoors he looked much less rustic; it was far easier to believe he'd been a figure with considerable responsibility when he was younger. 'If we've got people coming to see the brasses and willing to pay, why don't we charge them? Not just to look, of course – but if they wanted to rub them. And I've seen prints of rubbings in other churches – they sell them, and at a handsome profit, I dare say. And if there's one thing we need, it's a handsome profit.'

'That still means having someone on duty,' Mrs Mountford objected.

'Or having a regular stream of visitors,' I said, 'which I believe is one of the things the Church of England itself recommends. In other words, an open church.'

Even from the corner of my eye I could see Theo's smile, which contained as much love and encouragement as I could hope for. As he opened his mouth to respond, however,

Mrs Mountford thumped the table. The crystal glasses jiggled musically.

'Absolutely not. I resisted it all the time I was warden, and will do so till I die. It's bad enough all those bicycles getting stolen – and lawnmowers now, I hear. And have you heard of the JCB raid on that post office over by Canterbury? And in Loose? What if someone stole the silver? Or the brasses? Or if they defaced the tombs? They're not ours – they're only ours in trust for future generations.'

At last she'd said something I couldn't deny.

'The church insurance people would probably give advice,' George said. 'We've got to have something in this village,' he continued. 'No post office; no shop; no pub the way things are going; a school teetering on the brink; a village hall so cold you could store bodies in it; and a church only used for Londoners' weddings. We need something we can call our own and be proud of.'

I looked Theo full in the eye before replying. 'George is right. Domino effect. If we lose the first three, we'll lose the last three. I'm not really part of this meeting at all, I know that, and I just ask you to bear with me for a second. I'm about to suggest something you'll possibly loathe. It's been done with huge mutual benefits in other parishes, but it is a risk. On the plus side, it will mean someone will be in the building all the hours of the day. On the minus, you may say the world will come too much into what should be just a spiritual place.'

I thought Mrs Mountford would have a seizure. 'She *is* suggesting a drinks machine!'

'Actually, I'm suggesting something much more radical than that.'

'I propose we ask Mrs Welsh to leave the room this instant. I will undertake to finish the minutes.' She stared at Ted Vesey, willing him to act.

Before he could do more than open his mouth, however, Mrs Cox, a grey and gentle-looking lady who was probably given to crochet work, raised a hand. It might have been that she was asking permission to speak; in fact, it looked disconcertingly like an authoritative demand for quiet. 'I

understand from George that Mrs Welsh's background is big
business—'

'Exactly so! So why on earth our vicar should have taken
it into his poor innocent head to marry a—'

'That's quite enough, Mrs Mountford.' Theo overrode quite
a number of words I'd rather not have had directed at me.
'More than enough,' he added as she continued to warm to
her theme.

'What Theo does is his business,' George Cox said. 'I'm
beginning to think in Jodie he's made an excellent—'

'Not if he brings the church into disrepute. Which is what
I will tell the bishop.'

There was a shocked silence. That was a very serious accusation. If she did indeed make it to the bishop, even if it was
clearly in simple malice, there had to be an enquiry. Mrs Cox
rode in again. If only I could remember her first name. 'The
Bible tells us that we should be using all our talents, and Jodie
clearly has experience we don't.' She smiled encouragingly;
only I could see her wink. 'Why don't you continue, my dear?'

'Thank you. I don't even know if it's within your scope as
PCC to approve this. But what I would suggest is that we
consider offering accommodation to the post office and shop in
that spare space that no one ever uses between the chancel and
the bell-tower. I've done some preliminary sketches to show the
layout and a possible glass screen to separate the secular from
the spiritual.' I passed them round. 'You'd have to come to
some arrangement about lighting and heating bills, and so on.
The insurers would have to approve. But it would mean that
there was someone at hand to sell the prints of the brasses that
George suggested, and permits to make rubbings if people were
that way inclined. Postcards; someone could write a booklet
about the church – its history and architecture; maybe other
spin-offs. As Mrs Mountford rightly says, we're not dealing
with any old building. We're trying to preserve the house of
God; maybe we need to use the fabric to save the fabric.'

From the faces of some, I might have been proposing satanic
rituals. Though he smiled encouragingly at me, poor Theo was
probably wishing himself comfortably inside one of those
ornate tombs in the Lady Chapel. There was obviously no

need even to take a vote. Willing myself to show no emotion, I returned to my role as scribe. But suddenly – perhaps prayer does work – there was a minor miracle. The only person in the room under fifty was the treasurer, Jackie Simmons. Despite her responsibilities, she'd been unaccountably as quiet as a Trappist to that point. Now she produced the accounts sheets. Thank goodness for colour printers. The vivid red figures spoke for themselves. It was fortunate, because although Jackie was a qualified accountant, she spent most of the time hiding behind a curtain of beautifully straightened blonde hair.

She must have been rehearsing her contribution in her head; it came out in a continuous paragraph: 'Unless someone can come up quickly with an alternative solution, I suggest that we must, however reluctantly some of you will be to accept my advice, actively consider Mrs Welsh's suggestion. Since some of our debts are pressing, and we do not have the luxury, therefore, of further full meetings at two-monthly intervals, I would suggest a small working party to explore her proposals with the other interested parties.'

'A point of information, Chair: we don't yet know if the other parties are interested. It would have been premature of me to sound them out,' I said, my humility probably failing to hide my satisfaction. I knew that since I wasn't on the PCC I couldn't join the working party unless I was co-opted, but surely there would be members with vision. A glance at Elaine and at Mrs Cox – yes! Alison Cox! I'd remembered at last – suggested there were.

Mrs Mountford declared she would have nothing to do with such devil's work, adding, with a venom that almost scared me, that she would never forgive me if it came to pass, but Elaine, Jackie Simmons, Alison Cox and Tim Robins, a tubby bald man in his late fifties who made Jackie Simmons look loquacious, agreed to report back within a fortnight on Violet's views and the general viability of the idea. George Cox volunteered to contact colleagues in parishes that had already tried the same thing. Theo, his face suffused with joy, would check the C of E website for information and approach the diocesan office for their views.

In the space of minutes he had ceased to be a poor priest

deserving nothing but pity for being entrapped by a harridan, and become a man with a wife who might be useful.

I might have been a positive angel during the next agenda item: the bells. Ted Vesey was suddenly quite effusively keen on my offer to find a lawyer friend to deal with any legal action. Alison Cox wondered if a good PR person might be worth more just now. Did I happen to know anyone . . .? Another of her kind, warm smiles. And another wink.

I wasn't so sure about friends offering *pro bono* publicity, but promised to consult my dear old Rolodex. 'Actually,' I said as if it was an afterthought, though I knew exactly who'd be forking out the cash, 'there might be someone I know willing to match-fund any monies you raise. Teddies, whatever.'

'I for one would certainly sponsor you to run a marathon,' George Cox said.

'This year, make it a half-marathon and you're on,' I said. 'A marathon next, when I'm properly fit again.'

'A half-marathon. And I'll organize sponsorship forms and make sure every single one of us has a fistful to get signed,' he added. 'If someone's prepared to match-fund, let's ensure he or she has to fork out a very great deal.'

I'd not just be running but paying myself to do it: so be it. Then Alison Cox undertook to revive the defunct flower and produce show, and an auction of promises and babysitting were added to the list.

Theo's closing prayer sounded very relieved.

As the group trickled out into the hallway, talking about leaving if not actually doing so, I kept Jackie Simmons back for a minute to pass her an envelope. No one was meant to see. But very little escaped Theo – a hangover from his teaching days, he'd said.

He cornered me as I washed the glasses.

'And you gave Jackie . . .?' The interrogation might have been loving, but it was clear he was troubled.

'A contribution to funds. Confidential, before you ask, between her and me. And I asked her to Gift Aid it – and find that supply of envelopes for the church.'

He kissed me. 'And did you eke this contribution from your parsimonious housekeeping budget?'

'Eke. What a lovely archaic term! As is parsimonious. But a good one for a clergyman. Alas, there's nothing left to eke so I put a few things on eBay. My Louboutins, for a start.'

'But you loved those with a passion!' He looked – probably felt – deeply guilty.

I shook my head. 'Not since I left that one in the aisle grating. And to be honest, my knees and back are much better off without them. The Mulberry bags were far too heavy: my shoulders won't need so much physio now. It's just a case of matching common sense to the church's need.' I took his hand. 'We both know that, if you asked, I could fly in like a cross between Superwoman and a fairy godmother and fix everything. I could simply write a cheque and pay for every last repair to be done. Oh, Theo – please!'

'That would just be a short-term gain. Bringing the shop into the church – that would be such a blessing. For everyone. Churchgoers and non-churchgoers alike. What better way to bring God's love into the community? As for this match-funding – I suppose I'd better not ask who'll be doing it. Thank you.' His eyes said more than his words.

We embraced. But then I realized I was almost holding him up; it had been another dreadfully long day for him.

'Look, I kept back enough smoked salmon for you to have a decent supper, and there's still a bottle of the Chablis in the fridge – let's go and raise a glass to poor Rupert. Did he go gently?'

'So gently we hardly knew he'd left us.' He straightened his shoulders. 'It was an honour to be there, to assist a lovely man whose life had revolved round the church to a good Christian death. He's gone home.' At last he managed a smile. 'But we must also drink to something I'm sure he'd have supported: the open church project.'

FOUR

No horse's head appeared in our bed overnight, but two decapitated pheasants appeared on the back doorstep early next morning. I knew I'd annoyed people the previous evening, but hadn't expected quite such a vivid response. Hurtling to the downstairs loo, I bade farewell to my breakfast. I didn't want to see the corpses again, but I'd made it a rule never to ask other people to do things I couldn't do myself, not unless I paid them handsomely for the privilege. So, donning rubber gloves, I was ready to carry the bodies – at arm's length – to the bin. But Theo arrived just in time to do the deed himself. Except that he didn't. He seized on them with glee.

'How lovely! I wonder who left those for us.'

'A fox with razor-sharp teeth?' I shuddered.

'I take it you won't be dressing them?'

'Or more to the point, undressing them! Or taking their insides out!'

He shook his head as if trying not to laugh at me. 'I'll show you.'

'You can do it in decent privacy, thank you very much. I don't even have any recipes for pheasant,' I added mutinously.

'I'm sure we'll find one in Merry's old files.'

I hoped he wouldn't notice my half-swallowed gasp. According to Mrs Mountford, Merry had been a perfect vicar's wife and helpmeet. In addition to those regularly left by Theo, there were always fresh flowers on her grave. More expensive ones than Theo's. I wished he'd talk about her, so I could get a clear idea of her as a woman; all I could deduce from his silence was that he still found it too painful to talk about a perfect woman. Much as he loved me – and I didn't doubt that – he must see me as an inferior replacement model. The longer I spent in her depressing kitchen the surer I was that I was a pretty poor substitute.

'I'll go and check,' I said. He didn't understand how painful it was for me to go through her beautifully annotated ring-binders full of recipes clipped from magazines or newspapers or carefully transcribed in lovely clear handwriting.

Before I could do so, however, Burble hove into view. 'Road kill,' he said, as if that explained everything. To a country person au fait with game laws, it probably did.

'That's very kind – thanks!' Theo enthused, in a tone suggesting he'd been afraid they might have come from some-one's private estate.

'Owe you one for Violet – right?'

Heavens! Jungle drums or what?

'Sending the rubberneckers to the shop. Made a few bob. Ta, Jode.'

So it was nothing to do with my proposals. What would he bring if that little deal came about? A whole ostrich from Port Lympne Zoo?

'Lock your garage last night?' he asked. 'Shed? Look, just 'cause you're the vicar don't mean your gear's – what do they call it? – sacred?'

'Sacrosanct?' Theo prompted.

A grin disturbed Burble's piercings. 'Nice word, that, innit?' He rolled it round his mouth a couple of times. Suddenly, dropping the machete I'd found in the shed in question, and some leather gloves and goggles I'd bought him ('Elf and Safety, after all), he said, 'Know what you need,' and disap-peared. For the rest of the day, as it happened.

So did another couple of lawnmowers, this time from the estate the rectory backed on to – people who'd assumed that living in a village meant they didn't need to lock their sheds. At one point, before my arrival, it had meant you didn't even need to lock your front door. Now, as I discovered when I went for my next run, dotted all around the village were vans from burglar alarm companies, including the one Ted Vesey used and which he had no doubt recommended.

Until the dust from the PCC meeting had settled, I changed my route, avoiding the more picturesque part of the village which included Mrs Mountford's domain. Instead I ran through the small area of social housing, right on the edge of the village. Some houses were obviously in private hands, with owners making what Mrs Mountford would probably call An Effort. Others were less well maintained, but I'd seen far worse estates in London, and it hardly qualified for Ted Vesey's description of it as a sink estate. As I ran I made sure I greeted everyone I could, even the bunch of disaffected youths lounging near a car without a tax disc. One or two – Burble's mates, perhaps – returned my wave and smile. One actually detached himself from the group and stopped me to ask about my Porsche. He was sorry I didn't have it any more.

'Come on, they're already nicking bikes and mowers,' I said. 'Someone might fancy a Porsche!'

He shook his head sadly. 'Only to key it, like.' He fished one hand out of his hoodie pouch to mime vandalizing paint-work with a sharp object. 'Some people don't like fancy motors. Best with what you've got, maybe.'

'You don't think a six-year-old Focus is going to offend anyone?'

'What do you think? Make 'em shed a tear, more like.' It seemed the conversation was over. But he suddenly asked, 'What's it like, having lots of money? And why did you come down to this dump instead of spending it?'

'The second question's easier to answer,' I said honestly. 'I came down here because I love Theo, and since his job's here, he's not going anywhere.'

'But a lot of folk hate your guts, see, you being a banker.' That hurt. But at least I had the consolation that it wasn't personal. 'Might have been better if he'd got a job near you.'

'The church doesn't quite work like that. And if I say having money's nothing compared to loving the right person, I dare say you'd laugh in my face. Just for the record, I wasn't a banker. Ever. And I never had huge bonuses or any other stuff.'

'What was you then?' He looked taken aback, as if denied his right to be resentful.

'I worked in computing.' No need to specify the firms I spent most years with, since their tax arrangements appalled even me. 'Recently I did short-term contract work.'

'Used to like computers. At school. Then at the library. Then they shut the library.'

'And they shut the youth club, too.'

'Yeah, but the computers there were crap. And it was just for kids, really. The club, I mean.'

I was beginning to have the glimmer of another idea, but wasn't about to talk it over with him. Not just yet. Rather than come out with a platitude, however, I looked at his feet. 'Pretty sound shoes: are you up to running with me for a few hundred metres? Only I don't know your name.'

'Malcolm Burns. Mazza. OK. You're on.'

After some warm-up exercises he clearly thought were beneath his dignity but certainly weren't beneath mine, I took him on a gentle circuit round the estate, so he wouldn't feel bad about dropping out on the excuse he'd got to pop into a mate's house or something. But he kept going: he had the right build for a distance runner, whippy, and he ran in a neat economical style. So we circled the better-heeled parts too. Wouldn't you know it, halfway round the village green we overtook not the dreaded Mountford, who might have expired with a seizure at our feet, but Ted Vesey and his wretched amorous dog. Only it didn't seem too loving when the feet and ankles it saw were moving. Guessing what the dratted thing would do, I shoved Mazza hard enough to make him stumble away; I'd had enough practice of dealing with snappy dogs to jump clear. But I'd reckoned without the extended lead Vesey favoured, which acted like a tripwire.

Vesey's apology, when I fetched up on my hands and knees at his feet, was courtly enough, and I accepted it graciously, despite his acrid glances at my running partner. Fortunately I'd escaped with no more than bruises. In the summer, with shorts and no gloves, it might have been a different matter.

Dusting myself down, I trotted after Mazza, who to my horror was busily filming everything with a mobile even more expensive than mine. So what was all that about not being able to use a computer? 'Please promise me that won't go on YouTube or whatever,' I said. 'Just delete it.'

'Bastard tightened the lead deliberately,' he said. 'I'll make him smile the other side of his face. Could have hurt you bad. Sue him: he's fucking loaded.'

'Let's not start a class war over my knees,' I said. 'Keep it to yourself, please. Or I shan't train with you tomorrow. Mind you,' I continued, as I set us going again, 'I bet you'll be too stiff.'

'Bloody won't. What time?'

'Half-seven? At the rectory? We'll do some warm-ups and add an extra kilometre.'

He winced. At the time, I thought, rather than the distance I'd suggested.

'Or would half-one be better?' I asked with a grin. 'But let's see you getting rid of that footage first.'

'No way. That sort of bugger's likely to accuse one of us – OK, me – of kicking the little rat. But I won't put it on YouTube.'

'Nor on your Facebook page. Or anywhere else. Now for our warm-downs . . .' I started mine. As I stretched, I asked casually, 'Have you seen Burble? He popped off first thing this morning after bringing us a brace of road-kill pheasants and I've not seen him since.'

'Probably foraging,' he said tersely. 'Though he knows some weird—' His phone bellowed some music I didn't know. 'Got to take this.'

'I gather you're spending your time making young criminals fitter,' Theo said as we washed up before heading to bed that night. Oh, for a dishwasher. Oh, for enough space for a dishwasher.

'Ah. Ted Vesey's been in touch.' I put down a wine glass very carefully on the draining board.

He picked it up with equal delicacy. 'No. Not Ted. Someone else. You know every wall in a village has eyes as well as ears. Was it wise to kick Ted's dog, Jodie?'

'I'd have kicked Vesey's balls if I could have reached. Actually, the running shoe, as it were, is on the other foot. I tripped over the dog's lead, that Mazza swears—'

'As much as Burble?'

'Almost – Mazza swears that Vesey tightened the lead deliberately. He got footage to prove his point too, and to prove that my feet were flailing in the air, not kicking anyone or anything. I made him promise not to distribute it, though.'

'Thank you. Rector's Wife Assaulted By Churchwarden –
that would have looked good on the Internet, wouldn't it?'

'Quite. Though how Mazza comes to have such an upmarket
phone, I'd rather not know. I doubt if he'll come tomorrow or
I'd get him to show it to you. The clip, not the phone.'

'Sweetheart, you don't need to do that. I believe you. Without
any evidence.' Laying aside the tea-towel he kissed me thoroughly enough to convince me.

I returned the compliment, but not totally satisfactorily given
the blue rubber gloves. 'It'd be nice for you to be able to show
other people though. Or rather, tell – I'd be happier him not
knowing my personal number, which isn't the most Christian
thing to say, I know.'

'You're not the priest in charge, sweetheart; you don't have
to put your details into the public domain. But I'm interested
that you don't entirely trust this Mazza.' He put away the glass
and looked at me quizzically.

'I don't *dis*trust him. After all, he's not uploaded it yet: I
checked ten minutes ago. It's more – a matter of *distance*
between him and me. I'm not sure if I'm making sense. It's
one thing to get him running, to give him something to do,
but another to have him thinking he's my friend. Though I
think he might have tried to give me a veiled warning about
the folk Burble hangs out with. I'm not sure . . . But he did
give me one idea,' I added positively.

'You seem to be having a lot these days!' Turning from me
he hung up the tea-towel.

I flushed. I detected a distinct note of – was it simply amusement or was there criticism there too? No, just amusement. 'I
just thought that since I know quite a lot about computers,
maybe I should give the unemployed kids some lessons. In
the village hall or somewhere. A sort of ASBO club,' I added
with a rueful grin. 'It'd make them more employable, if ever
there are any jobs in the future.'

He took my hands and kissed me. 'That's a brilliant idea.
But what about the computers they'd need?'

'Ah. I suppose I couldn't just buy . . . No? OK, I wonder
if the village school would let us use theirs . . .'

'I know what Mrs Mountford would say: *No doubt the*

ne'er-do-wells would download material you wouldn't want a child to see.' He had her face and her voice to a T.

'As if I couldn't stop that. Filters, Mrs Mountford, ma'am! Still, one thing at a time: let's not try to run before I can walk.'

He turned his mouth down, Eeyore now. But he couldn't keep the joy from his eyes. 'You may have a lot of walking coming up, too. Jodie, I can't wait any longer: your shop in the church idea's going to get the bishop's approval. But don't say anything until everything's firmed up.' We danced round the kitchen like kids.

At last I pulled away. 'But it's not down to us, or even the bishop, is it? It's the PCC that has to make decisions. Speaking of which, I'd love you to circulate my PR friend's free idea – he wants the bells to be recorded and used on the church and the village websites and Facebook pages.'

'My love, as far as I know, neither has either. But you're right, before you say anything – both should have both.'

'Mrs Mountford notwithstanding.'

'Quite. So we don't tread on anyone's toes or even reinvent the wheel, I'll phone the chair of the parish council tomorrow and tell her what we've been talking about. Julie's a sensible woman: her husband's very ill so she's not been as active as she'd like. I'm sure she'd love a joint website – we have to sneak into the twenty-first century somehow!' He put his hand in the small of my back to propel me upstairs. 'I bet you've got a friend who can get us there, at least as far as the website's concerned.'

'I could do it myself, Theo, standing on my head with one hand tied behind my back. But remember what you said about fishing and teaching how to fish.'

'And to whom are you planning to give fishing lessons?'

I said mildly, 'It would be good if someone from the village could be volunteered into having them. Mazza, for instance . . .'

'Mazza!' But then his parson's instincts overrode his middle-aged, middle-class ones. 'Yes, Mazza. Perfect.'

Or not. I was ready to fight my corner when his face was transformed by the sweet smile that had turned my heart over the night we met.

'I'm so glad you've come to St Dunstan's. He'd be very

proud of you. Dunstan,' he repeated as I shook my head in incomprehension. He took my hands in his and kissed them in turn.

'I thought he was all about white sticks and guide dogs.'

'He gave up his worldly life and retired to Kent. Nothing, they say, gave him more pleasure than teaching the young.'

FIVE

Who had taken a jemmy to our garage? Someone, I assumed, that didn't know that one thing Mazza had enjoyed at school was whatever they called metalwork these days. Though not friends – Mazza, it transpired, was a year or so younger than Burble – they rubbed along enough for Burble to have told him how casual we were about our outbuildings' security. So Mazza had found a piece of metal and fashioned it into a backing plate for the edges of the garage doors. He'd also sneered at the padlock we'd hoped would guard our shed, sending me off to B&Q to upgrade it to something suitable for protecting the Tower of London. If, of course, we could remember the combination, which he insisted was not written down anywhere obvious or kept on my phone.

'We only keep old spades and flowerpots in there,' Theo had protested.

'Look, Vic, double glazing this old, locks this weak, all you need to do is shove a spade under a door frame and Bob's your uncle.'

'Or in these enlightened times, your aunt,' Theo had murmured, with a wry grin at me.

But we'd been glad of the boys' activities when we saw the scars on the garage doors. And – bother having to wait for a faculty – I brought in a locksmith to improve as far as he could the security of the rectory itself. It was actually Theo's idea. He'd counselled enough victims of crime to know that even if thieves didn't get away with hundreds of pounds' worth of loot, just having someone break into your home could leave you feeling violated.

'I assume it won't break your bank?' he said.

'I hope not. Though I could always sell a Monopoly money house,' I said lightly. It would worry him to know that the little terrace house I'd first lived in in Primrose Hill, the very first property in my portfolio, would probably fetch over three million pounds. Its next-door neighbour had. It's nonsense, the London property market. And getting crazier by the minute.

'A green one or a red one?'

'The red ones are hotels, darling. I'll never make a capitalist out of you.'

Without explanation, three scraps of newspaper arrived on the back step. In the first were a dozen repellent-looking fungi, which might equally be mushrooms or toadstools; next came what looked like a cross between bulb leaves and spring onions and smelt strongly of garlic; and in the third were green things I simply didn't recognize.

'Very Shakespearean,' Theo said, picking up the green things. '*King Lear*,' he said by way of explanation. 'The scene where Edgar pretends he's on the cliffs of Dover, with samphire gatherers down below.'

I dimly remembered. 'But what's all this to do with us? Apart from nourishing our new worms?'

'I fancy it's the result of some forager's activities.'

'Foraging? Mazza said something about Burble foraging; is that just another term for scrumping?'

'Not if by *scrumping* you mean stealing food from people's private property. Foragers claim they only take food from public areas – woodland, verges, the seashore. Which could well be true of this – wild garlic: smell! – and the mushrooms, assuming that's what they are. I might just check on the Internet before you put them in a risotto.'

I did. They were delicious. We lived to tell the tale.

Meanwhile, the bramble patch got smaller, Burble having apparently twigged at last that regular hours brought in regular money. He went quite pink with embarrassment when I thanked him for the food, and offered to pay for the vegetables.

'Nah. Free to me, free to you.'

'Your mum must be grateful for what you bring in.' He'd never talked about his family, so I knew I was taking a risk.

His face closed completely. He was ready to walk away. In other words, I knew what I could do with my nosiness. I'd save asking about his dad till another day. Meanwhile, I had to make the first move: 'Look, how about a bit of digging – it'd be a change from brambles.'

Apart from helping Burble, if indeed that was what I was doing, I made sure Mazza and I ran further each day. He had a real talent that someone should have spotted when he was younger. Soon I'd be able to get him on the hill circuit with the lovely views, not that I expected him to break into raptures and compose a sonnet even if, as the country greened up and even got a powdering of blossom, I was increasingly tempted to do.

The day he and Burble had to sign on at the Job Centre, both oozing resentment at what they clearly felt was a futile bureaucratic exercise, happened to be so temptingly bright and mild that, with Theo at some diocesan meeting, I allowed myself the luxury of a private run. I would do my complete circuit, even though the comparative lack of action over the last few days showed on my timing. Then I found something to slow me down even more. Yes, the view. But this time I wasn't about to wax lyrical about the countryside's delicate colours and the sweet scents and the fact that this time the birds were definitely singing. I was peering at the deep valley where I'd seen heavy plant – as in serious machinery – being used to clear what looked like mature trees. Now the same site was busy with workmen: what were they up to? Surely that nice bit of historic-looking woodland wasn't about to become a building site? Apart from the fact that none of them sported regulation yellow hard hats, it looked very much like the activity I'd watched from thirty storeys up as builders squeezed another skyscraper on to a spot previously occupied by a perfectly usable but not sufficiently prestigious tower of office space. The higher you meant to go up, the further you had to go down – and bother the priceless Roman site you were destroying. But no one was going to build a Shard in Kent. No, my eyes – or my ignorance of agricultural buildings – were deceiving me. Surely. But the lack of hard hats was a shame – safety issues aside, they'd have looked like bright buttercups in the sunshine, an image I thought Burble would like.

I pushed myself reasonably hard down the hill and didn't drop my speed to a jog, as I usually did, as I hit the village.

I was too keen to get to my computer to see if I could discover what was going on.

Zero information.

Clearly I needed to tap into a local grapevine, or bring my ear nearer the jungle drums.

So when Elaine, the Lizzie Siddal lookalike from the WI, phoned to ask me over for a cup of tea that evening I accepted with alacrity. Theo was taking a confirmation class in one of his outlying villages, and I still found it hard to relax, either with music or a good book, in a house that didn't feel as if it would ever welcome me. Perhaps it had heard about the changes I wanted to make and resented them.

Theo bit his lip when I told him I'd be setting out on my own, and on foot, too, since he needed the car. The only car. I'd just have to change his mind on the matter of one for me; not a key-attracting Porsche, however.

'You will be careful, won't you?' he asked. 'You city types tend to rely on your street lights, don't you?'

'As if there aren't lights in Birmingham! Come on, you tell me to be careful every time I go out alone,' I said, hugging him. 'I've got my trusty torch, the one that's a cross between a cudgel and a lighthouse, and I'd back myself to outrun most assailants.'

'But in the dark, on uneven pavements?' He shook his head in resignation. 'If only that guy on the parish council wasn't so keen on astronomy and didn't veto every single proposal for street lighting each time it comes up at their meetings.'

'I suppose there's a lot to be said for reducing energy consumption and light pollution,' I said, adding more honestly, 'in the summer at least. But I shall be all right. I'll even wear my high-vis waistcoat over my jacket if you want.'

I might have been half-joking, but clearly, from the intensity of his gaze and the fierce grip on my arms, he wasn't. He said, in the tones of a man who'd lost one dearly loved wife and didn't want to lose her substitute, 'I do want, Jodie. Very much.'

Elaine's house was in the old heart of the village, in what had once been the main shopping street (I didn't get the impression it was ever quite Bond Street). Now many of the houses had names like The Old Co-op, Bakery Cottage and The Brewer's House: they were older and less elegant than The Old Rectory. From the outside, Elaine's – The Hops – looked like a typical Kentish cottage, complete with peg-tiles; inside, Tardis-like, it was bigger than you could imagine, with a rather dark, narrow hall leading to a kitchen as up-to-date as mine in St John's Wood. *Ours* in St John's Wood.

As I'd expected, Elaine's kitchen smelt of baking, but I'd not expected the overlay of good coffee from a machine to die for. Instant decision: my next bit of expenditure must be on something like that. I'd had enough of instant or half-cold cafetière coffee. I'd even turned to tea, but since my taste in tea was as expensive (in proportion) as my taste in cars, I didn't drink too much of that either. Water? In this part of Kent it was so hard you could almost chew it. Perhaps that was why the tea and coffee tasted so bad?

Since she seemed embarrassed about something, I jumped in with my query about the building work I'd seen. 'Surely no one's trying to build on green belt land,' I concluded. 'It may even be an SSSI.'

She blinked at all the sibilants.

'Site of Special Scientific Interest,' I explained, now into alliteration. 'Maybe they've got rare orchids over there. Or a newt?'

Laughing at my ignorance, she said, 'I'll ask around for you – see if anyone else has spotted activity.'

'Discreetly, if you wouldn't mind, Elaine. Rectors' wives are supposed to be like Caesar's. Only in this case, it isn't *above suspicion*, more *above suspecting.*'

'I'll talk to George Cox's wife, Alison, she's used to being discreet.' She added, 'You know she was once a prison governor? In charge of all sorts of notorious inmates. She still practises martial arts, by the way – I think she's a senior champion at something or other.'

If only I could learn not to stereotype people. 'You might give me the low-down on some of the others one day – Ted Vesey, for instance.'

'Assuming I ever get to find out anything about him. Maybe you shouldn't ask George Cox, though. No love lost there.'

I nodded. 'Is there any reason why they loathe each other?'

I'll swear she hesitated; she did know something. 'No idea. Just a mutual antipathy, maybe. And now it's my turn to pick your brains,' she said, putting a pod into the coffee-maker. Ah, that must be a point against the things – not very environmentally friendly. Unless I could get one with pods the worms could eat . . . 'In fact, you gave me the idea the other night, and I've been mulling it over ever since.'

'Eh?'

'At the PCC meeting. I blurted something out and Ted Vesey shut me up. About all that food left over after WI meetings. We're compulsive bakers, Jodie, and very competitive, though none of us would admit it.'

'My poor cupcakes.' I recalled them with an embarrassed sigh.

'I'm sure you're good at other things,' she said briskly, not bothering to deny that they were substandard. 'This business of the shop moving into the church, for instance. Brilliant. What you said about the domino effect of one institution closing was spot on. Unless they turn the pub into a gastropub and simply attract incomers for a posh meal, the Pickled Walnut will die. Of course we lose the pub either way. Try these biscuits – they're a new recipe.'

'Thanks,' I said, absent-mindedly trying one: it was warm from the oven and so wonderfully full of bad things I wouldn't let my Theo within fifty yards of one. 'These are excellent, Elaine! Sorry. You were saying . . .?'

'I was wondering if the WI could sort of take over the pub – out of licensed hours, at least – and turn it into a tea room. What do you think?' She looked genuinely anxious.

'Have you talked to the landlady about it? What's her name – Suze?' Why should I be involved? It was between the WI and the pub, surely.

'I think the idea might . . . might have more credibility . . . if it came from you.'

'As the local business guru?' I snorted. 'It might, Elaine, but what it gained in credibility it would almost certainly lose in popularity. Think about that PCC meeting,' I added ruefully, helping myself to a second biscuit. Instant addiction. 'I'm persona non grata with at least a third of the members.'

'But you won the day. Or you will when we've presented the report, anyway. Violet's absolutely desperate to move; the post office will make no objection so long as a fully trained clerk continues to work for her, which isn't a problem because the existing one is afraid he'd never get another job, the way things are. Her nephew reckons he can fit a decent glass screen—'

'That's one job that has to be done professionally!' I warned her.

'He runs his own kitchen and bathroom installation company. Knows all the safety and fire and building regulations. Says he'll compete in open tender against anyone.'

'Excellent.' It was. And so was the third biscuit. 'All the same, Elaine, I'm an incomer and I've made enemies. For a project like the teashop, you might do better to get Mrs Mountford on side.'

Elaine paused to let me make my own deductions. 'If you were to get involved,' she continued, in a somewhat wheedling tone, 'where would you begin?'

'You'd need a business plan for starters.'

She looked appalled. 'Even if we're volunteers?'

I nodded firmly. '*Especially* if you're volunteers. I know you'd be amateurs, but there mustn't be anything amateurish about the way you do it. Opening hours, rotas for cake-making, substitutes if someone's ill. Is it just cakes and coffee or would you do light lunches too? If you did, would lunches come with alcoholic drinks? It's a brilliant, brilliant idea, Elaine, but so that you all stay friends – with each other, with Suze and with the customers – you must all know exactly where you stand and what you're committing to. Not just cooking the cakes, either: waiting at table, washing up, cleaning. And sourcing – do you buy wholesale, go to a supermarket or effectively subsidize the village shop, wherever that's located, by buying there?'

Her face a picture of despair, she tossed back her hair. 'It sounded so easy, just baking a few cakes and biscuits.'

'I'm sure when you get into a rhythm it will be. Actually, I may be able to suggest a washer-upper or two, not to mention some waiting staff – but they'd have to be paid, and at the national minimum wage, too, if not the living wage. And you'll have to watch the number of hours they work, so they don't try to work full-time and still claim the dole.'

'Not those awful kids you seem to have taken under your wing? Oh, Jodie.' Her mouth turned down quite comically.

'Something to discuss with your colleagues.'

She looked at me sharply. '*Our* colleagues. You're a WI member too.'

Having agreed, with as much enthusiasm as if I was signing up to root canal work, to attend a special WI meeting the following week, I walked home as briskly as Theo would have wanted, my high-vis jacket like a buckler against the dark forces he feared might beset me, the torch a sword. In reality, the beam cast a broad clear light. I needed it. What pavements there were disappeared from one side of the road only to reappear twenty metres or so later on the other. They were uneven too, a mix of flagstone and tarmac. At least I was sure-footed enough in my new flat-heeled loafers, though my former colleagues would have gaped in disbelief that I could bear to wear anything so unfashionable. There were hardly any cars on the roads, and no sign of any of the youngsters who would have alarmed most people but whom Mazza and Burble had assured me were their mates and would therefore never harm me. A couple of elderly dog walkers (the ambiguity is deliberate) greeted me with a cautious wave. Only another three or four hundred metres to go and I'd be within sight of home.

There was one section of my journey I didn't even like by daylight: a K-shaped road junction, the upright of the K being the main street. Any signal a motorist gave couldn't be clear: was the car heading into an acute or an obtuse angle? A pedestrian needed eyes in the back of his or her head.

Even as I leapt backwards faster than I knew I could, I found time to wonder why on earth the car had no lights. I don't think I hit my head as I went down, but I certainly landed hard and awkwardly in a banana-skin pratfall. I blinked hard at the pitch darkness enveloping me. If I hadn't hit my head, why couldn't I see? I had a nanosecond of panic: had the fall somehow detached my retinas? Both of them?

While I talked to myself sternly and found my feet, at last my eyes grew accustomed to the dark – there! I wasn't blind! – and I was able to pick out on the street the squashed sausage that had once been the torch. It could, I reflected soberly, as I picked up the pieces, have been one of my limbs.

There was, of course, no sign of the offending driver.

Theo, whiter and shakier than I was as he checked me over for anything more than bruises, went into middle-aged mode. 'It must have been one of your young protégés too busy nicking a car to look where he was going. I'll get on to the police.'

'Would they be interested? A near miss? And in any case, sweet one, I had a sense of a big, powerful car. I think. I couldn't give any sort of description. I never saw the driver's face – it could even have been a woman. You know the way some of these incomers drive when they're off to collect their spouses from the station. Shame about the torch, though. Now, you tell me how that confirmation class went and pour me a drop of that Sauvignon Blanc while you're about it.'

'And we'll also talk about a car for you – Monopoly money permitting.' He added with a grin, 'I suppose you could always sell Piccadilly Circus.'

SIX

The weekend is the busiest time of the week for the average clergyman, especially poor Theo, with so many churches to keep an eye on. Of course he had support: there were a couple of people called lay readers who were allowed to read services and even give sermons, but not to give Communion. There was also a priest who'd retired from Bradford but now lived free in a house in the furthest flung village; in exchange for his accommodation he gave up three or four days a week to parish work. I'd devised a simple program for Theo to work out who was at which church at any given service.

I hardly saw him on Sundays, when he had to take at least three services; I simply had to accept that for parsons Sunday was the opposite of a day of rest. I still found it disconcerting, however, after a life involving concerts, opera and theatres every weekend, to be on my own on a Saturday evening, and I longed for Theo to be able to sit and share an hour's peace with me. Was it acceptable to pray for the phone to remain silent? I was always embarrassed to ask for something that would benefit me; in any case, my prayers would rarely have been answered. Tonight it rang just as Theo had picked up a glass of wine. The sound of the voice at the other end made my stomach clench: clearly someone was desperate. It turned out to be a young parishioner whose husband had just announced their marriage was over; he hadn't, he said, signed up to being the father of a disabled child who simply took over every aspect of his mother's life. Kissing Theo as I waved him off, I reflected that Merry would have had a pie or cake for him to take with him for the harassed mother. When he'd tried to counsel and pray with the couple, he said he'd drop in on a lonely old lady in one of the alms houses in the same area of the village. But he wouldn't be late home.

Back home in St John's Wood, Saturday evenings were the

most convivial of the week. If I wasn't involved with music, I'd be eating with friends at the latest trendy restaurant. If for some reason I found myself alone, I'd simply have donned my running gear and pounded round well-lit streets with lots of CCTV to keep an eye on me. But after last night's incident, however much I'd played it down, I was a little jittery. It would be an evening in for me. On my own. Did I dare admit I was lonely?

Come on. I was a grown woman. Self-sufficient.

I checked my iPod. Beethoven? Mozart? But how could I luxuriate in an evening of my favourite music when Theo was working his pastoral socks off? I tried to shut out the nasty, niggling voice of conscience, but halfway through the slow movement of Brahms' D minor Piano Concerto I had to give in. Work for me too. And that meant parish work. But not till the end of the movement: no one could leave Brahms' Requiem for Schumann half-heard.

Unable to face cake-making in the user-unfriendly kitchen, I went for another form of punitive homely activity. I'd been cajoled into making fabric bags, some forty centimetres by thirty, to fill with things that would keep children quiet during a service. Had there ever been any children young enough to enjoy the contents it would have been a really good idea. But nothing loath (actually, that's quite wrong: I hated the chore), I accepted the job, and was supposed to have bought up some remnants from a shop in Canterbury. Needless to say I'd forgotten. I was sure Merry would never have been so remiss. In any case, if one of the kitchen drawers was any indication, she'd probably had a whole bag of scraps of material that might just come in useful one day.

I hadn't, of course. Or had I?

I'd brought down to the village a couple of dresses that I'd hoped to wear at suitable social gatherings. So far there'd been a big round zero. In desperation I'd organized a supper party myself, only to find people turning up in trainers and fleeces and staring at my London gear as if I was a sideshow. Furious with myself for having the wrong expectations and making such a mess of everything, I dragged the dresses from the back of the wardrobe where I'd shoved them and cut them up. Then

I settled down with Merry's old electric machine. There were, I have to say, at the end of my evening, some very grand-looking bags indeed – even if none of the corners was quite a right angle. No wonder I'd been banned from domestic science at school. Still burning with undirected anger, I stuffed each one with scribbling paper, crayons, and a couple of puzzle games, all from pound shops. I'd also raided charity shops for cuddly toys, each of which I'd washed to within an inch of its life. A row of twelve hopeful-looking bears, depressed lions and even a baleful hippopotamus regarded me from their new lodgings, temporarily on the long and fiendishly uncomfortable sofa that dominated the living room. At last I managed to laugh – at them and, more importantly, at myself.

At last I heard Theo's key in the lock. But his face told me he'd find nothing to amuse him in the sight.

Monday morning saw Theo back at the old lady's, with a casserole I'd made; I was better with savoury food than sweet, which wasn't saying much, of course. There was also one for the newly-single mother.

Then I spent half an hour online, striking while Theo's conscience was still warm. If he now thought I needed a car, I could indulge in something – ah, something that wouldn't attract Mazza's keys or vociferous condemnation from Mrs Mountford. So no Porsche. On the other hand, I wanted a little more oomph than the poor Focus possessed. What sort of cars parked here for PCC meetings? I discounted the huge environmentally unfriendly four-by-fours immediately, and a couple of elderly Fiestas. But there were no fewer than three mid-range Audis, if that's not an oxymoron. So I could have something similar, preferably one that looked mid-range but actually had more under the innocent-looking bonnet than you thought.

And according to the Internet there was one apparently sitting waiting for me in Ashford, though its twin exhausts would give the game away to anyone in the know. Within minutes I'd fixed a test drive for Wednesday: much as I wanted that jolly red A3 now, now, now, I didn't want to load Theo with further pressure, and I certainly didn't want to sacrifice our free day.

When Burble arrived, not long after ten, which was pretty early for him, I joined him in the garden, hoping to make a final assault on the brambles. In the fine drizzle he made no more than a half-hearted effort; had he not looked so ill and careworn, I'd have snarled at him. At last, as damp as he was, I brought out a mug of drinking chocolate apiece and a packet of biscuits from Violet's. He helped himself almost mechanically, while I asked him if he knew anything of the valley building developments. He cocked a half-closed eye at the horizon, as if seeking inspiration, finished the chocolate and declared the green wheelie bin too full for anything else. Since I'd already been told off by the binmen for trying to get rid of bags of green refuse, bags with sharp prickles moreover, I could do little more than agree. He made to leave, but turned back.

'This here website, the one Mazza's on about – what would it have on it?'

'The sound of the church bells for a start – background music. A list of village activities—'

'Blank page there, then,' he snorted.

'Announcements about things like the fête. An appeal for funds for the church repairs.'

His interest was clearly waning, and why not?

It was time to think on my feet and come up with something I should have thought of at the start. 'And a montage of photos of people and places. Not just the pretty-pretty cottages and the ducks. Real people. Mazza's phone's got a camera. Has yours?'

'Mine's run by a hamster on a little wheel,' he snarled, clearly thinking of his peers' superior models.

I laughed at the image. Reluctantly, but nonetheless sincerely, I think, he joined in.

'How about you borrow my camera?' I asked, as casually as it's possible to ask when offering a piece of kit worth – well, probably more than Theo's poor old car. 'It's pretty straightforward. It's not point and shoot, but you'd pick it up pretty quickly.'

He tried to look bored and insouciant, but the inner little boy won hands down. 'You sure, Jode?'

'Let's see how you get on with it. Leave your shoes by the back door, will you?'

Shouldn't have asked that. He had trainer foot in spades.

His eyes rounded when I produced the camera, putting it on the table in front of him. 'Telephoto lens and all? I mean – bloody hell, Jode.'

'Let me just change the memory card – there, that's a couple of gigabytes for you to play with.'

He picked it up tenderly, but put it back down again. 'Worth nicking, that.' He looked me in the eye, having, I guessed, assessed its value to within a hundred pounds. 'What if someone thinks I robbed it?'

'Stole,' I said, automatically. 'Easy. I can write a note on a bit of paper saying I've lent it to you and you can take a snap of it. That way you've got evidence you didn't steal it.'

'Bloody hell. Never have thought of that.' He stared at the note I wrote, on a piece of rectory-headed card. But his hands seemed paralyzed.

'It won't start till you take the lens cap off.' I talked him through the various obvious functions. 'Now, snap that card. Ah, it may want extra light – can you work out how to get it? Good. It's often better than flash because you don't finish up with people with red eyes.'

'But doesn't pressing that get rid of red eye?'

It didn't take him long to work his way round it. All my years in computers and this undereducated kid picked things up more quickly than I did.

At last he wound himself up to ask a couple of salient questions. 'Are you really sure, Jode? I mean, what if someone nicks it off me? Or I drop it or something?'

'Insurance,' I said blithely, but wished I hadn't. What if I was leading him straight into temptation and a chance to make money for drugs? 'But it won't come to that, will it? Got a lot of sentimental value, that little beastie.' I patted it as if I was telling the truth.

At last he took himself off, but he doubled back. 'Green bin,' he said, tenderly putting the camera back in my hands while he trundled the bin round to the front of the house.

When Theo came back, much later than I expected, he was

quietly furious. His bicycle, which was pretty well as old as he was but which nonetheless occasionally, when he felt the need for exercise, got him round the village for house calls, had disappeared from outside the old lady's bungalow. As instructed by Ted Vesey, wearing his Neighbourhood Watch hat, he reported it to the police before he even sat down, but his announcement was greeted with little more than a sigh. 'Of course I'd locked it,' I heard him say. 'I'd chained it to a lamp post. But someone simply smashed the padlock.'

Time for a cup of tea, I'd say, and a suggestion that on Wednesday we might nip into the nearest Halfords en route to the Audi dealership. But as soon as I turned my back, the sound of voices snarled in from the garden. It seemed Theo'd taken it on himself to do a spot of detective work, with a loudly objecting Burble having his hands checked for oil. What on earth was Theo doing? Even vicars aren't supposed to demand the truth in that sort of voice. He was clearly about to threaten the kid with divine retribution. But Burble could always make a counter claim of common assault. I must step in, with cups of drinking chocolate.

'I tell you, Vic, I was helping this poor bastard biker. Leathers and all. BMW, for your info.'

'And I've been helping the Queen of Sheba!'

Burble's voice squeaked with indignation. 'Big bloke. Bigger than you, Vic. Looks like a bloody great badger,' he persisted. 'Said he was looking for Jodie, like. Only he's got to wait for someone to pick up his bike. Imagine, a fucking Beamer going belly up. Asked me to bring one of his panniers for him,' he added, his spotty face aglow with righteousness as he pointed to the proof of his story.

'A biker? Looking for Jodie?' Theo repeated bitingly.

'Right. Over by the Pickled Walnut he was. He's probably heading this way now. Dead slowly. Not dressed for walking.' Then his voice got quite tight. 'Hey, Vic, what's all this about the missus getting run over? She never said nothing this morning. Look here, anyone hurts her, I'll make sure the bugger never walks again.' He was so incensed he forgot he wasn't supposed to swear in front of Theo, and used a plethora of words I'd expressly forbidden. But before I could run out and chew his ears off, I realized his voice was cracking. So much for the macho and offhand image he liked to project. At this point there was a thunderous knock on the front door. The tall dark stranger, no doubt.

Tall and dark he might have been. But he wasn't a stranger: he was my cousin, Dave. Dave was the sort of man who'd make even our living room sofa look small. He was not only taller than Theo, he was broader too, though probably with muscle rather than fat. We soon worked out that we'd not seen each other for all of two years. It wasn't that we'd argued or anything; we just weren't that sort of cousin. We were the wedding and funeral type of cousin, retiring to a quiet corner to exchange sardonic family gossip and to wonder aloud why we didn't keep in touch a bit more often.

Dave grabbed the morning's *Guardian* and, turning to a page of ads, spread it out and sat on it. Theo passed him a wad of kitchen towel for his oily hands and he gave them a cursory wipe before absent-mindedly accepting some of Theo's truly awful coffee. He left black prints all over the mug, which almost disappeared in his hand. The other tugged at a piece of expensive material that had sunk between two cushions. It was a leftover from my bag-making activities, but it was clear he recognized it from the last time I'd worn it, at a snazzy wedding for his side of the family, though he merely raised an eyebrow in my direction.

Editing the episode very heavily lest I worry Theo, I explained that I'd recycled some clothes I no longer needed.

Possibly Dave saw through me. 'I didn't think vicars' wives had to be Lady Bountifuls these days. Thought they were supposed to have independent careers. Especially high-flyers like you.'

'They clipped my wings, Dave. Made me redundant.'

'Not that you couldn't have pulled in a few quid here and there as a freelance consultant,' he observed, before adding more sombrely, 'It's getting quite fashionable, isn't it?'

'Oh, Dave – surely not you too!'

Theo said, 'I didn't think the police were allowed to make people redundant. Not front-line officers, that is; I know they've been getting rid of swathes of back-room staff.'

'They don't call it "making redundant". They simply enforce
the thirty-year rule, which says you can retire when you've
done thirty years' service. In this case *can* equals *must*. So it
was thank you, DCI Harcourt, and goodnight.' The bitterness
in his voice suggested he needed Theo's counselling skills
rather than my simple sympathy. 'I took the money and ran,
of course – any day now I can see the government abolishing
lump sums, can't you? Since then, I've actually been all round
the world on that old bike. I come home – and it dies here.'

'Round the world?' My eyes widened. Dave had never been
one for adventure, but this was embracing freedom with a
vengeance.

'And back again. That lad who says he works for you –
fancy you having outdoor staff, eh, Jode! – did his best, but
in the end I had to get a BMW dealership to cart it off for
radical surgery.'

'We've got a spare room and a washing machine at your
disposal, Dave, if you care to stay until the bike's back on the
road,' Theo said. 'You and Jodie have obviously got a lot of
catching up to do, and I don't suppose she'd object to a bit
of company anyway . . .'

'I'd be very grateful for some,' I confessed, hoping I sounded
sociable, not needy. 'Theo works six days a week, from breakfast to late supper. And sometimes after that too. Theo'll show
you the guest room. While you clean yourself up, I'll get some
lunch. Are you still vegetarian?'

To my relief he shook his head. 'Devout carnivore these
days.'

But there was a snag, wasn't there? Monday was our night
off. We wouldn't be here tomorrow. First there was lunch with
an old friend I wanted to wheedle into providing the equipment we needed to record the peal of bells for the website.
And in the evening we'd got tickets for an LSO concert at the
Royal Festival Hall; fond as I could become of Dave, I didn't
want to sacrifice them on the altar of family unity.

In the event, Dave, registering the fact that we only had one
bathroom and a bitterly cold downstairs shower-room, declared
himself quite happy to have sole occupancy of the house for
thirty-six hours. Having mastered the washing machine, and

expressed horror at the absence of a tumble dryer, he even promised to help Burble – or perhaps compel Burble – to finish off the bramble for good, motivating him with the promise of a bonus.

'I liked the kid,' he declared through the game pie I'd forced myself to make with Burble's birds and had frozen for just such an unexpected lunch as this. 'Did his best with my bike, though I'm not convinced he learned all his skills honestly. What's his background?'

'Anything and nothing. I'd say his main problem is lack of stickability, which probably has a proper psychiatric name. He learns quickly, but just when you think you've pressed all the right buttons, you don't see him for a couple of days.'

'Don't you indeed? We'll see about that.'

SEVEN

Our thirty-six hours of R and R were always over all too soon. I revelled in the warmth of the apartment, the furniture I'd chosen, the pictures I'd bought from artist friends, and once Theo had shaken off the guilt he always brought with him, he enjoyed them too, probably even more than I did. There was the spectacular sight of London, Lord's particularly, spread out before us; the rectory must have been the only house in Kent not to have a view from any window. Here we could oversleep or pad off mother-naked to get breakfast to eat in bed without fear of Mrs Mountford knocking at the front door and peering through the letter box to see why we didn't respond instantly to her summons. All visitors could be screened by the charming security staff in the foyer if you asked them; since I was now away from home so much – and what a Freudian slip that is! – I made it a firm request. Today, having had a leisurely shower, with as much hot water as we wanted, we lunched with an old friend who flashed credit cards, expertise and promises of equipment with equal ease, punctuating the conversation with delicious gossip. We had a mid-afternoon slot at the latest exhibition – as a Tate Friend I could get us a quiet preview time – and then the most superb concert rounded off by an uninterrupted late supper *à deux*.

The only thing to alarm me in the whole break was a quiet word from Ravi, who wore his security uniform as seriously as he took his responsibilities, as we left for Kent: 'Doctor Harcourt, someone was asking the other day if you lived here.'

'If?'

'Quite. An odd question, I thought. So I put on my most pompous voice and told him that it wasn't our policy to disclose the identity of any of our residents, nor to confirm or deny that they were indeed residents.' He grinned. 'I pretended I was playing Jeeves.'

'One day, Ravi, one day. If not playing Jeeves, you'll soon be back on the stage where you belong.'

'I hope so, Doctor Harcourt. Though I must say this place is wonderful for people-watching.'

I always dragged my feet as we returned to the cold village and colder rectory. This time I was more than reluctant: I simply dreaded the moment.

There was no reason, of course. Dave would have kept an eye on things; his presence was better than any burglar alarm, all the upgraded locks. And he'd have kept the central heating going full blast, if I knew him.

He'd done more. At eight-fifty the kitchen already smelt of fresh ironing. Not only was the bramble gone, but the garden now had a couple of official beds, newly dug. As Theo headed to his study to pick up phone and email messages and I carried our overnight bag upstairs, Dave erupted through the front door, talking loudly to someone whose voice was so quiet I could hardly hear it.

Dumping the bag on the landing, I ran down again to resume my daily triage duties. Theo's time was spread so thinly that people couldn't just barge in and demand to see him. I had to filter them – like a doctor's receptionist – or he'd never get to see the parishioners in urgent need. A bereavement had to trump someone wanting a bit of theological chat over why God had allowed the latest natural disaster, important though such issues were to the person concerned.

But Dave said this woman wanted to talk to me, not Theo. 'Burble's mum,' he said in an aside, as she hesitantly introduced herself as Sharonammond, running the two names together into one continuous strip of sound.

I sat her down in the kitchen, pressing on her coffee and shop-bought biscuits. It was almost impossible to put an age to her – she could be anything between forty and sixty, though given that she had a son in his teens the former was more likely. She was so thin I suspected anorexia. Her hair was colourless and thinning; her teeth were as poor as her complexion. Burble had never mentioned she was ill – had snubbed me when I'd mentioned her at all. And I'd never found a chance to press him, however gently, again. What about his father, too? Domestic skills, people skills – despite my years telling senior management exactly what their multimillion-pound businesses needed, I had such a lot to learn, didn't I? Especially as I hadn't a clue how to put the poor woman sufficiently at ease for her to tell me what she wanted. She sank the awful coffee as if it was nectar, but although she couldn't keep her eyes off the biscuits, she accepted only one, as if in response to a long-ago instruction to remember her manners.

At last I found myself asking point-blank, 'Is Burble all right?'

She blinked hard. Then it seemed to dawn on her. 'Burble? Oh, you mean Bernard. Named after my grandfather. I call him Bernie. But he made so much noise as a kid – you know how they won't shut up – I used to yell at him not to burble on so, and he seemed to think it was his name, so that's what his mates call him. And he still won't shut up. I tell him sometimes, why don't you just shut the fuck up? But the little bastard always has a bit of cheek for me. Mind if I smoke?' She produced a battered pack, her hands shaking so much I was almost inclined to say I didn't.

But I did. Very much, in fact. 'Burble always smokes out here in the back garden,' I said, getting to my feet. 'Do you want to see what he's been up to? He's achieved so much.'

I might have been asking her to fly.

'Thing is, you been paying him, right?' The cigarette crept reluctantly back into the packet.

'Oh, Lord, I haven't messed up his dole, have I?' The blood rushed to my cheeks as if I was a teenager again. I sat down.

'Just wondering if . . . if, like, you owed him anything. So I could give it him,' she added in a rush.

I was about to embark on a probably boring explanation that I'd not seen him when Dave materialized.

'I paid him in full yesterday, Mrs Hammond. Didn't he tell you?' he said implacably, resting his hands firmly on my shoulders. It may have looked like an affectionate, cousinly gesture, but there was also no way I could reach, as I'd intended, for my purse.

Not surprisingly the poor woman quailed. 'Just wondering. You know.'

'Yes. I do know. So I'm sorry, Mrs Hammond, we don't owe him anything. And of course, since he's an adult in the eyes of the law, we could only pay him direct in any case,' Dave declared, almost lifting me to my feet so I could – had to – usher her out.

Theo emerged from his study just as I turned to Dave, wringing my hands. 'I could have given her something anyway. I wouldn't have missed it!'

'On the contrary,' Theo said, 'Dave was quite right. If you'd given her money, sweetheart, it would have gone straight on drugs. Giving an addict food's one thing, but it's so dangerous to give cash. Right, Dave?'

'Right. I just hope she doesn't have to earn it on the streets. She needed her fix, that one. I don't think you noticed the needle tracks all over her arms, did you, Jode?'

I shook my head. 'It never occurred to me to look. But you didn't need to pay Burble, Dave, that's my responsibility.'

'As it happens, I didn't. He worked for an hour yesterday, no more. Then he said he'd see you this morning, soon as he got up. And he buggered off – noon, I suppose.'

'After what passes for him as a full day's work,' Theo laughed sadly.

'He did say he had another errand to do as it happens. Photos. You were a bit trusting to lend him that camera, by the way, Jode – a couple of grand there, just waiting to be nicked. Or more likely, from what I've seen, for his mum to get her hands on and flog.'

Theo nodded. 'I hope she doesn't – she could get more than enough heroin or whatever to kill her.'

'What do you actually know about Burble?' Dave asked. 'I know he's not keen on anyone meeting some of his mates,' he added ominously.

'Very little. He was just drifting past when I needed a hand and he gave it to me. So it was just a spot of casting one's bread upon the waters,' I said, trying not to sound as defensive as I felt.

'Jodie's managed to uncover a side of that young man which

no one seems to have found before,' said Theo, in a suspiciously pulpity voice.

'Someone ought to have,' I said shortly. 'If only he'd been allowed to burble more – he probably got clouted into silence – he might have done a lot better at school and not got into bad company. He's got an unexpected way with words sometimes – it quite takes one aback. He said you looked like a large badger, Dave.'

'Without the TB, one hopes,' he said, running his hands over his black and grey hair.

The next female to present herself at the front door also wanted me. From her very strong facial resemblance to my new running partner, I gathered before she even spoke that she was Mazza's sister. It turned out her name was Martina. I wondered – but not aloud – whether someone in her family had wanted her to be a great tennis player. Curiously her nickname was Sian. Maybe one day I'd get the back story. But clearly not now.

''Bout this website,' she said, 'for the village and that. Mazza reckons I can't do it. I reckon I can. With a bit of help,' she added, honestly if not quite audibly.

'Shouldn't you be at school?' I asked, stepping aside to let her in.

'Suspended,' she said, wiping her spike-heeled boots carefully. I wasn't sure if the ladders in her tights were intentional. She didn't have any piercings and her hair was a reassuringly natural-looking blonde, so I deduced she was neither punk nor Goth. 'Only a couple of weeks,' she continued, pulling down her crop-top in case a clergyman's wife might be embarrassed by the sight of a navel. 'But they were teaching me fuck all and—'

'Uh, uh. Mazza should have told you about my no-swearing rule.'

She looked me full in the eye. 'I thought that just meant blokes. 'Cos I heard that old bugger Vesey saying you swore like a trooper. Which means like Burble, doesn't it?' Before I could even attempt to explain the difference between Vesey's perception of swearing and mine, she added, ultra-casually,

'He seems to have fucked off somewhere again. Not answering his phone, little sod. Sorry.'

'Burble? He makes a bit of a habit of it, doesn't he? Perhaps he's off foraging.' Deep down I knew I mustn't ask point blank if he was her boyfriend, but I could tinge my next comment with a hint of sympathetic enquiry. 'It must drive his mates mad.'

She agreed that it did. In as many words. Or perhaps a few more, by way of embellishment. 'Not that you want to know about his mates. Some of them,' she added hurriedly.

'What's the problem with them?' I asked crassly.

'Oh, you know . . . But this website, miss?'

I could have told her that I couldn't help her with her computer skills just yet, because Theo needed his lunch. But I saw no reason why the two men couldn't bond over a raid on the fridge, and every reason to get busy while she still had the urge to learn.

Half an hour later, I turned to her. 'Do they know at your school how good you are – and might become?'

'Don't know shit, that school. And they can't teach shit, neither. They just stand there yelling at us to keep quiet. Mind you,' she added, as if determined to be fair, 'that's all I could do with some of them monsters. Not just the blokes. The girls too. Talk about fucking tarts! I'll swear one of them was sucking this kid off in the back of the class last time I was there. And filming it on her phone.' She caught my eye. 'Sorry. That's swearing too, isn't it?' She squared her shoulders. 'Now, thing is, Jodie, I can't spell. They did these dyslexia tests – don't worry about that, because if it is, it means extra money or something for the school, like people having free dinners. But it's not dyslexia. It's just I wasn't there very much when I should have been learning. So I need you to put the words in right.'

'Uh, uh. You do it and use the spell check. What do you want to type?'

'Apart from what a crap place it is?'

'It's very pretty,' I began. Actually, it was. Despite myself, I had to admit that.

'Who wants to live in a picture postcard?'

The answer rang strong and true in my head: *I don't!* But

I didn't let it out. 'Perhaps we should be thinking in terms of what might bring visitors here. Once we've got money coming in, then the community should flourish and be able to afford facilities—'

She stared outside, pointing. 'Look, there's another one!'

'Another one what?'

'Another flying pig, of course. The only folk wanting to come here are illegal immigrants or people from Eastern Europe wanting the jobs and undercutting our wages. Not that there are any jobs, of course.' She punctuated her BNP rant with as many expletives as Burble. So much for my dearly held belief that the young were liberals at heart. I'd have to try to persuade her to share my *Guardian*-reader's creed at a later date. 'And if there was any money, you can bet your life they wouldn't spend it reopening the youth club. And they couldn't anyway, not without a youth leader.'

A youth leader! That was another thing on poor Theo's bucket list, another I could pay for and not really notice. But he insisted it must be a benefice effort: until his flock perceived a need, they'd resent anyone swanning in with a handful of cash, no matter how good the donor thought the cause. I was coming to see that he might be right. Perhaps if the kids did a good job on the website, I might be able to point not just our PCC but all the other PCCs in that direction.

Might.

Eventually, largely because I was about to fall into despair as deep as hers, we agreed on some safe headings: the school, the church, the people, and so on. I floated the idea of campaigning to save the village shop – or more accurately, move it into the church.

'So we need pics of the shop, and of Violet. Oh, and the church and where the shop might go. Got a camera, Miss?'

'Burble's borrowed mine. But Mazza's phone's pretty good. So why not join forces with him? The light's not bad now; why not spend a couple of hours snapping?'

'I thought he was running with you? You missed yesterday, he said. Had to go out on his own.' She made it sound as if I'd made him walk barefoot in penance to Canterbury Cathedral.

Or perhaps that should be me, for letting him down. 'We

could all three run?' As if. 'Have you got a phone like his?'
I tried, ever hopeful. 'No? You could tell him you're borrowing
his while we're out running; there's not a lot of coverage on
the route we take.'

'Tell?' Her eyebrows shot up. 'Suppose I could try,' she
conceded.

I set a pace that left Mazza with too little breath to moan
about lending his kid sister his most prized possession. We'd
had a minor disagreement about the previous day's arrangements, or rather lack of them, but when he got to the sulky
gravel-kicking stage, accompanied by, 'I just thought . . .',
Dave and I lost patience and set off without, it has to be said,
the proper warm-ups. I wouldn't even let us pause for breath,
not until I'd got to the top of the hill from which we could
look down on the valley once filled with trees and now clearly
a building site.

A big building site. Occasionally the rumble of the heavy
plant carried all the way up here, though some birds were
blithely ignoring it. One day I'd learn to identify them.

Dave goggled. 'If anyone ever asked me what an eyesore
was, I'd point them at that. What on earth's going on there,
Mazza?'

'Shit knows.'

Dave didn't seem to move, but there was suddenly no doubt
that he was six foot five tall. 'When I want swearing, I want
it at the right time and in the right place – and I want it more
original than that. When you're old enough, kid, I'll give you
some lessons. Meanwhile, I asked a civil question. What's
going on down there, Mazza?'

'Replacement for Dungeness Nuclear Power Station?' he
snarled sarcastically.

Dave clapped him on the shoulder. 'That's better. So you
don't know either. Hmmm. I wonder how they got planning
permission for that. Assuming they did. Any idea whose land
it's on?'

Mazza swallowed, his Adam's apple suddenly active. 'Sorry,
I don't. But there's a track down.' He pointed at a faint
sheep-trail.

Dave shook his head. 'With grass as thick and slippery as that you'd need proper walking boots, not light shoes like these. Another day.' He picked up as quickly as I did what Mazza wasn't saying. 'Trouble is, I've not got my boots with me. And Theo's wouldn't fit, always assuming he's got any, that is. Fancy a trip to Ashford Outlet, lad? There's a shop there often does two pairs for the price of one and I've only got two feet.'

Mazza looked at me sideways under his lashes. Now what? Was he checking if it was all right by me for him to go and have a boys' day out? Or was he . . . surely he couldn't suspect Dave's intentions? But why not? A good-looking biker with something of the Freddie Mercury about him and no female in tow?

And what did I know, who'd only caught up with him at family gatherings?

'Sounds good to me,' I said. 'Look, I'm due in Ashford with Theo at five. We could drop you off at the Outlet and pick you up on our way back.'

I set a smacking pace homeward, so once again neither had any breath to argue.

We reached Ashford a little later than I'd arranged with the dealership, not because of our run, but because of some parochial business that took Theo longer than he'd intended. In front of the others he couldn't tell me the problem; I suspected, since he drove like Jehu, that it might involve Mrs Mountford or one of her allies. I just hoped that side-taking wouldn't lead to outright schism.

But the outing itself was successful: a new bike for Theo, the car for me, and boots for Dave and Mazza. I even popped a coffee-machine on my credit card. So there was a lot that was good to look forward to. That evening I celebrated by buying a leaf-blower cheap on eBay. Really, really cheap. So cheap it brought a smile to Theo's face and would possibly do the same to George's. I hoped so. He was one villager I was really coming to like. And I suspected – very much hoped – he and his wife were coming to like me.

Even I had to admit that running in Thursday's driving rain wouldn't be pleasurable, and Dave vetoed the expedition down the steep valley he and Mazza had promised themselves until they'd walked their new boots in. In any case, the large-scale maps of the area Dave had ordered online still hadn't arrived. Clearly – and to Mazza's obvious frustration – Dave was taking this very seriously indeed.

There was no sign of Burble, of course – if gardening in fine weather wasn't his idea of heaven, working in the wet was probably his idea of purgatory. I sorted out the insurance for my new Audi, tackled the housework and set myself the challenge of working through some of Merry's cookery books.

Friday and Saturday brought a load of photos, the combined efforts of Sian and Mazza on Mazza's phone, and the arrival of my car. The bell ringers put in an extra couple of hours' work on Saturday afternoon, their efforts recorded by my contact and put on the brand new village website. Sian and Mazza worked in comparative harmony as they cropped their photos and adjusted colour and structure, rightly proud of the result. The site was almost up and running.

All we were waiting for now was Burble – plus my camera and a lot more photos.

EIGHT

By Monday evening there was still no sign of Burble, although the weather had improved enough for him to do more work in the garden had he been that way inclined. Without exactly telling us that he was postponing his departure, Dave let it be understood that he'd mind our house again while we took our precious day off.

No one, least of all me, said anything about Burble's protracted walkabout, but I was certain the men were as worried as I. Mazza and Sian had condemned him roundly for pushing off (or words to that effect) just when he was needed, and for refusing to answer his hamster-wheel phone, but hadn't evinced any concern, either for his safety or for the fate of my camera. Burble was clearly doing what Burble did.

But Burble didn't usually have a nice cashable asset with him. He'd probably not get the full value if he sold it, but a kid with nothing wouldn't mind if he got a cool thousand, would he? Even five hundred.

Halfway through Tuesday afternoon, just as we emerged from an overcrowded British Museum exhibition, Theo said, 'You'd rather be back home, wouldn't you, sweetheart?'

Yes, yes, yes – even if it wasn't home. 'To prepare for tomorrow evening's meeting about the shop in the church?'

'Uh, uh. To see if Burble's back. You've been checking your phone every half hour; I take it you're hoping against hope for a message.' He cleared his throat. 'Sometimes one has to face unpalatable truths – I did when I was a teacher, and I still do. Humans are weak and fallible. Sometimes they reward our trust a thousandfold; sometimes they let us – and themselves – down badly. I'm sorry, I truly am. All I can suggest is that you put it down to experience.' He kissed me. 'Have you got enough Monopoly money for us to go and buy a replacement camera?' He gestured: as we stood on the BM steps, we were surrounded by expensive cameras round the necks and in the hands of people from all over the world. Some had seemed to see the whole exhibition through a lens, with accompanying raised elbows or extended arms almost designed to stop others seeing anything.

I smiled at a tourist who was glaring at me for standing in her way. She backed off as sharply as if I'd flourished a machete. 'I could put it on my credit card,' I said mock-seriously. 'The one that makes a donation to Oxfam every time I use it. No, let's give Burble a few more days . . . How long is it before he becomes a missing person?' I tucked my hand into his and set us in motion.

'You'd have to ask Dave. But I suspect that if he's eighteen, he can go where on earth he wants. And with his mother, who could blame him? Provided he'd got hold of some cash legally, of course,' he added gloomily.

I tried to think positive. 'You're assuming he has flogged the camera. He might just have lost it or broken it and be too ashamed to confess. Though I did tell him I could claim on insurance if he did. Big mistake, eh – I practically told him he could nick it.' Clearly this wasn't the place to stand stock still with your hands covering your face. 'Let's go and have a coffee and forget about all this. And assume he'll be back tomorrow, anxious to show off his handiwork. After all,' I added, recalling Theo's new-found love of chamber music, 'there's that Cadogan Hall recital this evening by my old friends; we wouldn't want to miss that.'

Missing an exquisite performance of the first Brahms sextet and the Schubert octet wouldn't have saved Sharon Hammond's life, either.

Mazza and Martina-Sian were sitting at our kitchen table when we got back home. Although Mazza's running had brought a healthy outdoors glow to his skin, today he looked pale. Sian, who was usually exemplary in her make-up, hadn't so much as a slick of mascara and looked as waiflike as her brother. It was all I could do not to gather them to me in a group embrace, but I was sure it would unleash emotions both would rather keep in check.

Dave was watching coffee from our new machine bubble

into first one mug, then another. The toaster was working overtime. Passing them butter and jam, he nodded Theo and me back into the hall, and thence into Theo's study.

'They decided they'd had enough of Burble dossing around in bed when he should have been helping with the website. So Mazza broke in. Poor kid. Found the body – no, not Burble! No sign of *him*. His mother. According to a mate of mine up in Maidstone, there's a load of bad heroin come into the country all of a sudden. Looks as if she might have taken some.'

'When did they . . .?'

'Late last night. They spent a lot of it talking to . . . the police.' He smiled sourly. 'Strange to call them that. Eighteen months ago it might have been me who was the SIO. Senior Investigating Officer,' he added, in case either of us was unfamiliar with the term. 'If I were, I'd probably be telling the coroner it's not really a suspicious death. I wouldn't be setting in motion a huge investigation. Anyway, they both decided that here was where they wanted to be, so they kipped down in the living room and—'

'What time did they arrive?' Theo asked.

'About three. Apparently their mother works nights and they didn't want to be on their own. And before you ask, their mother needs the job and they didn't want her to take time off. So they nominated me as the adult they wanted with them.'

Theo made little rewinding gestures. 'So they rang here as soon as they found . . . Mrs Hammond?'

'Yes. I called the police for them. And went to the police station and stayed with them through everything. Don't look so guilty, Theo – I've probably forgotten more about the procedure than you even know. But it's over to you now – I need to shower and shave.'

He was halfway out of the door when Theo asked what I found I couldn't: 'There's no suggestion, is there, Dave, that Burble could have had any part in this?'

'Not on the basis of what I saw and heard. But one thing's certain – whatever he's up to, wherever he's gone, we need to find him. I suspect there's no love lost between him and his mother – *was* no love lost – but I'd rather he heard the news from one of us, not from one of my overworked mates. Former mates.' Still in the doorway he added, 'Theo, it's none of my business, but I reckon those kids would be better off occupied. It's a sin Sian's not in school, Mazza too, because counsellors apart, there'd be plenty to keep their minds off last night.'

'I'll get on to her head teacher,' Theo said.

'If that's what she wants,' I said, raising a cautionary hand. 'And her mother, of course. But what about Mazza? I don't think he's seen the inside of a school for months. I can't imagine anyone . . . you know, league tables and attendance figures and A-starred GCSEs . . .'

'What about Mazza indeed? You could be about to run a lot of miles, Jode – and if you don't mind my hanging around a bit longer I can get him using those walking boots, too.'

'Mind you hanging round?' Theo said. 'My dear Dave, you're a godsend.'

Dave shrugged off the compliment. 'Burble's mates, Jode. Did you ever meet any? I gather from Sian they weren't the sort you'd invite to tea on the rectory lawn. Not the average rector's wife anyway.' He looked at me quizzically. 'I was just wondering if he might know a few drug-dealers, you see.'

'He must know at least one. The one he bought his cannabis from. A mate, he said. As far as I know he only tried to smoke it here once,' I assured Theo, who'd literally gone white. 'I told him off when he tried to dispose of it in the green bin in case the media got hold of the story.'

'You knew! And condoned it?'

I'd never thought to tell him about my pot-smoking activities when I was younger, because everyone in my group had done it. They'd all have grown out of it, just as I had. Though I might confess later, now certainly didn't seem the time.

'Keep your hair on, mate. It's what kids do, for heaven's sake,' Dave said, putting a very policemanly hand on Theo's arm. 'Come on, you've got a druggy mother, you're likely to be a druggy kid. But nothing Class A, Jode? Come on, it could be important.'

'He certainly didn't take any drugs here, not after the aborted spliff,' I said, stung. 'As for it being a symptom of something more serious, I didn't even realize what was wrong with his mother, did I?' I protested.

'I need you to remember everything – anything – you might have known about his mates. Was he the sort of lad to show off the camera to them? One of them might have . . . well, maybe I'm getting ahead of myself.'

Theo said, 'I've got friends in the Salvation Army – far better than the police for running missing people to earth. I'll phone them now.'

I needed something to do too. 'And I'll go and talk to Violet. I know Sharon Hammond was only distantly related to her, but even so . . . I'll ask her if she knows anything about Burble's absent dad while I'm at it.'

Dave nodded approvingly. 'And I'll talk to an old mucker of mine – but I think I'll do it face to face. I'll have to tell him about your camera, Jode,' he said, almost apologetically.

'I know just what he'll say. I was daft to hand it over, and Burble's just done a flit with it. But you know something,' I said rather too loudly, 'I don't believe he's nicked it. I really don't.'

Dave shook his head kindly. 'Know what I think? We find the camera and we find Burble.'

'It's just surprising she lasted so long, to be honest, God rest her soul,' Violet said briskly, in response to my murmured words of sympathy. 'As for Bernard – Burble – she used to say he was born to be hanged. You know, his own mother says something like that! So God alone knows where he is, and He isn't telling. If only the lad had met someone like you a bit earlier – if only he'd got a few exams behind him.'

'Did no one ever try to improve his life? Social Services? I'd have expected them to worry about his living with a drug addict.'

She looked genuinely shocked. 'How would they have known? No one from the village would have let on – and look at all the mistakes they make, anyway, these social workers.'

I wasn't at all sure which sentiment to tackle first, so ended up giving a feeble – possibly feeble-minded – smile. Yes, I was ashamed of myself. At least I managed, 'I don't suppose you know what happened to his father.'

'Si? Drank himself to death long since, I'd imagine. Or drugs. Total waste of space. We all heaved a sigh of relief when he left the village. Ten years ago it must have been. Maybe longer.'

So poor Burble had been on his own with his mother since then.

'And no one kept in touch with this Si?'

'Why should they?'

If Theo had the Sally Army, for all my ignorance when I saw a real drug user face to face, at least I had a few contacts in drink and drugs rehab: there was one charitable trust I supported that might provide information that wouldn't necessarily reach the authorities. So I fired off a few emails.

When I could drag the kids from the TV they'd colonized, I floated the idea of school. If either was interested, I'd phone their head teachers myself. Sian grumbled, but secretly, I think, was relieved. I left her tweaking the website while I made the call. She didn't need to know the choice words I said to the headmaster about his staff's failure to recognize her IT skills, though she might have been impressed that it was possible to make a strong point without raising one's voice or using a single swear word.

As I'd feared, Mazza had no school to return to, so I was glad when Theo lent Dave his car so they could head off to a coastal path to walk their boots in; Theo retired to his study to pray. Borrowing Dave's newly arrived large-scale maps, I went for a drive in my new toy. But not just any drive, of course.

At one level I was doing what I ought to have done long ago – I was exploring what everyone agreed was one of the most beautiful counties in the country, the Garden of England, no less. Parts of the coast gripped even me, not just the stirring White Cliffs, but places more subtle in their appeal, like the shingle banks round Dungeness. Today, however, I was staying much nearer to home. I picked my way purposefully through blossom-filled lanes, narrow and narrower still, around the steep-sided valley the other side of what I was coming to think of as 'my' hill. To my uneducated eye, there was nothing to show that anything other than farming might be taking place, and plenty to show what I assumed was proper agricultural behaviour. There were picture-book sheep in one field, and horses, all in their own taped-off mini-fields in others. I couldn't pick up any birdsong over the rumble of the low-profile tyres, but I was sure that if I'd stopped and rolled down the window I'd have heard a veritable pastoral symphony of avian melody.

But Mazza, Dave and I had all seen alien activity in that valley. Seen it. Industrial, not agricultural activity. I needed to investigate further. However, I couldn't just drive up the tracks in the right direction, could I? I couldn't press the entryphones of Double Gate Enterprises or Elysian Fields to enquire about illegal building activities. Could I?

Not without someone to watch my back. And not, come to think of it, with all those CCTV cameras ready to take snaps of anyone crossing their path. They'd probably taken mine already, come to think of it. Reversing cautiously, as if I'd simply taken a wrong turn, I headed whence I had come, embroidering the mime a little more by pulling over and peering in furious disbelief at the satnav screen.

On the way home – and funnily enough I found myself checking my rear view mirror just in case, though I never admitted to myself what it was just in case of – I called in to see Mazza and Sian's mother, Carrie, a woman of about forty whose plumpness owed more, I suspected, to the wrong food than simply to too much. I'm sure Merry would have known exactly what to say. And bring. Of course, I hadn't got a cake or anything. Should I have done? Or would bringing one have seemed patronizing? We smiled at each other appraisingly as I introduced myself.

'I was just wondering if Sian is OK, Mrs Burns? And Mazza, of course,' I began. Give me a PowerPoint presentation to make to a CEO any day. 'After last night.'

'They could have called me. Should have. You'd best come in. Cup of tea?'

'Only if you're making one.'

I braced myself for the sort of cliché that some of the media tell you to expect in social housing homes, or even the Dickensian poor-but-honest converse. In the event it was neither foul with unwashed pots nor so clean you could have eaten your supper off the floor. There weren't many books, true, but neither was the living room dominated by a huge TV. There was one, but it was smaller than ours, and she switched it off as she moved a pile of freshly ironed sheets from the sofa and asked me to sit.

The ensuing conversation was no more inspiring than the opening lines, but we somehow established a mutual trust. She was afraid her kids were bothering me; I assured her they weren't, that I really liked their company. We talked a bit about Mazza's running; she worried about clubs and the cost of shoes and so on. Clubs! He really had got the bug then. Lying through my teeth I told her most clubs had sponsors who paid for the gear for talented members; I made a mental promise to keep him in footwear wherever Theo's job might take us. As for Sian, I could reassure her that the girl had academic and tech-nological ability the school must develop. I suspected, I said, that she'd only played up so much because she was bored.

We parted with a cautious hug. It was only as I headed down the path to the car that she said, 'That Burble. Any news of him yet? Only I hear on the grapevine that one of the local dealers has taken off fast.'

'Burble *deals*?' I asked, too horrified to keep my voice down.

'Not that I know of,' she said, motioning me back to the house. 'I'm just worried – you know what they're like, these bastards. If they thought he couldn't pay, or that all this time he spends at the rectory means he's going to blab . . . Well, you never know, do you?'

'Did you see much of him?'

She gave a crooked smile. 'Too much, sometimes. But before I got this job, there were times – well, to be honest, I couldn't always put food on the table. And he brought all sorts of strange foraged stuff. A lot of it went in the bin, mind you, but it was the thought, wasn't it?'

'It was indeed. When did you last see him?'

'Let me think . . . A week ago? And him not knowing about his mum. Not that he'd care much, I dare say.'

'Did he ever talk to you about her?'

She pulled a face: what was she about to say? But then she looked beyond me, and I turned to see Sian, in what I can only call a vague approximation of school uniform, coming round the corner. 'Look at that muck all over your face, my girl – I'm surprised at the school letting you in like that. You go and get yourself cleaned up, missy, or I'll know the reason why. And before I go to work we'll go to Tesco's and buy a skirt that's halfway decent.'

Now was obviously not the time to ask Sian about her afternoon – but I sensed a great deal of love in that ongoing rebuke.

NINE

Tonight there was to be the follow-up PCC meeting about the shop's move to the church. We had an early supper, because I suspected that the meeting might run very late. Once again it would be held in the rectory dining room.

'How do you think it will go?' Dave asked, as we cleared the kitchen table at which we'd eaten.

'Well, I hope— drat! I'd better take that.' Theo put down the tea-towel, and went off to answer the phone.

'I think poor Theo's got some sticky tape to cover my mouth,' I said, squirting washing-up liquid. 'But I'll try to be professional and simply minute everyone else's ideas.'

'It'd be fun to make up a few, wouldn't it?' Dave began.

'I'm afraid she won't be able to do that this evening,' Theo interrupted him, returning to his tea-towel. 'That was Mrs Baker to say her arthritic hand was better, and she would be present to minute the PCC meeting. I'm so sorry, Jodie: I can imagine how much you wanted to be present.'

I managed an insouciant shrug. 'They'll speak more freely without me. And no one will be able to accuse me of trying to influence any voting. So long as that poor arthritic hand of hers can manage to open the wine bottles and fill the glasses.'

Undeceived, he gathered me into his arms. 'I'd no idea how much you were investing in this. Not money. But will and desire. Commitment to the future.'

I was ready to protest that I was doing it for him. But it dawned on me that I was doing it for other people too – Burble and Mazza and Sian, for instance, and all the other villagers I'd not yet met; even, perhaps especially, for those who'd never have dreamt of going into a lovely building but would now buy their stamps there. Perhaps something would, in Theo's phrase, rub off.

With an exhausted Dave for company, I adjourned to the living room, defiantly turned on another bar of the electric fire (to turn the central heating up might provide enough comfort to prolong the meeting) and poured rather better wine than the PCC would be getting.

'I'd just barge in if I were you,' Dave said, as I looked at my watch for the umpteenth time. 'Your idea, your effort – you should be in on the final call.'

'But I'm not a member and I've not been co-opted. And Theo's got to live with the result. And with me. So if I do something to cause problems, they'll come back not on my head but on his.' My would-be smile might have been a grimace. 'At the risk of sounding as if I'm changing the subject, has Mazza got any theories about Burble's disappearance?'

He snorted. 'If all Mazza's theories are as sound as the one he had about me, I wouldn't build too much on any of them. He's got the idea I must be gay, and possibly predatory with it, on account of not having a wife and getting on well with my cousin.'

Swallowing the slight question mark I'd raised myself, I said mildly, 'He's probably not had much adult male company before – doesn't know how to take it. Probably very few male role models in his life at all.'

'Even so – how would you have felt being asked if you were a lesbian?' He stood. The room shrank.

'It would surprise me, given my married state. But it wouldn't be a problem.' Though I suppose it might be if you'd spent your life being a macho policeman. 'There was one accusation that hurt, however: the villagers thought I was a banker!'

He put his head back and roared with laughter. 'My God, how did you get out of that one?'

'Evidence: I'd already ditched the Porsche. And I told Mazza the truth.'

'What? All of it?' He frowned. 'Your annual income, for instance?'

'Hell's bells, no – what do you take me for?'

Before he could answer, the door opened and Theo came in. His shoulders were shaking so much I was afraid for one dreadful moment he was in tears. Perhaps he was. Tears of laughter. He leant on the back of the sofa.

'Poor Mrs Baker's hand can't cope with the speed at which she's required to write. I don't suppose you'd care to help out, my loved one? Oh, bring your glass with you. We'll be stopping for refreshments any moment now.'

'Don't go,' Dave urged, already reaching for the TV zapper. 'They made their bed – let them lie in it.'

'I'd guess that Mrs Mountford made this particular bed – and I've no desire, sexual orientation apart, to share it with her!' I darted back for my wine, which Dave had obligingly topped up, and for the pad and biro we kept beside the phone.

'What was all that about?' Theo asked, waiting for me in the hall.

'I'll tell you later. Or better still, Dave will.' I kissed him before following him into the dining room. Taking the tediously apologetic Mrs Baker's place, slightly behind George Cox, who was chairing the meeting, I prepared to become demurely secretarial.

There was a loud knock on the door, Dave putting his head round it simultaneously. 'Theo, I'm sorry to interrupt but the police are on the phone – won't let me take a message, of course.'

Theo went white. His eyes held mine: this was going to be really bad news, wasn't it? He put a hand on George's shoulder. 'Just carry on.'

It was hard to concentrate, let alone take notes, although it was clear that the meeting was going what I still thought of as my way. A glance at Mrs Baker's beautiful if shaky writing – unlike my scrawl, vile and shapeless after years of using nothing but some sort of keyboard or another – told me that at the start it looked as if Mrs Mountford's cohort had the edge, despite the absence of Ted Vesey, who'd sent apologies. What on earth could have kept him from what he knew was a very important meeting? Now, however, wasn't the moment to speculate. But as each report was presented, from Violet's impassioned plea to the calm tones of the diocesan office, it was clear that more and more people wanted to have an open church. And if accommodating the much-needed shop was the only way

forward, so be it. Any moment now, George ought to wrap
things up by calling for a vote – but he wouldn't want to
do so without Theo. On the other hand, he probably
wouldn't want to lose impetus by adjourning the item and
moving on to the matter of the website, a late addition to
the agenda.

Theo's return resolved the situation before it could become
a crisis. His face showed both relief and exasperation. He
raised a quizzical eyebrow in my direction before asking
George's permission to speak.

'Goodness knows why the police needed to speak to me in
person: they only needed to tell me that they thought they'd
found my old bike. And a couple of others, so brace yourselves
for "urgent" calls too.' He gestured ironic quotation marks.
As he sat, he produced a weary smile. 'OK. Where have you
got to?'

'I was just about to call for a vote, Theo – if we need such
a formal measure.' George smiled around the table, making
sure he included me, to whom I'll swear he added a wink.

I suspect Theo was going to suggest that we did, but someone
else was louder and quicker.

'I certainly want my opposition put on record,' Mrs
Mountford declared, glaring at those whom she suspected of
changing sides. 'So perhaps Mrs Welsh would be kind enough
to note not just the numbers but also the identities of those
voting.'

'Overruled,' George declared. 'We are a committee; we
behave as a committee; we take committee responsibility.
Just a show of hands, please. All those in favour? Against?
Abstentions?'

As I dutifully wrote down the results, trying to suppress the
smile of triumph on my face, George leant back in his chair.
'As if anyone ever bothers to read the minutes, apart from us,
that is. And sometimes, when we're asked to approve them at
the next meeting, I really doubt if any of us has read them.'
He knew as well as I did that minutes were a legal require-
ment, but I took his point.

He returned his attention to the rest of the committee, saying,
'And now item twelve on the agenda: the village website. I'd

like to thank and congratulate all involved in getting St
Dunstan's on to it. I thought the wording of the appeal for the
fabric was particularly effective against the vivid pictures of
the cracks.'

'I don't recall our giving permission for any of this,' Mrs
Mountford said.

'Julie Cole and the parish council authorized the village
site; it only took a phone call. As to St Dunstan's presence,
how could we have a village site that didn't mention the
church?' Theo asked, quite deliberately avoiding the question,
which was a valid one, after all.

'It seems . . .' began a middle-aged man whom I saw so
rarely it took a moment to recall his name. Tim Robins, that
was it, breaking his apparent vow of silence. 'It seems terribly
sad that to access the St Dunstan's pages one has to go to the
village site. Our own might just have been preferable.'

'It was cheaper to have just the one,' I said. 'And quicker.
If you're prepared to authorize funds for a second domain, I'll
happily separate them. Unless you happen to think that the
church should in fact be at the heart of the village?'

Jackie Simmons, the normally silent treasurer, suddenly
emerged from behind her sheet of hair: 'Could someone remind
me when we approved payment?'

'You've got me there, Jackie,' Theo said affably. 'I paid out
of my own pocket.'

He'd done no such thing, of course, but I didn't see anyone
challenging him. So I added cheerfully, 'I gave him a considerable discount for cash. Actually, all the work was done by
volunteers. All we had to pay for was registering the domain
name: twenty-four pounds, valid for two years.'

'I note the term "we", Mrs Welsh,' Mrs Mountford said. 'Whom
do you mean by "we"? And who were these volunteers?'

'I should imagine they were those splendid young people
who've been dashing round the village taking photos,' Alison
Cox said, with a wink. Did she and George spend their evenings
together communicating with their eyelids? 'Did they help
build the website – or whatever the correct term is? Such a
good idea to fill their time with something constructive. Well
done, Jodie.'

'There may be one volunteer less, I should imagine,' Mrs Mountford said, 'when they run to earth whoever stole your cycle, Theo. If ever there was an obvious delinquent it's the young man who's been helping in your garden.' Taking the shocked silence as encouragement, she added, 'Did I not hear on the grapevine that the lad has done what I believe is called a runner? Or perhaps that's more directly connected with the sad and very sudden death of his mother.'

Theo didn't exactly slam his hands on the table, nor did he raise his voice. But he radiated anger. 'Are you implying that young Burble is both a thief and a murderer? Because I tell you straight, unless you have any evidence, let alone proof, such an accusation is unworthy of you. Please withdraw it and please don't make it again.'

I would have said a great deal more, including a firm recommendation that she leave the meeting and indeed my home. Preferably for ever. But then, Theo was the professional Christian, and I just did my best.

George turned to me, laying a firm hand on my notepad. 'I don't see the need to minute any of this, Jodie, from beginning to last. Let Alison's congratulations be noted, however. Is there any other business?'

Elaine raised a hand. 'Just a point of information, George. The WI will be holding a special meeting tomorrow—'

'Not the blessed WI and its excess of confectionery again,' someone from the Vesey cohort muttered rather too audibly.

Elaine flushed with what looked like a mixture of anger and embarrassment, but she turned his rudeness to her advantage. 'The excess of confectionery, as you so eloquently put it, is going to be channelled into helping the pub to survive, thank you very much. What Jodie said about church visitors needing somewhere to eat struck home. We're hoping to come to an agreement with Suze—'

'That would be the esteemed Mrs Fellows, as well-met as her name implies,' yawned Mrs Mountford, inspecting her nails.

By now Elaine was scarlet. 'I'm not sure what you're implying by that, Mrs Mountford, but to continue, we are hoping to come to an agreement with Suze to provide morning coffee and afternoon teas in the Pickled Walnut. Thank you, George.'

'Thank *you*, Elaine. I hope your sterling efforts will be sampled by all here. Do let us know if there's to be an official opening, won't you? We'll all want to be there. And now, Theo, I wonder if you'd be kind enough to wrap up our meeting with a prayer?'

TEN

Mazza appeared at the rectory at nine on the Thursday morning: he must have thought it a truly ungodly hour. I sensed his mother's influence, and maybe a well-directed shove out of the door, but perhaps I misjudged him.

'Thing is, Jodie, I was thinking maybe we could go and talk to the filth. Now his mum's gone, and she was fucking rubbish as a mum, you gotta believe me, there's no one to report him missing, like.'

I put my hand on his shoulder. 'Don't you think Dave's already done all he can to interest what I think we ought to call the police? After all, Dave was an officer himself,' I added, ambiguously. 'And Theo's been in touch with the Salvation Army.'

'I'll bet the *police*,' he began, now angry with me too, 'think he's done his mum in and legged it.'

'I don't imagine so for a minute.' It was time to treat him as an adult. 'The timings don't work for a start. According to Dave's contacts, forensic pathology suggests that she died well after anyone last saw Burble. What I think they suspect is that he nicked my camera and did a runner, and that it's pretty much my fault for giving him the means to get out of the village.'

'You're joking. I mean, he'd have guarded that bit of kit with his life, wouldn't he? He's . . . I mean, when people expect you to nick things or smash them up, it's like, why not? You look down your nose at me, I'll really give you something to worry about. But, see, you treated him like a mate. Well, you know . . . He wouldn't want to fuck up. Wouldn't admit it to anyone. But I saw him practising – take a pic, delete it, take another of the same thing, delete it. Takes maybe half a dozen of the same bloody house until he's got one good enough to show you.'

'Which house might that be?' When he just shrugged at

the apparent stupidity of the question, I continued, 'What if he'd just lost it – felt he'd let me down, somehow, and just took off?'

'Nah. Told me how you'd got it insured. But he did say,' he admitted, 'that you were fond of it, like. He was treating it like his baby, Jode, and that's the truth.'

Suppressing a flicker of irritation – only Dave and Theo had ever contracted my name like that – I nodded. It fitted what I'd briefly seen. 'So what do you think has happened to him?' When he shifted his weight from foot to foot like a kid about to fib, I continued, 'Would it be bad drugs? Or pressure from his dealer?'

'What do you mean, pressure?'

'You tell me. Someone tells me a well-known dealer's done a runner.'

He looked around to check no one could be listening. 'Coincidence, I'd say. Burble didn't really do hard stuff, not any more. Just pot. He's got a mate – that's who he gets his skunk from. And the guy's too spaced out to harm a fly, Jode, honest. He's his own best customer, believe me.'

'I'd like to talk to him.'

His face was so expressive he didn't need to speak.

'He might prefer me to the police, Mazza. Come on. Unless you think Dave might be better?'

'But Dave'd have to tell his police mates, wouldn't he?' He sighed and chewed his lip. 'OK. Pill. Short for Philip – geddit? He drifts past the Walnut about seven some evenings. Drives a yucky green Corsa.' He took a deep breath: this was definitely an end to this part of our conversation. 'Is Dave up for a walk today? Can't use the new boots as an alibi for ever, can he?'

'Actually,' Dave said, appearing over my shoulder, 'you mean excuse. Alibi means being somewhere else so you couldn't have committed a crime. Like Burble, when his mum died.'

Mazza's face froze. But not at having his vocabulary corrected. 'What if,' he said slowly, 'he just stocked up on her stuff and fucked off, knowing it'd kill her?'

Neither Dave nor I spoke.

'Nah,' Mazza answered himself. 'He never hated her. Not

enough to kill her. Just ignored her. Even when she stole his pocket money – yes, his dad used to send him some, years back.'

'His dad?' I exclaimed, grasping at a straw not even my drug charity mates had offered. 'Is he still in touch with him? Mazza, you don't think Burble's gone to see him, do you?'

'Don't see why. Hasn't been in touch for years, so far as I know. Not even birthdays or Christmases. Probably as bad as his mum. Don't know where he lives, in any case. And Burble's still not answering his phone, is he?'

Dave said quietly, 'I guess you'll be too busy for a run today, Jodie.'

Would I indeed? It was news to me.

'What do you say to a decent walk, Mazza – now our boots are walked in, I really haven't any excuse, have I? The forecast's good; we could walk Jodie's running route with a bit of a detour to look at the building activities. Is your phone charged, by the way? We might want to take some snaps.'

They drifted inside talking walk-talk, raiding my pretty well empty kitchen for supplies, no doubt. Which left me no option, really – if I'd been told I was too busy to run, I might as well make use of the hours freed up to do the other sort of run, the supermarket one. Which meant visiting Violet first, to make sure I bought everything I could from her before plunging into BOGOF territory. Or, since I didn't want to be greeted like a cross between Mother Teresa and St Joan, I could always send Theo there instead when he got back from collecting whatever might be left of his newly recovered cycle.

I'd not sorted the Bluetooth connection in the Audi, so I left my phone off. I filled my Sainsbury's trolley with a huge supply of food, as well as a non-stick sauté pan and a wok, neither of which Theo need know about. Was I being overly touchy? Did he really mean to give the impression that the kitchen and indeed most of the house was some sort of shrine to Merry? Those awful pans . . . the dingy crockery . . . At least I'd turned the thin grey tea-towels into dusters without his noticing. To be fair, I'd had rapturous praise when I'd bought bales of thick fluffy towels, though of course I now had the concomitant problem of where to dry them on wet washing days. No tumble dryer, remember, and nowhere to put one either.

Only after I'd loaded the car did I switch the phone on again, to watch wide-eyed as a stream of texts appeared. The gist was I must be back in the village by noon. Must, must, must! Theo added nothing more, so I spent the journey worrying about the reason for the urgency. Surely if Burble had turned up he'd have told me. Or if he'd been found . . . dead? No, that'd be a face-to-face job, wouldn't it?

My new best friend the satnav told me the M20 was blocked by an accident and that the A20 was struggling to cope. How about some nice empty country roads? For the next few minutes, if I hadn't been worried sick, I'd have been in car bliss.

Theo was waiting for me on the doorstep, just like a Victorian papa for an errant daughter. He was also extremely smart, dog-collar agleam against a royal blue shirt. He grabbed my car keys. 'I'll unload. Get into smart casual and put on some make-up if you want. We've got five minutes.'

He'd already turned the car and was ready to drive by the time I reappeared. 'You look lovely, sweetheart. Beautiful. Just what the TV cameras will lurve.'

So here I was, being filmed for TV. Fifteen minutes of fame. Rather less after the edit, of course. I talked about the shop's move to the church: why the shop needed new premises, and why the church was in desperate need of an income. I plugged the website as a means of giving to the church appeal. And then we all adjourned to the Pickled Walnut, opened specially for the occasion, according to Suze, the landlady. It was in fact, I suspect, to take sensible advantage of the desire of the assembled media – well, one agency reporter and Dilly Pound, a BBC South East news reporter in her thirties, and her silent cameraman – for food and drink. Perhaps Suze had summoned assistance from Elaine: there were elegant canapés as well as rather too hefty sandwiches.

As I took a glass of champagne – on the house, it seemed – I thanked goodness that Theo had made me change; I might not be as young and beautiful as Dilly, but at least my clothes and my make-up declared I knew my place in the world.

Apparently pleased with the way the piece had gone, Dilly was as friendly and affable off-screen as she was on, though when she was off-guard her face was unexpectedly sad.

'And you've only been married two months?' she asked with a dimpled smile, over the champagne. 'And you've lived here . . .?'

'Two months. Living in sin – what a wonderful old-fashioned term! – isn't really an option for a clergyman, is it?'

Her face dimmed. What had I said? But she straightened her shoulders. 'I suppose not.' You could see her bracing herself until the smile returned. 'So here you are, as we said, living in this blissful place and doing good works.'

I laughed. 'You make me sound like a heroine in an improving Victorian novel.'

'Not *Middlemarch*, I trust,' Theo observed, edging towards us and taking my hand. 'My Jodie might be as lovely as Dorothea but I hope I'm not a Casaubon!'

'Surely you'd be more like the handsome rector – or is he just a vicar? – in *Candida*,' Dilly declared, fluttering her long eyelashes at him.

He moved to put his arm round my shoulders. It felt protective rather than possessive. 'The Reverend Morell, fighting for my marriage as Eugene Marchbanks dallies with my wife? My lovely wife's wonderful with some of the village's disaffected youth, but I don't think any of them has got round to wooing her with poetry.'

They'd lost me a couple of sentences ago, but at least I could pick up on the cue about young people. 'I dare say they're tweeting about me even as we speak,' I joked. And then I couldn't smile. 'Apart from the lost one, that is.'

'A lost parishioner? That sounds very biblical, Theo. Can I expect to do a piece about you: the pastor carrying home the wayward sheep on your shoulders?'

It was as if someone had rolled me in snow. I could see a modern male Pietà: a weeping Theo carrying in his spread arms Burble's body, head and legs lolling in death. Closing my eyes didn't shut out the image. Well, it wouldn't, would it? The image was in my head.

'Be careful what you wish for,' he said, changing emotional gear as quickly as I had. Had he had the same vision? 'Off the record, Dilly, what I really fear is that some other reporter – maybe even you – will be doing a piece to camera about an unknown young man's body being found.'

She switched off flirtatious and became as serious and professional as I could wish. 'What do the police say? I used to have a couple of really useful contacts but they've both retired. Not entirely voluntarily, I have to say.'

'My cousin used to be in the police – he got retired too,' I said. 'The trouble is, Dilly, as I'm sure you've seen in your profession, that if you pare resources to the limit, there's equally a limit as to what you can do. I understand the police are now operating some triage system: they only investigate a crime if they think they can solve it. A teenager goes missing – what's news, when London's so close? A lot of lads of that age want to disappear. That, according to Dave, was the line they fed him when he reported that Burble's not been seen for a week.'

I thought for a moment she was about to faint, and pressed her down on to the nearest banquette. She swallowed hard, took a decided swig of champagne and looked in a business-like way at her watch. 'I've got contacts in the Smoke,' she said briskly, getting to her feet in an easy movement that suggested time in the gym. 'If that's where the police think he might have gone, I'll get my friends to keep their ears open.' She looked from me to Theo. 'But there's more you haven't told me, isn't there? Is there a family angle?'

'His mother died soon after he left home,' Theo said. He didn't go in for euphemisms like 'passed away' or 'is no longer with us'. *Why bother*, he'd once explained, *when I don't think death is anything to be feared?*

'So this poor kid doesn't know . . . What about his dad?'

'He left years ago.' Why were we telling her this?

'Thank God he's got you two then,' she said. She dug in her bag. 'Look, this story's touched me.' As if we couldn't tell. 'Let me know how it ends. If it ends here. Meanwhile, I promise I'll do all I can with my contacts.'

Theo's attention was claimed by someone else. I drifted

outside with her. Her cameraman, sucking deeply on an elec-
tronic cigarette, was engrossed in a phone call.

'Are you sure you're all right, Dilly?' I asked.

'I'm fine. Absolutely fine.'

Or not. 'I thought you were going to pass out in there – and
you can't blame the heat. That business of Burble's disappearance really got to you, didn't it?'

She clutched my hand. 'It's just the thought of someone
. . . anyone . . . dying totally alone. Once—' Her mobile trilled.
'Shit, I've got to take this.' She turned away. I had a clear
sense that she was glad to end our conversation. But at last
the call was over and she looked up to find me still hovering,
although politely out of earshot. Her smile was by now
dismissive: friendly, kind, professional – but dismissive.

It took, however, rather more than a beautiful smile to deter
me. 'Dilly, you mentioned missing person contacts. You
wouldn't have any other contacts who know about building
developments, would you? Local ones, I mean.'

'Would this be something . . .?' She rocked her hand so all
three rings on her engagement finger flashed in the sun. Dodgy,
she meant.

'I think so. But I've really no idea. And since I'm new here,
I don't know who to ask, confidentially at least.'

'These bloody hamlets! Fart and the whole world knows
you've eaten beans!' she exclaimed with an anger that sounded
personal. 'Have you got a card?'

'Here you are.' At least my rustication hadn't completely
dulled my professional edge. 'Or you can always find us via
the church page on the village website.'

ELEVEN

To our post-champagne, lust-filled dismay, within seconds of our return to the rectory, Dave turned up, inclined to be surly. And no wonder: Mazza had waited until two miles into their walk to remark, ultra-casually, that he was supposed to be signing on at the Job Centre.

'As Burble wasn't there to go with him the little bugger wanted to forget it and keep walking,' Dave grumbled into his lager, 'but I told him it was the last he'd see of me if he did. I got him there with three minutes to spare. Anyway, if he's a good boy, etcetera, I'll take him another day. Tomorrow, actually. So I ruined your run for nothing. Sorry.'

'I'd have had the same problem and taken exactly the same action, Dave, so don't worry.'

'Anyway, since it was such a nice day I went back on my own. I didn't have time for the long route I planned, so I took another – just because it was there. If it happened to take me towards that excrescence of a building site, so what? Anyway, nice day, birds singing – actually heard both a cuckoo and a lark, would you believe? – and there I was, walking along, happy as Larry. Not a care in the world. And then,' he said, reaching for his rucksack and grubbing inside, 'I found this. No, don't touch it. It's in my sandwich bag for a reason.' He grabbed my wrist.

'But it's my camera!' I prodded the polythene bag, which he'd turned inside out.

'So is that good news or bad?' Theo asked, his arm tight round me.

'One theory is that he lost Jodie's camera and felt unable to face her. So he scarpered. That might be right.'

'What if it isn't?' I asked, suddenly changing my mind. 'What if . . . Surely, Dave, you must know someone who could – you know, check it over.'

'Looking for what?' Theo asked. 'Blood? Fingerprints? I

can see a bit of a dent. I still cling to your original idea, Jodie – he was so chagrined at having damaged it he simply couldn't face you.'

'But he knew it was insured. He'd have brought it back to me with some rigmarole about how it wasn't his fault. He wouldn't have chucked it away. You should have seen the way he looked at it, handled it. If it's possible to love an inanimate object, at first sight, too, he loved it.' I looked from face to unbelieving face. 'He couldn't wait to use it. And he wasn't just snap-happy, content with rubbish, according to Mazza – he was meticulous. Mazza said he took one house again and again till he was satisfied with the results.'

'Why don't we look at the pictures he took?' Theo said reasonably. 'You've got those lightweight disposable gloves somewhere.'

'In the kitchen.'

He nipped off.

'I used to wear them for cleaning the church brass. That was on the days I had manicures to worry about,' I added ruefully.

'And still should, if you ask me,' Dave chipped back unexpectedly. 'No need to let yourself go, you know, Jodie. Menopausal woman and all that.'

'I beg your pardon?' It was more an explosion than a question.

Theo returned in time to stop a cousinly row. 'Are these the ones? One size?' We separated a pair each. He peered disbelievingly. 'Are they really going to fit Dave and me?'

They did. But though the men were kitted up, I was going to be the one to pick up and examine the camera, which I did as tenderly as Burble had done. Apart from the minor dent on the lens cap, all seemed fine. But it wouldn't let me review what he'd taken. I was ready to exclaim that he must have thrown it down in a fit of pique. Then I read the on-screen message: NO MEMORY CARD.

Stupidly I looked anyway.

The battery was still in place. Well, it had to be, for me to get the message. But the slot beside the battery was empty. I pointed.

'Could it just have fallen out?' Theo asked.

I passed him the camera. 'See if you can make the battery fall out? Go on, a really good shake . . . No? That's why I bought it. Idiot proof.'

'Not that you're an idiot,' Dave said, so sharply Theo blinked at him.

'Was the battery cover open or closed when you found it?' I asked.

'It was just as it was when I gave it to you. So no, I didn't look round for anything – I'd have been hard put to with all that gorse.' He displayed a badly scratched arm. 'But I did mark the spot. Just in case,' he added meaningfully.

'In case this finally interests the police?' Theo asked.

'Quite. Unfortunately, in this economic climate it'll take a lot of information to interest them. Which is why, Jodie, I think you're right about getting it checked. I've got a contact who's a freelance forensic scientist. Let's just get a nice clean polythene bag – you need some more by the way, Jodie. I had the last of the cheese—'

'What a good job she did a supermarket run this morning,' Theo said, in a tone I couldn't quite register.

'Meanwhile, I'll take the camera to my forensic scientist friend. It'll cost you, I'm afraid; she needs to earn a crust.' He paused, possibly embarrassed.

A *her*: ho, ho. I jumped in. 'Whatever it costs, Dave – whatever!'

He nodded, adding casually, 'I'll probably eat with her this evening, so don't wait for me. Or wait up. OK if I take your car, Jodie?'

'Of course. You know where the keys are. Any idea when your motorbike will be back, by the way?'

He looked embarrassed, even shifty. 'Actually I wouldn't fancy leaving it in the open round here,' he confessed. 'It's got every alarm going, but if someone came and picked up the whole thing bodily on to a truck, they'd probably get away with it.'

'Not if you put it in the garage,' Theo said firmly. 'In a village like this Jodie needs wheels, just as I do. Now, I don't mind leaving the Focus out – it'd almost be a mercy if someone

did nick it – but I think you need your own transport. When
it's been repaired, that is. One of us can give you a lift to the
garage whenever you need to pick it up.'

I had a feeling I should have said that. After all, I would
have done if someone had been employing me to say it.
Sometime, somehow, I'd lost my edge, along with my
pampered and painted hands.

Theo had retired to his study with a strong cup of coffee. I
donned some of those gloves and attacked the oven. After all,
I'd sunk too much alcohol to run, and I had to find some other
way of working off excess energy which avoided the villagers,
not all of whom would have been impressed by what some of
them would certainly have inaccurately called a media circus.
There'd be no point in telling them that I'd had nothing to do
with organizing it, and it would be demeaning even to try. If
the young man angling for the contract to install his aunt's
shop in the church had wanted to float the news, then so be
it. I thought he might have been a little premature, but, as I
told the putative vegetable patch, there was nothing I could
do now. And refusing to give an interview would have been
churlish and hurtful to Violet, who no doubt would even now
be telling all her friends to watch the six thirty news.

Which, of course, we did ourselves. The piece about the shop's
move to the church was on, but bumped right down the order
because the lead story was of a raid on a village post office near
Dover. The thieves had brought up an official-looking low loader,
rolled a JCB off it, and then driven the JCB into the front wall
of the post office, scooping out the safe. Then, safe still aboard,
it had trundled back up on to the low loader and been driven
away. The low loader's number plate was illegally but credibly
obscured by mud. And there were no witnesses except the
shocked and outraged post mistress, because all the villagers
commuted out of the village to work. Hmm. That sounded
familiar. So the link between that and our shop's proposed
move to the church was equivocal, to say the least. On the other
hand, they'd got a spokesman from the diocese to comment very
positively; perhaps he had his fingers crossed behind his back.

*   *   *

Tonight was a WI meeting, but since it wouldn't start till seven thirty, I had time to speak to Pill, assuming he and his Corsa were where Mazza had suggested. They were. Uninvited, I got in. The young man, who looked like a young John Lennon, nearly died at the wheel.

'You're Pill – right? No, I'll ask the questions. When did you last see Burble? Did you sell him anything bad?'

'Weed. Only stuff I use myself. Well, some skunk.' He might have been auditioning for the BBC, his delivery was so RP. But he looked even less healthy than Burble.

'Anything stronger? You know his mum died: bad heroin.'

'Shit, no. I never touch chemicals. What about Burble? I've not seen him for a bit.'

'You're sure?'

'He owes me sixty quid, so of course I'm sure.'

'You say you use yourself. Do you grow it yourself? Hydroponics?'

He looked as if he might embark on the sort of paean you'd expect an expert gardener to give on the subject of runner beans.

'Look, Pill, have you heard of this latest pot-detecting device – sniff cards that tell people if someone's growing illicit cannabis in their neighbourhood? Because if I have, other people keen on a reward will have done too.' I let the information sink in. 'Tell me, why start growing something like that in the first place? If you don't nick someone else's electricity, it can hardly be profitable.'

'Someone I knew had MS. Cannabis is great for that.' There was a long pause. I suspected the patient had died. 'And the job situation.'

'What's your background?' I managed not to groan as he told me. 'So you have a biochemistry degree, student debts and no job? Look, Pill, you dry out, right, and kill your plants, and then take this card to the guy whose name's on the back.' I printed clearly. 'Read it back to me. Right. Now, if you haven't contacted him within the week and also got back to me to tell me what job he's offered you and what you've accepted, I shall grass you up – pardon the pun. OK? I said, OK? Seems like a good deal to me. No gaol and a decent job, a reasonable way from here so you get a proper fresh start. My friend will find you accommodation.' I got out of the car but leant back in. 'I didn't hear you say OK. Of course, I could just call the police now.'

'OK.' He checked the card, and added with a smile with a decent hint of humour in it, 'OK, Doctor Harcourt.' Then his voice got cockier. 'Of course, nature abhors a vacuum, doesn't it? So even if – even *when* – I give up, there'll be a dozen others ready to take my place.'

'Not if I have anything to do with it, Pill. Or perhaps from now you should become Philip again. Now, my friend there will check that you do have the qualifications you say you have. Please don't disappoint him. Or me.'

He looked like a kid suspected of stealing sweets. I was asking a lot of him, wasn't I? I'd ask a bit more.

'Who is it dealing heroin round here?'

'I daren't tell you. He might . . . OK, I won't be round here, will I? He just calls himself Wiley. I think that may be his surname. And I fancy his initial's D. But I . . . you know how it is, Doctor Harcourt.'

I did. 'How are you for cash?'

'Eh?'

'You might be short, since you obviously won't have time to collect any drug debts you may be owed.'

He took a deep breath. 'If this mate of yours gives me an advance, I should be OK.' He looked at his hands, as if not quite sure they were his; after a while, he stuck the right one in my direction. 'Thanks. I think.'

'No problem.' I made as if to leave. 'You'll need a new phone. You wouldn't want your old clients to be able to contact you and turn you from the path of righteousness, would you?' I held out my hand for the phone, which I put right under his front wheel. I flicked him some nice used notes: 'Get yourself a new phone – different number, right?'

'I'll text you as soon as I've spoken to this guy.'

As would my contact, so I'd know he was telling the truth. I watched him put the Corsa into gear and solemnly squash the phone.

And so, seamlessly, to the village hall and the WI.

As I'd suspected from the lunch nibbles, the WI link with the pub was being nicely firmed up. It turned out that one of the other members, Tina, who'd given the impression of being ditzily impractical in an old-fashioned feminine way, had actually been a lawyer in her pre-retirement life, and a sharp one at that, at least if her skills with the contract between the WI and Suze of the Pickled Walnut were anything to go by.

'So it'll be just morning coffee for a trial period of a month,' Tina told us, wild hair and hands whirling. 'Softly, softly, catchee monkee, and all that. Then we might want to give up altogether or add in afternoon tea. And if everything works, we might want to join up the sessions by offering light lunches. But everything is subject to month by month agreement, which can be terminated with a month's notice on either side.'

'Time to draw up a rota, then,' Elaine said, looking encouragingly – or compellingly – around the room at each member in turn.

Including me.

'But I can't cook to save my life!' I wailed in the privacy of our bedroom an hour or so later. 'And I can't excuse myself by claiming to have a full-time job.'

'You're pretty busy anyway,' Theo said absently, attacking a hangnail.

'Not so busy I can't set aside a few hours.' There were times when I was desperate for occupation, after all, though he wasn't to know that. 'It's what I do in those few hours that worries me: imagine trying to pass off my poor cupcakes on paying customers.'

By now I had his full attention. 'Does it have to be cupcakes? What about jam or chutney? You could sell half of what you make for the church appeal. Which is, I have to point out, still very much in need of funds. I think we've got so jubilant about winning a battle, we've forgotten there's still a major financial war on. And no, I'm not suggesting that you instantly raise some Monopoly money.'

'What if I did what that vicar did who gave each of his flock a tenner and told them to go away and make money from it? No one simply walked off with the cash and most doubled or tripled it . . . I could provide the cash for the initial investment.'

He cupped my face in his hands and kissed me. 'You have a generous soul, my dear one. I'll float the ideas to Ted and George; technically it's their problem, since I'm just the incumbent.'

My heart leapt: did this imply he was ready to go somewhere else? But now wasn't the time to leap up and down humming the theme from *The Great Escape*.

'Wave a few fivers at them, it'll concentrate their minds beautifully. Meanwhile, making jam and chutney is a brilliant idea.' Even though it would raise pence, not thousands of pounds. 'I'll put it to the WI committee. Meanwhile, it has to be cakes.'

'But not necessarily cupcakes? I have happy memories of your cherry cake. Very happy. Not all of them to do with baking, I admit,' he said, obviously enjoying the memory so much that he decided to rekindle it – though without any culinary ingredients.

The following day my wave to Mazza and Dave, who'd returned about half an hour earlier, was perfunctory. It was time to call the police with the possible ID of Sharon Hammond's dealer, Wiley; they didn't overwhelm me with their gratitude, but a few minutes' conversation persuaded them that they shouldn't just write it down on the back of a shopping list and forget it. Then I forced myself into the kitchen. Surrounded by flour, sugar and eggs, I sat at the table, Merry's files in front of me, the neat writing a constant reproach to my appalling computer-eroded scrawl. As far as Theo's parishioners were concerned, she'd only failed on one count, as far as I could see: there were no children in the rectory. I know Theo regretted not being a father, but apparently she'd been adamant. As for me, the biological clock had not just ticked but struck midnight, so no joy there for him either. Childlessness apart, she'd clearly been a paragon. She was even able to manage on the pittance that was a parson's stipend. Not just food and heat, but even her clothes. Perhaps she didn't take to charity shops, she bought from them.

To be angry and resentful about a woman who'd died in a motorway pile-up six years ago was simply unreasonable, I told myself firmly. As well as being pretty unchristian. After all, as Alison Cox had pointed out, we all have our gifts. Mine was for making money, not saving it.

All the same, clearing my head with a run didn't seem a bad thing at all. Theo was going to be busy all day, and had asked me not to leave anything except a sandwich for lunch. The sun was shining. I would run.

No, I wouldn't. When I'd finished baking I'd make another attack on that vegetable garden and maybe later on treat myself to a trip to a garden centre to buy some plants to put in it.

I'd be a proper rector's wife if it killed me.

TWELVE

The rectory was used to unexpected visitors, but usually, of course, they were for Theo. So when one arrived for me, even though it was Elaine and I expected a drubbing about my cake quota, I was delighted, particularly as I hadn't started cooking and was still relatively clean and tidy. Although I meant to install her in the living room, she drifted into the kitchen with me when I went to make coffee.

She sat, looking expectantly at the machine, like a dog waiting for its bone. When I placed the mug of mocha in front of her, she savoured the aroma with closed eyes. 'Oh, how wonderfully chocolatey. I bet it tastes . . . mmm . . . heavenly. Whoops! Sorry!'

I waved aside her apology for a pun best avoided in a clerical household, perhaps. On the other hand, when I bought chocolate I couldn't resist the Divine brand, which had the double bonus of being Fairtrade and delectable.

'Golly, I was bracing myself for some of Theo's vile brew,' she continued, 'and I get this nectar! Actually, his was better than Merry's. She always bought the cheapest possible and never put enough in the mug. This is coffee bliss.'

'Thank my new best friend.' I patted it affectionately before I sat down. 'It was yours that inspired me. I wish I could say it was your biscuits that inspired these, or even that I'd bought them at Violet's, but I can't. The posh range at Sainsbury's. Let's be frank, Elaine, I'm going to ruin this brilliant idea of yours. Unless I bake an endless supply of cherry cakes.'

'There's no reason why you shouldn't. I've never seen so much wonderful fruit in one cake. But I can't help wondering if that's the best use of your talents.'

I spread my hands in a gesture of surrender. 'OK. I'll make chutney and jam to sell to punters. Theo's suggestion last night,' I added. 'I gather he's been talking to you.'

'No. Why should he? WI business, not the church's. And we hadn't bargained on selling goodies, not at this stage.' Her look was quite penetrating. We sipped in silence till she pointed at the pile of cake ingredients and the files waiting balefully at the far end of the table. 'Don't get the idea that Merry was a domestic goddess, Jodie. She wasn't. She was a nice, quiet, conscientious woman, whom Theo married straight out of uni – but I guess you know that. What you wouldn't know, because he's a decent, loyal man, is that a number of us thought that had he not been a parson, the marriage would have ended long before he moved here.'

'But—'

'I don't think she had any idea of what she was letting herself in for when she encouraged him to give up teaching and enter the priesthood. At least, that was what she always claimed. And actually, it would have been hard to do it without her support, financial and otherwise. But then, all of a sudden, she gave up her job. Just like you did.' She looked at me with appraising eyes.

'Actually, my job gave me up, Elaine. Redundancy.' I didn't need to tell her about severance packages and the contract work. That was Theo's business and mine. 'Merry was a civil servant, wasn't she?'

'A revenue inspector. I think Theo would, biblical allusions to tax gatherers apart, have been happy for her to carry on working – he had a suburban parish somewhere near her work. But then she suddenly got a misty-eyed yen for a roses-round-the-door village life; God knows what she thought of this place when she actually got here. Not to mention this house, of course.' She looked around her expressively. 'Talk about sackcloth and ashes! She had all sorts of money-saving ideas; I think she even kept hens for a couple of months until some commuter bastard complained that the rooster crowed too early in the morning. She made curtains with not quite enough material so they didn't meet in the middle – well, you've seen. Those great piles of recipes were a substitute for putting a decent meal on the table. All this is between you and me, of course. Because I think her meanness somehow guilt-tripped poor Theo into being equally cautious with money – tight-fisted, if you don't mind the expression.' She smiled. 'But I'll bet that he was the one who got the coffee-machine out of its box and read the instructions and set it working, and that he's the one who can't live without it. Give the poor man half a chance and he'll take over that car of yours, not because he begrudges you the fun of driving it but because he's sick of being dreary. I bet he loves the day's life in London you've got the sense to maintain.'

'We both do.'

'Of course you do. I bet you love wearing nice clothes again. You looked really good yesterday, by the way. It takes really expensive clothes to look as elegantly understated as that. Which is why we need you to do something other than make jam and chutney or whatever.'

What did good clothes have to do with anything? Best not to ask. 'Not even a cupcake?'

'Bugger cupcakes. How this craze for over-decorated mouthfuls of refined sugar, refined flour and cholesterol came about I don't know and I don't care. What I need you to do . . . Well, now I come to say it aloud it seems a bloody cheek.'

'I can deal with cheek,' I said coolly.

'We may have a wonderful team of bakers, and all the women have the best and kindest hearts you could imagine. But how many of them could do front of house stuff? And I'm not for one moment suggesting, before your jaw hits the table and breaks, that you become a waitress or even the maître d'. Well, only for a couple of weeks,' she conceded. 'We need to recruit waiting staff. I think we discussed it before. So I thought of some of your young protégés.'

Or rather I had, a week earlier. But it was always good for people to believe they'd had a brilliant idea all on their own. So I simply beamed enthusiastically. 'Recruiting kids like Sian and Mazza and their mates would be wonderful. Absolutely admirable. I know they'll need training on the job, but they'll also need a wage.'

Her face fell. 'Wouldn't their tips cover that?'

'What if they had a load of tightwads one week? No, it's got to be a proper wage, the national minimum at least. Wasn't that part of Tina's business plan? No? Oh dear. Though,' I added with a smile, 'I know someone who could sponsor their wages until the concern built up. And someone like Tina should look into tax credits and things I know nothing about. I don't want them to miss out on their dole.'

'I think you'll find it's called welfare now,' she said tartly, surprising me. But then I remembered what daily paper she read, and blamed that for the narrowing of her outlook.

All the same, I couldn't let it pass. 'Whatever happened to Social Security? That was a good name. Not so patronizing to the recipients. Anyway, you asked for my advice and that's what it is.' I knew I was being confrontational, which was the quickest way to antagonize someone I needed as an ally. 'I'm sorry, Elaine. I always get on my high horse when people aren't paid properly – like all those poor interns working their socks off in fashion houses and law firms for nothing except expenses if they're lucky. I've been there, believe me. Being a drudge is not good.' I didn't need a shrink to tell me what had driven me to uni and my doctorate and all the way up to the corporate ceiling, which I'd duly crashed through. But I'd never turned my back on my roots. I might have made fistfuls of cash, but they were honest fistfuls, and I'd never knowingly underpaid anyone. Or sacked anyone to save money, whatever the size of the organization or the pressure from the board or the shareholders. Never, never, never.

'Anyway, I'll find a sponsor, and I'll certainly talk to the kids for you. Mazza's got a good head on his unemployed shoulders – he'll know who could do it and who not. And I'll help train them. And then if the scheme works, you've got local staff – always a bonus – and if it goes belly-up, then at least they've got something for their CVs.'

She obviously recognized my olive branch. 'I hear you got Sian to help with your website – would she be a good option?'

I laughed. 'Technically she's back at school, so she could only do a Saturday morning shift. In any case, I think she might have her sights set on something else now.' And if that school of hers didn't develop those talents, I'd want to know the reason why. If she didn't get many formal qualifications, there were always some of my old mates who might take her on anyway and make her an unqualified success. 'But there must be other capable young women.'

'And these sponsors – they wouldn't just renege on the deal if they felt like it?'

No, I wouldn't! I shrugged what I hoped looked like high-finance shoulders. 'You're asking them to sponsor five or six kids, if that. Four weeks. By then the WI will have made a decision about whether the project continues for another month, right? I presume that'll depend on its profitability. If there are profits, then the kids should be able to draw wages. End of sponsorship. Peanuts to the organization I have in mind.'

She might be laughing but there was more than a hint of asperity in her expression.

'What have I said?'

'You always speak as if the WI is some external body. It isn't, Jodie – it's us. You're an integral part of it.'

Why did it sound more like a threat than a simple statement? It was enough to make me stow all those unopened ingredients in the cupboard.

As I dug another row in the future vegetable garden, I caught a glimpse of my reflection in a window. I didn't like what I saw. Had there been a hint of surprise in Elaine's voice when she'd remarked on my TV interview outfit? Ditching the Louboutins and the posh bags had been sensible, but – apart from when I was gardening – did I need to look such a mess? What had happened to the Jodie of only two months ago? The sort of metaphorical sackcloth and ashes Elaine had mentioned in connection with Merry, that was what had happened. Heavens, I wasn't even wearing gardening gloves! I, who used to have a manicure at least once a week, and a regular pedicure too.

I was inspecting the pretty poor job I'd made of painting my fingernails when the phone rang. I couldn't leave it, of course, in case it was important. Why on earth didn't we have one of

those modern phones that showed the caller's ID? Next thing
on my list, obviously. Meanwhile, I picked up.

'Jode, one of your rich mates got a helicopter we can
borrow?'

'No, Dave, but I know some of your friends who have.
They're called the police, remember.'

'I know to the nearest pound just how much a shout they
cost. Twelve hundred an hour. So I haven't a snowball's. Come
on, you must know the odd millionaire – bloody hell! OK, I
suppose we'll just have to have a closer look ourselves.'

'Where are you?'

I think I knew the answer; in any case, I wasn't going to
get it from Dave, who'd clearly switched off his phone. I'd
better go and see what they were up to. I smeared nail varnish
all over my running bottoms as I dragged them on.

I popped my phone and fresh water into my lightweight
rucksack, in which I always kept chocolate and a first aid kit.
If I drove to the start of the footpath it would win me ten
minutes, and correspondingly save my energy. Why had I let
so many days go by without really taxing myself?

Fortunately for road safety the village streets and the lane
leading to the downs were deserted. In fact, the first car I
saw belonged to Ted Vesey, who gave a most courteous
salute in response to my wave. I slung the car into a lay-by
and set off uphill without so much as a sensible warm-up.
However, it quickly dawned on me that my going lame
wouldn't help anyone, so I slowed and stretched. Only then
did I run on, and up. It was only when I'd been striding out
– second wind! – for some ten minutes that I remembered
I should have brought heavy walking shoes too: if Dave and
Mazza were heading down that tiny sheep track it'd be hare-
brained to the point of foolhardy to try to follow them
without boots. That was what had stopped our previous
expedition, after all. On the other hand, I had such a strong
sense of trouble that I pressed on, ready to deal with the
problem of the track as and when I reached it. It didn't help
that I usually ran down, not up, this particular path; the
incline was much steeper than I realized, and I'd never, even

when I was younger, had the legs and lungs to be a cross country runner.

I was really struggling by the top of the hill. It wouldn't be a case of stopping to admire – or speculate about – the view. I would simply have to stop to gather myself together.

And then worry about that track.

THIRTEEN

The track was even more overgrown than I remembered, full of spiky young shoots at ankle height. In places where the soil showed through, however, there were clear boot tracks heading downhill. And I had to follow them. In running shoes. And with my calves exposed. I was about to regret this.

About fifty painful, scratchy metres down I heard the sound of other walkers: laboured breath, the occasional grunt, not much conversation. They were coming my way. Dave and Mazza. But side by side? On this track?

Then I realized Mazza was almost carrying Dave, who was struggling both with the steep slope and an injury. Ankle? Knee?

Dave raised a hand: I was to stay where I was. For once I was pleased to do as I was told, although I could see that his hand was streaming with blood, as if he had stigmata. It would be best if I simply turned round and made my way back up again; there was no way anyone could administer First Aid here. I did – and promptly stumbled so hard I nearly went base over apex.

Despite the running gloves, falling hands first into gorse was not a pleasant experience.

Clearly Dave hadn't had even that minimal protection. I sat him down on the nicely greening grass on the edge of the path along the brow of the hill, from which we could see the steadily growing building in the valley below.

Like an obedient child, Dave held his hands out. However, as I tore open the first antiseptic wipe, he reached for the wipe himself, wincing as the alcohol touched raw flesh. But he declared bravely, 'I think I'll live.'

So did I.

'What about that ankle?' Mazza asked. 'And how are we going to get you back down to the village?'

'Why didn't you buy a four-by-four, Jodie?' Dave grunted.

'Because I'm not in the habit of trying to ferry people up and down hills. And I don't think four-by-fours are allowed up here.'

'You don't usually let minor considerations like rules and regulations bother you.' He'd finished wiping the blood from his hands and was inspecting the deeper cuts. I passed him a selection of sticking plasters. 'Or you didn't till you became a vicar's wife.'

Was that regret or anger? But this wasn't the place to have a row, especially as Mazza was cocking an eyebrow.

I asked quickly, 'How did you come to fall, anyway, Dave – someone who prides himself as being as sure-footed as a camel?'

His eyes narrowed. 'Didn't I see you trip earlier? Mazza, you've got the sharpest eyes – go and check. Careful, mind!'

'What's he supposed to be looking for?' I asked as Mazza moved cautiously down the path, stopping abruptly more or less where I'd tripped.

'Yeah! Got it!' Mazza bent, and then straightened, flourishing something over his head as he made his way back up, as slowly as a pensioner looking for a paper clip on a pavement. 'And another one!' he called. 'Look, Jodie,' he panted as he triumphantly laid some scraps of wire on my rucksack.

'Tripwire,' Dave said.

'That's how he got to be a DCI – recognizing wire when it trips him up,' I observed. 'Or are you reading too much into it, by any chance?' But then, jeering no longer, I answered my own question with another. 'Or is this the physical equivalent of all those CCTV cameras by the entrance to Elysian Fields and Double Gate Enterprises? The properties on the far side of the valley,' I added impatiently.

Dave frowned, as if I were some rookie constable. 'I didn't know you'd been out there, Jodie. On your own?'

'I was just enjoying my new car,' I said. 'And found my way there quite by chance.'

'I wish you'd been enjoying a nice anonymous hire car instead,' Dave said. 'And don't let that give you any ideas. Someone really doesn't want chance visitors down there, do they? Are you sure you can't summon up a chopper, Jodie?'

'I bet Double Gate and co would have ground-to-air missiles to deal with it if I did.'

'Have you really got mates with helicopters, Jodie?' Mazza gasped.

'Only in Dave's imagination,' I said, not quite truthfully. 'Or I'd summon one to get him down this hill. I've got some serious strapping here, Dave. If we bind up your ankle, do you think you could manage to walk if you leant on the pair of us? Or shall I dial nine nine nine and see what happens?'

'Air ambulance?' Mazza gasped again. 'Really?'

Dave eased his boot off and waggled his foot.

I watched carefully. 'I don't think anything's broken – not that that's any consolation: sprains can take as long as bones to heal.'

'OK, avert your eyes – I'm about to take my sock off. Tape, please, Jodie.'

I've never been one for male feet, but I knelt in front of him, taking the weight of his leg on my lap and applying the strapping myself. 'There, you look like second cousin to a mummy. Let's get your sock back on. And your boot. And I've got paracetamol in here. Water?'

Down went the tablets. 'I could have done with something stronger. OK, let's get me upright.' We took a hand each and got him vertical. And then it was time for the long stagger back, Dave's height and weight making it hard for him and his human crutches. We were all glad to see my car. Until we realized it now sat heavily on four flat tyres.

'Bastards. If I get my hands on . . .' Mazza embarked on a diatribe that Burble would have been proud of.

'I'll call the Audi helpline,' I said wearily. 'Before that I'll summon Theo. I'm sorry, both of you, to offend your sense of style, but it's got to be the five-year-old Focus that rides to your rescue.'

Theo insisted on staying with the Audi while I ferried Mazza home, and Dave, protesting loudly, to the nearest A&E, where he received the promptest and most courteous treatment one could wish for. They even provided him with free elbow crutches, though he was instructed firmly to keep the offending limb off the floor for at least five days. 'And elevated above head height for the rest of the day,' the casualty nurse said by way of valediction.

And to think that Theo had been urging him, almost literally, to get on his bike and take himself off home. Truly, the dear man would need the patience of a saint for the next few days.

It wasn't until Dave was settled for the night that Theo and I had a chance to catch up on our day, which we did in the privacy of our own room. I thought Theo would be concerned by my hilltop adventure, but he was far more interested in my conversation with Elaine.

'So you're going to pay any kids you manage to recruit out of your own pocket?'

He sounded more stern than delighted, I thought, as he relished the last drop of the red wine I'd prescribed as a nightcap.

'Not me. A trust fund. It's helped young musicians, actors, artists . . . Now it can help a few waiters.'

'What if it won't play ball?' He seemed determined to see the bleak side I was coming to associate with the rectory. Or was it with Lesser Hogben?

'It will. It might be quite independent of me legally—'

'Ah, so you are involved!' he exclaimed, with a quizzical smile.

'Did I ever deny it? It meets every last Charities Commission regulation, but since I set it up and help fund it, I can nominate up to ten applicants a year.'

Back to stern again. 'And if people find out?'

'You're saying they won't like it? In any case, they'd be hard put to discover anything. The trustees are household names, the accounts immaculate. And the name Jodie Welsh doesn't appear anywhere. Josephine Diana Harcourt, yes. So unless someone nips up to St John's Wood to check the names in the register of marriages, I'm in the clear.'

'You make it sound as if you're committing a crime!'

'You make me feel as if I am.' Heavens, where had that come from? Theo looked as shocked as I was. 'And I'm not. I'm trying to do good by stealth, that's what, and if I can't cook and I can't garden, and I can't even paint my own finger-nails properly . . .' I wasn't sure how I was going to round off that lot, but I didn't need to.

'Why do you want to do any of those?' Since he was kissing the messed-up nails in question, it didn't feel like an interrogation.

'Because I've never been a wife before. I've never even lived with anyone before, or at least not for twenty-five years when I was young and adaptable. But now I am a wife, I want to be a good one. And being a rich one with no talents doesn't seem to endear me to your parishioners.'

'No talents? You're the most amazing— Oh, bloody, bloody phone! I'm not here and you don't know where I am,' he hissed as I reached reluctantly for the handset. 'Unless it's the children's hospice – poor Carol and Wayne's kid. Not expected to live through the night.'

It was. He dressed without a word and left.

Finding the bed miserably cold, I did what I should have done earlier: using the council website I reported the extensive presence of wire on the hillside, and the injuries it had caused. I asked for immediate action, adding the rectory address by way of a spuriously authoritative bonus.

Still no sign of Theo or of sleep. So I switched on our trusty fan heater and spent the next hour giving myself the best pedi-cure I could – which was not great given that the distance between my eyes and my toes was just wrong for my contact lenses. Eventually I fished out the lenses and drowsed off. At one point I registered the sound of a car door slamming: he must be back. Should I go down? If the child had died, would he prefer to be left on his own to pray? Would he like to have me beside him, or would he consider it an intrusion? We'd never faced anything as serious as this in our short time as a couple.

Theo had always said that in a tricky situation he asked what Jesus would do. I found myself asking what Merry would do. Sometime, while I was agonizing, I must have fallen deeply asleep.

Then I awoke suddenly. What was that? There was still no Theo beside me – but from somewhere in the house came unmistakable bedroom noises.

By now thoroughly awake, I found slippers and dressing-gown once more and headed to the kitchen – making far more noise than I needed, I admit – in search of hot chocolate and those good biscuits. The kitchen door was closed, but light showed underneath, so I went in. Theo, head in hands, sat at the table staring blindly into space. He switched his gaze to me, staring in what looked horribly like disbelief. And then relief.

'Don't dare say you thought that involved me,' I hissed, jerking a thumb up the stairs.

'I wondered whose the car was.' Which didn't seem to be an answer to anything.

'My secret lover's, for goodness' sake?'

'Whose, then?'

Arms akimbo, I said, 'I should imagine it's some friend of Dave's, shouldn't you? His forensic science mate, perhaps. I just hope whoever it is has come to sweep him back into his or her arms on a permanent basis. It's bloody freezing in here. I'll make some chocolate. You go upstairs. Put the fan heater on – oh, and Classic FM. Loudly.'

He was deep in prayer when I got upstairs, but it didn't seem to bring him any joy. I knew better than to ask him how he felt. Here in the rectory he'd simply clam up. I'd have to wait till he was safe in my apartment before he'd talk. But at last I felt him relax in my arms, and then we slept the sleep of the just.

FOURTEEN

There was no sign of Dave the following morning when we finally surfaced, much later than usual, probably because I'd forgotten to set the alarm. Presumably whoever had been here the previous night had taken him away: I couldn't imagine he'd have found much to excite him in the rectory over the weekend. So the conversation I'd planned to have with him would either have to be put on ice – in other words would probably never happen – or would take place over the phone. Naturally I was put straight through to voicemail.

Bother that for a game of soldiers. Cleaning the house from top to bottom was better than standing in the kitchen emulating Burble's rich vocabulary, and at least when Theo came back from his morning's rounds to spend the afternoon in his study working on the following day's sermon, even he could tell the difference. And he had a choice of home-made curries when he knocked off for the day – except he didn't, as there was a problem with some travellers on the edge of the village and the police thought a gentle answer might be better than wrath at turning them away.

On Sunday I broke with my habit of worshipping at St Dunstan's, whoever preached. I just wanted to be with Theo, and sat beside him as he tracked between early Communion in one tiny church, with two communicants, morning service in St Alphege's, some twelve miles away, with sixty bottoms on the pews, a farewell barbecue (with the temperature struggling to reach ten Celsius) for a choirmaster in a third parish, and evensong in a fourth. Each time he asked for Burble to be added to the prayers of intercession – that is, the prayers offered in addition to the ones set down for the day, sometimes by the person taking the service, and sometimes by a member of the congregation. Our own daily prayers hadn't been answered yet and I confess that I doubted whether a mass effort would impress the Almighty any more. Even so it was illogically comforting to hear the poor kid's name spoken with loving kindness by so many decent people. I just hoped whoever was responsible for the prayers at St Dunstan's had remembered him too. But I had an idea that it was Ted Vesey's turn, and didn't hold out much hope in that quarter.

'What in hades do you think you've been up to? Missing the whole weekend without so much as a word. Though, of course, perhaps on Friday you didn't need words!' I addressed a bleary Monday-morning Dave as he ensconced himself in the kitchen, propping his leg on a spare chair.

He pushed his badger's crop back, looking insufferably smug. 'A friend of mine dropped by some spare clothes – I needed trackie bottoms, not jeans – and we took advantage of the moment. And the house key I'd happened to leave at her place,' he added less confidently, as he picked up the chill emanating from me. 'And then – well, we thought discretion was the better part of valour.'

'You left the key I'd entrusted to you at someone else's place?' Any moment now I'd resort to the kind of language favoured by Burble and Mazza, not least because our free day had just been hijacked. Someone had phoned to ask Theo to take a funeral first thing on Tuesday, because the priest who was supposed to be officiating had gone down with shingles. I should have overflowed with Christian charity. I didn't, and would have loved to take out my bad mood on Dave. But I shouldn't, should I? Especially as Theo was busily cancelling meetings on Wednesday so we could still have some private time. 'Perhaps,' I continued more coolly, more my old management self, 'you'd be happier staying full-time at this person's place.'

'I wouldn't have thought so,' he mused, quite ignoring the subtext. 'After all, she's out all hours and her house is all twists and stairs. Not suitable for a peg-leg at all.'

'Oh, what a shame,' I said with mock sincerity.

'In any case, I'm expecting my visitor here again today.'

'I beg your pardon?' It was my icy, reduce-them-to-tears voice, but Dave smiled blandly.

'Rosemary's getting hold of some waterproof covers for my leg so I can have a decent shower.'

Still fearing I was about to lose my temper irretrievably, I dug in the back of one of Merry's drawers, an Ali Baba's hoard of all things useful, or that might conceivably be useful one day. Plonking on the table in front of him a roll of heavy-duty polythene bags large enough to accommodate even a size twelve foot, I headed for the garage and returned with my next prey. 'There. Gaffer tape. Make sure you pull it off in one swift movement – any hesitation and take it from me it's absolute murder. OK?' I looked him straight in the eye.

It didn't take him long to get the message.

He was still in the shower when Elaine paid another unannounced visit, her wonderful hair set off by a green top with tiny coppery flecks: it must have cost her a bomb. As for me, I was horribly underdressed, wearing jeans that were scruffy without the prefix *fashionably*. Shoes not slippers, at least. I'd washed up but not got round to drying the breakfast things; apart from that the kitchen was neat and clean enough to welcome her, and the thought of a special coffee attracted me too.

'Cow sheds,' she said as she settled herself at the table. 'I've been doing some asking around for you, all very discreet of course, and discovered that's what they're building out at Double Gate Farm.'

'But the site's huge. I thought cow sheds were just big enough to hold the cows while they were being milked. Mocha again?' I patted the coffee-machine.

She nodded. 'Please. I think you mean milking parlours. These aren't milking parlours. They're sheds large enough to accommodate the whole herd pretty well year round. And they've got a lot of cows. I think the idea is that if they keep them in optimum conditions – in other words, warm and indoors, with lights on pretty much all the time – they can milk the animals three times a day instead of twice. Fifty per cent more yield.'

'And I always thought cows lived in fields and ate grass and buttercups and daisies. Silly me.' I put her cup in front of her and waited for the machine to give me mine. 'Gives a whole new meaning to the term *poor cow*.'

'The world's a hungry place, Jodie,' she declared. 'And supermarkets want a cheap product. So it's up to the farmers to maximize production. I checked: they do have planning permission.'

'Just for the building?'

'Oh, no. It's not as straightforward as that. There'd be some sort of assessment of the effect the development would have on the environment. I looked it all up on the Internet. There's slurry storage to worry about, you see—'

'Slurry being the – er – end product?'

'Right.'

Would I end up like this? Passing my time checking on slurry? On the other hand, there'd have to be a lot of slurry to fill a building the size of the one I'd seen. I gestured with arms stretching backwards and forwards: how big?

'Oh, it'd be about the same depth as the shallow end of a swimming bath. Not that you'd be thinking about diving in, of course.' She gave a comic shudder. Recalling news items about people dying in slurry fumes, I found it hard to join in. 'You've got an access ramp for vehicles when you have to clear it out.'

While I tried to work out why I hadn't found all this myself when I searched the Net, I had to say something. 'Talk about cleaning the Augean Stables.'

'Quite. And poor old – was it Hercules? – who would also have to clear out any extra storage for the stuff. Maybe a lagoon.'

I couldn't resist humming the music that introduces *Desert Island Discs*: 'Sleepy Lagoon'.

'Or maybe,' she continued, ignoring my townie's snigger, 'according to the Internet, a great big metal tank above ground level. They've got to make sure nitrates don't seep into rivers or the water table. Farmers have to be really environmentally aware these days.'

'Good,' I said almost absently. None of what she'd said made sense of those foundations, though, deep enough for a double or triple decker shed, like a multistorey car park. Were cattle really kept underground? The thought was enough to make me sign up to the RSPCA. 'So, these here prize milkers – do they get to see the light of day or are they kept like battery chickens? You know, do they live in flats?'

She looked genuinely shocked. 'That'd be inhuman!'

I thought of some of the mammoth social housing estates I knew in London. Inhuman indeed. 'So it's just one vast flat concrete field, as it were, with comfortable bedding and stuff underfoot and plenty of nice nutritious food.'

'Exactly.' She hadn't picked up my irony.

Clearly, if we were to remain friends, a change of topic was called for. 'I've contacted the trust about our trainee staff, by the way,' I said, reaching for plates and the biscuit tin. The plates were where they were supposed to be; the tin wasn't. Nor was it anywhere else, as far as I could see. Bloody Dave. But in fact its absence was a godsend. Before I could say apron, Elaine had rolled up her sleeves, raided my fridge and larder for the stuff I'd bought and never used, and embarked on a baking lesson.

The trouble was that when Dave limped in, attracted by the wonderful smells coming from the oven, the gleam in her eyes, the blatant body language, told me she was more than willing to embark on something else. A deeper acquaintance with my scapegrace cousin.

Any moves she might have wanted to make in that direction were stymied, however, by the arrival of Mazza, armed with enough computer games to keep them both off the street for a week. Where he'd got the money from I chose not to enquire – it wasn't my business so much as Dave's, was it? And having a chaperone for Dave seemed an entirely good thing while I worked out the most tactful way to warn Elaine that he already enjoyed a warm relationship with someone else. What she chose to do with the information was up to her, of course. Actually tact was more Theo's line than mine, but I felt a bit of sisterly loyalty was in order. Especially with those biscuits of ours on the cooling rack.

I wish I could have given her the chance to see what appeared to me a much more desirable piece of eye candy, but I could hardly drag the man to whom I answered the front door into the kitchen for her delectation. Six foot two, with broad shoulders and narrow hips, and the most gorgeous blue eyes, he was a good ten years younger than her.

'Daniel Baker, Doctor Harcourt.' He flashed his council ID. 'You made a serious complaint about dangerous obstructions on open land.'

'I did,' I said, my fingers crossed behind my back; although the ridge was certainly a right of way, I wasn't at all sure about those sheep tracks. 'I'm delighted by such a swift response, I must say. Come in, please.' The best place to speak to him, with Dave in the living room and the kitchen clearly out of bounds, was Theo's study.

As we passed the living room door, it burst open. 'Dan! What are you doing here? Come along in! Oh, leave this to me, Jodie, I'll fill him in. After all, I've more to complain about than most.'

And, alerted by the male voices, Elaine was already halfway out of the kitchen looking interested. So I didn't argue with Dave this time, and returned to my baking lesson.

Within minutes, Mazza slunk into the kitchen, sniffing optimistically. 'Seems Daniel's an old mucker of Dave's – something to do with motorbikes,' he said. 'So they're sort of wondering about coffee and some of those biscuits . . .'

I grinned. 'Elaine, this is Mazza, whom I was talking about earlier. Mazza, Elaine, who's putting together a team to serve tea and coffee at the pub.'

It was hard to tell which of them was more nonplussed.

Mazza recovered first. His mother had taught him well. 'Pleased to meet you,' he said, sticking out his hand.

She had to take it, of course, and return his polite smile. 'Jodie thought you might be able to recommend some young people who'd make good waiters and waitresses,' she said, disbelief creeping into her voice, which had become ultra-clipped for the occasion.

There was no doubt Mazza would have picked up on it.

'I said you were a good judge of character,' I explained. 'You'd know who was flaky and who could be trusted to put in a full shift on a regular basis.'

He pulled a face. 'Bloody dole might be a problem.'

'Jodie's got some ideas for dealing with that,' Elaine said.

I repeated all I'd told her about protecting the youngsters' benefit and waxed lyrical about their future employment prospects. 'I guarantee that everyone will benefit and no one will take any financial hit. The scheme will be backed by a trust fund,' I concluded. I'd said too much, hadn't I? Mazza gave me a knowing look and the tiniest flicker of a smile. He'd sussed out who was behind it all. Drat, and I'd really wanted to keep my part quiet. But I could surely trust him to keep mum. Surely.

Elaine was too busy overcoming her reservations about her new HR consultant to have noticed, I thought. With a visible straightening of her shoulders, she cast about for something to write on. As if he was a son of the house, Mazza passed her the jotter and biro from beside the phone.

There was a loud yell from the living room. It was Dave demanding to know what had happened to his coffee. For that he'd get standard cafetière issue. And, since he'd stolen the tin of biscuits, he could whistle for anything else.

Mazza looked from the tray I was loading to Elaine and then to the kitchen door. How about that for an exercise in working out priorities?

'So how many girls would you say would be interested?' Elaine demanded, establishing herself as the more important. 'Or do you think boys would be more reliable?'

'It's hard . . . Look, I can put it around to mates I can trust that there's a chance of a job, but I can't – you know – appoint people or check references and that.'

'But surely you could—'

His phone rang. Although he put down the tray, I think he was going to switch to voicemail, but then he double checked who was calling. 'Sorry. Got to take this.' He turned politely towards the back door. 'Ma? You what? Bloody hell no! 'Course I bloody didn't. You just go to bed. I'll be straight down.' He cut the call and turned to me, white-faced. 'My mum's just found a load of bikes dumped in our garden. Well, not so much dumped as hidden, like.'

'Hidden?'

'We keep all our garden chairs and stuff under an old

tarpaulin. Mum was just hanging out the washing when she thought it was bulging, so she took a look. And there were half a dozen bikes.'

Out of courtesy to Elaine and me he'd rationed his expletives, but there were still enough to make Elaine wince.

'You're being fitted up?' I asked, hoping the lingo was reasonably up to date.

'Bloody right I am.'

'By whom? Call your mum and tell her not to expect you just yet and absolutely not to touch the bikes, OK? And yes, to go to bed. She works nights,' I said in an aside to Elaine. 'And then you'll have a word with Dave. He'll know what to do.' For all I hoped to sound positive, I knew, as I took the tray into the living room, that this could have very serious implications for Mazza.

'Ah, mine hostess with the nectar I spoke of!' Dave declared, as expansive as if he were Falstaff and I a serving wench. 'No? Jodie, what's the problem?'

I told him.

'Shit.' He turned to Daniel. 'And tenuous as it may seem, I think there's a connection with the wires on the paths and Jodie's slashed tyres, too.'

'Tyres?' All too clearly he didn't know what Dave was talking about.

'Ah, I was getting round to that,' Dave said.

'Enough theorizing, Dave. Mazza's in big trouble. He's still talking to his mum on the phone – while I go and get him, work out what he should do to get out of it.'

By now off the phone, the poor kid was trying to escape Elaine's interrogation. The police might be slow and overstretched, but surely wouldn't pass up a chance to nab a whole load of stolen items and the person allegedly handling them; in fact the very pressure they were under to get good clean-up rates might make them act swiftly.

He couldn't have stolen those bikes – could he?

'I'm sorry, Elaine. Dave needs to work on a plan for Mazza right now. His police experience should be invaluable.' Putting an arm round Mazza's shoulders, I propelled him towards the living room.

Daniel was holding up a hand. 'Hang on, Dave. All this sounds like a job for the police, not me. There's no point in us getting involved if it's part of a wider investigation. Our budget—'

'Of course it's your budget, isn't it? Look, though I'm sure Jodie's right, for the time being forget what she said. Everything. And just take yourself up there and see if you can see any more of these – these *obstructions*. Go on, you say yes and I'm sure she'll give you a better cup of coffee.'

'*She* is here,' I said tartly, 'and so is Mazza. Just cut the cackle, Dave, we need a plan. Now, before someone grasses Mazza up. I'll send him back in here. Sorry, Daniel.'

Daniel took the hint. 'I'll take a stroll up there this afternoon, Doctor Harcourt, and get back to you.'

Back in the kitchen, Elaine was donning oven gloves. Offended as she might be by my behaviour, she couldn't do an Alfred and let everything burn. It was clear she wasn't happy with her efforts, however: half the biscuits were too pale, a quarter perfect and the last quarter clearly overcooked. I'd always had my suspicions about that oven.

Whatever the state of the end product, however, I owed her a profound grovel. 'I'm really sorry. I just had to get Dave on to this urgently. Or you might find you have to go to visit Mazza in gaol to get his advice,' I added quietly.

It was clear she was still huffed. 'Of course, Ted Vesey always did say it was him behind the thefts. Or was it that young man who did a bit of gardening for you?'

Happily for me, Theo chose that moment to enter via the back door. 'As far as I know, both are entirely innocent. As I said, Elaine, at the PPC meeting, such rumours are best not repeated. Now, sweetheart, I've had an urgent message from Dave, so you'll have to excuse me.' He kissed me on the lips and, grabbing a biscuit, joined the men.

FIFTEEN

Though I was desperate to be party to the discussion between Dave, Mazza and Theo in the living room, I didn't want to snub Elaine any more; despite her stupid gossip she was doing her best to help both me and, via the WI, the village as a whole. So, listening with more than half an ear for the front door – why the hell wasn't Theo dashing down to Mazza's house to sort things out? – I continued my initiation in biscuit making. Either Elaine was sincere in her determination to make me overcome my culinary fears or she wanted to get another glimpse of Dave, her own charms augmented by those of her Viennese whirls, their colour more or less uniform after she'd done some high-speed manoeuvring of baking trays in the oven. So at last I was inducted into the mysteries of some of the arcane equipment I'd found in rarely opened drawers. Finally, all the eggs, all the flour and all the butter were used up – and still the three men, wise as monkeys I hoped, were closeted together.

I could bear it no longer. I was just about to apologize for chucking Elaine out when she glimpsed the clock – some forty centimetres across and ugly with it – that dominated the kitchen, and rushed off, squealing about being late, my genuine thanks echoing behind her.

OK. Now for some action in the real world.

'What are you all doing here? Shouldn't you be down there supporting Carrie, Theo?'

Though huddled in a clearly terrified knot of arms and legs on the most uncomfortable armchair, Mazza shook his head. 'It's not like anyone knows, is it? She's only just found them.'

Dave was still sofa-bound, but looked as if he'd be happier striding round the room giving orders. Theo, in his pulpit-pose, clearly thought Mazza should present himself to the police and insist that he'd had nothing to do with the bikes' arrival.

'You're sure you've never even touched them? Ever?' I asked, gaining a look of approval from Dave. 'So your DNA or prints simply wouldn't be on them?'

'I never touched anything under that tarpaulin,' Mazza said, a bit defensively. He added more positively, 'I don't recall ever handling a bike at all, actually.'

'So if your prints or DNA appear on them, you're being framed.'

'You missed your vocation, Jodie,' Dave drawled.

Ignoring him, I said, 'If you're dead sure you're in the clear, Mazza, then Theo's probably right.'

Mazza wasn't happy with the idea, but interestingly from my point of view feared that if the police believed him – a big if, of course – then blame might fall on Sian or on his mother.

'No one would think Carrie capable of such a thing,' I declared forcefully. 'She's a good, hard-working woman.'

Mazza nodded. 'But Sian's got a bit of form. Only shop-lifting – lipstick and crap like that – but you know how that'll look.'

'I should imagine she wanted the lipstick, but I can't see her on a bike. Or several bikes,' I added, with what I hoped was a reassuring grin. And I did go and perch on his chair and give his shoulder a squeeze. 'Carrie ought to be in bed asleep, but I can't imagine that she is. So I'm going to go down and talk to her.' And maybe more. Why should anyone go to the trouble of dumping all those bikes if they weren't going to tell the police where they were? 'OK, Mazza?'

Like a kid without his teddy, he nodded.

I arrived at Carrie's to find three police cars outside. Whether it was the village gossip-machine or the more dangerous person behind the tripwires and the tyre-slashing, someone had, to use the vernacular, dobbed her in. Texting Theo to tell him what was going on, I surged in, aiming, with my body language and hastily assumed mantle of village guru (wasn't that what rectors' wives were supposed to be?), to look authoritative. It would have been better if I'd been wearing a business suit and heels, but at least the thuggish-looking officers stopped to look at me. If I'd hoped Carrie would welcome me as a potential rescuer, I was disappointed. As I strode forward to comfort her, she muttered, 'It was all right till he got tangled up with you.'

But though she was taken aback and clearly unwilling, I insisted on hugging her, whispering, 'You know he didn't do this. Someone's trying to frame him.'

'I can see that,' she whispered back. 'But this lot won't be bothered to find out who. Arrest. Guilty verdict. Result.'

'Not if I have anything to do with it. Have they arrested you for having stolen goods on your property?'

'Not yet, but any moment now.'

We were pulled apart. It was time for me to return to my dear familiar management mode. 'Is there any reason for you to have your hands on my shoulders, Officer? Thank you.' I refrained from dusting myself off. 'Now, how can I help you? I'm Doctor Harcourt. The rector's wife,' I added for good measure. Heaven forgive me for hiding behind Theo's cassock. 'Mrs Burns – Carrie – is a good friend of mine,' I continued, taking and holding her hand, 'as is her son. How can I help?' At this point I realized on the bottom half of my jeans there were drifts of flour where the pinny had stopped. I just hoped they wouldn't be noticed.

'We're looking for Malcolm Burns, Doctor,' someone with sergeant's stripes declared, not quite truculently, but nevertheless somehow implying that I was wasting everyone's time.

Mistake.

'I'm sure if you'd simply asked Carrie, she could have told you that he's at the rectory. He's helping another friend of mine – who used to be a DCI down here, so you may know him – with a problem they encountered when they were out walking together yesterday. DCI Dave Harcourt,' I added, with such a serene smile that no one would ever guess that he was an only half-welcome guest whom I'd had to bollock for his incontinent behaviour. I corrected myself – it was best to get the lingo right: 'An incident. I'm sure he'd like to talk to you about it.'

'Until we have an official complaint, Doctor, there's no action we can take.' He sounded unpleasantly delighted. Or was he simply relieved? 'So you're telling us we can find our suspect at the vicarage.'

'Suspect? My young friend is at the rectory.'

Another, possibly brighter, officer grinned sarcastically: 'I suppose he's asking for asylum or something. Or would that just be in the church?'

'I'll have to ask my legal team to check cannon law. But this is nonsense: he's neither hiding nor seeking asylum.'

'In any case, this is all very theoretical,' said the sergeant. 'Very well, Carrie, you're coming with us.'

'Are you *arresting* Mrs Burns?'

He tried to look down his nose at me but remembered I was a good inch taller. 'Just a few questions – not that it's any business of yours. *Doctor.*'

'Everything in this parish is my husband's business – and of course, that of his Boss.'

'He'll be the one that confirmed my cousin,' hissed a youngish man with the blue hatband of a community support officer. 'A bishop!'

Close, but no banana – or perhaps I should have said, no episcopal crook.

The sergeant shifted his feet, as if disconcerted by personal connections, which of course I hadn't meant anyway. 'I don't think there'll be any need for God-botherers to involve them-selves,' he said, as much to the community support man as to me. 'Very well, Carrie, time to be off.' He grabbed her upper arm; Carrie clutched my hand like a frightened child.

'There's no need for physical violence,' I said. 'Carrie, would you like me to come with you? No? Very well, officer, just let me know where you're taking her and I can arrange for my solicitor to be in attendance. Maidstone? Very well.'

Carrie straightened her shoulders and swallowed hard before relinquishing her hold on my hand. 'Just look after Mazza for me,' she whispered.

I hugged her again. 'I will, I promise.' And so would the fanciest solicitor money could buy. 'Just remember not to say anything till your lawyer arrives.'

Her eyes rolled. 'Can't afford . . . well, Legal Aid, I suppose.'

'I can,' I assured her, overriding all objections. 'And I will.' I whipped round to the sergeant. 'And what do your colleagues think they're doing with those bikes?'

'What do you think? They're evidence.'

'In that case they go in bags. I don't want them corrupted in any way. Bags, Sergeant.'

He was inclined to bluster, but his underlings were already obeying me. I suspected, however, that I'd won a skirmish but not the whole battle. I could do with Marshal Blücher and his forces turning up on the horizon. I got a white van.

'And who the bloody hell is this? The damned Archbishop?' the sergeant demanded.

'Do you really think he'd travel in a vehicle like that?' I asked in the most dulcet of tones, even though I was as puzzled as he was when a tall, angular woman not much younger than me emerged, white overall already in her hands.

'I'm Doctor Rosemary McVicar,' she declared.

The sergeant rolled his eyes. I could quite understand why.

McVicar, clearly used to this sort of situation, continued, 'Forensic scientist. Who's in charge here?'

The sergeant stepped forward. Then he asked, not unreasonably, 'And why might you be here? It's not like we've got a body on our hands.'

'*As if* you have a body on your hands, I think you'll find. I'm just here to see there's no DNA contamination, accidental or deliberate,' she said. 'You must be Jodie Welsh. I understand it's you I'm to bill,' she added with a slightly ironic curl to the sentence.

I could hardly respond with advice to be less vocal during the night, so I returned nod for nod. 'Of course,' I said smoothly. 'How clever of Dave to arrange it all. I've had the bikes bagged up.'

She grinned. 'Well done you.'

Almost despite myself I returned the smile. Then I turned to the police officers. 'Now, if you'll excuse me I have legal matters to attend to.' And with luck I'd get back to the rectory before they did. 'I could do with your name, Sergeant, couldn't I? OK, Sergeant Masters, I look forward to all this being sorted out soon.' What a pity I'd made an enemy for life.

'What about Sian?' Carrie called over her shoulder. 'Will they march into school and arrest her too?'

'I'll make sure they don't,' I said tersely, reaching for my phone again. 'In any case, I'll be there at three thirty or whenever it is she leaves.'

Back at the rectory, Mazza was jittery with fear, but managed to hear my news about his mother, not to mention the legal support I'd organized, without breaking down. This was possibly because he and Dave were involved in what looked like a pretty violent computer game. I hoped this was evidence that Dave was distracting him from any problems, rather than that Mazza didn't care. There was no sign of Theo, but I deduced, rightly, that he was in his study.

'One of us should go with him as a responsible adult,' Theo said, without preamble. 'He knows you best – trusts you.'

'But I promised Carrie I'd be at school to pick up Sian. And, like a Double Diamond, a dog-collar works wonders.'

'Dave's already called the police to say Mazza will be coming in to make a voluntary statement.'

'Good. I'll get a solicitor for him too. I've already fixed one for Carrie, and there'll be someone—'

'Carrie? Why should she need a lawyer?'

'Dragged in for questioning. Well, stolen goods on her property. No arguing with that. The only question is who put the bikes there.' I ran my hands through my hair, well overdue for a cut and colour. 'If only the village bristled with as many CCTV cameras as London, we'd have a very good idea who delivered them.'

'Assuming it wasn't Mazza.'

I shook my head. 'I believe him. He's a car man. And he runs. Cyclists aren't runners.'

'My darling, no one would steal bikes to use, would they? Unlike Sian and her lipstick. You're very pale: you need to eat before you set out to Maidstone. We've all had a few biscuits,' he said apologetically, pushing me gently into the kitchen. 'There are some left, but they might be a bit rich for you.'

Chin set, I rounded up what were left and crammed them

into a plastic box which I stowed carefully at the back of the freezer. 'Heart attack fodder,' I said, pointing accusingly at his chest. 'We eat properly in this household.' I reached for the bread crock for wholemeal bread to make sandwiches. It was empty. 'Bloody Dave again, I suppose!' I banged it down so hard it broke too badly for even a superglue repair. 'Oh dear. I'm so sorry.' I'd always loathed it, because it was chipped and ugly, but since it had come with the territory I'd said nothing. And now it was gone, and all because of my bad temper. I stood with the two main shards in my hands and choked back a sob.

'There's some bread in the freezer,' Theo said mildly, wrapping the crock in yesterday's *Guardian* and throwing it in the bin. 'I took the precaution of getting a spare loaf from Violet's. But this is the second time in as many days you've been in tears or near to it. Are you so very unhappy?' At last he enveloped me in a big soothing hug. Back home in London he was as tactile a lover as any woman could ever wish; here he seemed to have adopted a no touching regime well before Dave's arrival on the marital scene.

Could I tell him I was just lost? I didn't know where I was. I was still trying to lead someone else's life, and I didn't know how to make it mine. Especially not when Elaine had to show me how to make biscuits using Merry's equipment. I owed him some sort of answer, and what I said was true at least. 'Do you know, when I wanted to cow the police a bit, I announced I was the rector's wife? I've never had to hide behind someone else's authority before. Mind you,' I added sheepishly, attempting a grin, 'I've never been out with flour all over my jeans before.'

'But you've probably saved the day for three people, with or without flour,' he said, releasing me. 'For two at least.' He burrowed in the freezer and popped the loaf in the microwave to defrost. 'I'm not having you drive on an empty stomach . . .'

We set off at the same time, leaving Dave happily awaiting the arrival of Dr McVicar. At least, that was what we deduced from his smug demeanour, though as Theo gestured him towards the front door, Mazza declared that Dave had cheated in order to win, so there might have been another explanation.

'After all those years in the police, are you surprised if he cheats?' Theo muttered. 'Not that you can quote me on that. Ever. And especially this afternoon,' he added, as he put a comforting but authoritative hand on the poor kid's shoulder.

Sian, whose insouciant carapace had cracked only briefly in the car, was now ensconced in front of my computer, not playing games but developing her programming skills. She'd been engrossed for about an hour when she started to lose concentration. She agreed she might be hungry, though she swiftly declined biscuits: they brought her out in spots, she said. She wasn't keen on a sandwich that didn't contain ham, and eyed with the gravest doubt the basic hummus I whizzed up. Tinned chickpeas, garlic, lemon juice, salt, cumin, tahini and a blender – I couldn't go wrong there, because it was one of my party staples, as were my variants. I divided the mush into three bowls, adding chopped coriander to one, sun-dried tomatoes Sian herself had put through the blender to another, and puréed sun-dried peppers to a third. It was the culinary equivalent of finger painting, but it kept her mind off things.

'Bloody hell, Jodie, I thought Mazza said you didn't like cooking.' She stuck a finger in the first, scooped and sucked. She was just about to use the same finger to test the next when she stopped. 'Where d'you keep your spoons? God, these are great.'

It wasn't long before Dave dot-and-carried himself into the kitchen to join us. I was about to warn him that eating normally while you couldn't exercise normally was a weight-gain disaster, something I'd learned the hard way, but the expression on his face made Sian grab my hand with a scream. He made matters worse by saying in heavy police tones that he'd like a quiet word with me.

I put my arms round her and sat her down. 'She's not a child, Dave.'

'If it's . . . I mean, I need to—'

'Oh, I've not heard about your mum or Mazza yet,' he said, as if already bored with teenage emotion. 'But I have had a call from Daniel. It wasn't just tripwires he found on that sheep-track, Jodie. He found remains. They may be human.'

SIXTEEN

'Full marks for tact, Dave,' I said, as I tried to revive Sian, out in a dead faint on the kitchen floor. It could just as easily have been me, but feeling her slide from my grasp had somehow galvanized me and I'd caught her before she – or I – could fall. Now she was flat on the kitchen floor, legs raised on to the chair next to the one on which Dave had propped his leg while he sat giving me quite unnecessary first aid instructions. 'She and Burble were . . . close.' As were Burble and I, if in a totally different way.

'No one told me,' he protested. 'Might have guessed,' he conceded. 'Shit, Jodie, I shouldn't be here, dossing round like this. I should be out there with the recovery team. Would have been eighteen months ago.'

'Even if you were still working, with that ankle you'd be on sick leave or – what do they call them? – light duties,' I pointed out with admirable lack of logic. I was spared what I suspected would have been an extremely acid response when the doorbell rang. Rosemary McVicar. We exchanged the smiles of polite but cautious acquaintances. She blinked first.

'It was so good to meet you properly, Jodie. I'd heard so much about you,' she declared, with the sort of grin that made you think she was already a friend.

I nearly riposted that I'd heard so much *of* her, but buttoned my lip. We might have got over any possible embarrassment during our muted exchange this morning, and in any case I blamed Dave for assuming he could simply bring his partner here. And then I wondered why on earth he shouldn't. We lived in a house, not a church. Please, don't let me start thinking Merry's thoughts! Flinging the door wide with a welcoming sweep of the arm – that wasn't very Merry-ish; I felt better already.

As she stepped inside, Rosemary dropped her voice. 'Any news?'

'Not of Carrie Burns. And her son's gone along with Theo to make a voluntary statement, or at least say what his lawyer says he can say. But Dave's just had a phone call. They've found a body.'

She put her hand on my arm. 'Not that lad you've been worried about? Bumble? No, that's the cricket commentator.'

If she knew that, sometime in the summer I must invite her to my St John's Wood pad and let her watch the cricket from my balcony. Dave didn't care for the game, and Theo had only limited enthusiasm.

I flashed her a smile to show I'd registered more than a slip of the tongue, but shook my head. 'Our lad's called Burble. As for the . . . the remains . . . they don't know who it is. Even if it is a who, not a what. Just that . . . something . . . was found on the hillside the far side of the village. But Carrie Burns' daughter's in the kitchen, having fainted dead away thinking they've found the body of her boyfriend, who's been missing for some days now. Dave's keeping an eye on her.'

'Do you want me to make a highly unofficial call?' She flourished her mobile. 'See what I can find out? I might be freelance now, but I've got mates still working for the police.'

'I'll take over from Dave and send him into the living room. You can fill him in without Sian overhearing.'

She put a hand on my arm. 'Talking about overhearing – I'm really sorry. Poor old thing had lost his mojo after his enforced retirement. I reckon that's why he did that crazy bike trip. And then the thought of being crippled, if only for a few weeks . . . Anyway, as you'll have gathered, he seems to have got it back. But—'

'Forget it. I have,' I lied. 'More important things to think about.' Which was true.

Sian had regained consciousness, but Dave had ensured she stayed lying down by dint of pressing one of his crutches against her shoulder. '*Now* you can think about getting up, with Jodie here to catch you if needs be. Easy does it, both of you.'

'Yes, nurse,' Sian said with a cocky tilt of her chin. But she consented to be helped up and accepted a couple of squares of my favourite Divine chocolate. She even managed a pale grin when she registered the name. 'Didn't know vicars had to have special food,' she said. But she ended on a sob. 'It's not fair, Mum and Mazza being arrested for something they didn't do. And now – oh, what if it is Burble?' She clutched my hand painfully.

I dealt with the first point first. Easier all round. 'Your mum and Mazza have top class solicitors to look after them.'

'How come?' She narrowed tear-filled eyes. 'It's you, isn't it? Why?'

'Same reason as I got Mazza running and you working up your computer skills.'

'Ah. Your do-gooding,' Sian declared accusingly. 'That's what Mum says it is. Do-gooding,' she repeated. 'Same as when you lent Burble your camera. Which may be why he's dead.'

I couldn't argue – it was what I'd been thinking myself, after all. The front door opened and voices reached us: Theo, Mazza and Carrie.

'That's enough from you, my girl,' Carrie declared, surging in. 'Jodie's mates have saved us from a hell of a mess.'

Mazza had picked up the rest of what Sian had said. 'What's that about Burble?'

Theo, dazed-looking but perhaps on automatic pilot, had boiled the kettle and made a big pot of horrible vicarage tea-bag tea. Somehow all our guests sat down. But he stopped dealing out mugs to look at me, still standing.

I gripped the back of a chair, looking at the white knuckles as if they belonged to someone else, and updated them. 'Doctor McVicar,' I concluded, 'the forensic scientist who joined us this morning, Carrie, is here, trying to get some hard news for us.'

'News she'd rather hear in private,' Carrie observed shrewdly but not necessarily wisely, given the effect it had on her children, who, if they'd been white before, were now green.

'News she needs to be able to hear – there's a much better signal in the living room,' Theo said sharply. Then he grabbed the conversation and turned it in a slightly less sensitive direction. 'Thanks to Jodie, the police had to bag all the bikes they found in Carrie's garden. Then Doctor McVicar suggested they check them for Mazza's DNA – and Carrie's and Sian's, of course – before any charges could be brought. She, like Jodie, thinks that someone planted them there.' He paused to smile at me. 'As do the legal team who turned up mob-handed at the police station. They pulled together Dave's tripwire injury, your tyres being slashed, Jodie, and the speed with which the police arrived after Carrie's discovering the bikes, as evidence that something bigger might be in train. Oh, and I mentioned your being run down that night.'

'And were they impressed?' I asked.

'The legal team yes; the police no. They refused point blank to waste their budget – though they called it Public Money – on something as trivial as bike theft. So I'm afraid Doctor McVicar will have to do that privately.'

'How much will that cost?' Carrie was now as pale as her kids.

'Didn't you hear her say this morning that she'd bill me? Mates' rates,' I declared cheerfully. Or as cheerfully as I could manage – in reality, as we heard the sound of the living room door, our expressions froze and we held our collective breath.

Rosemary actually tapped at the door as she put her head round it. 'It's news and not news. The pathologist confirms that the remains are human so a PM will be held. They're also working on the person's ID. But at this stage I can tell you that they'll rule nothing in and nothing out. They simply don't have the resources to fast-track DNA and other forensic tests. So I'm sorry, there's really nothing more that I can tell you.'

Theo put three mugs of tea and a plate of biscuits on a tray. 'I'll carry it – years of training. After you, Rosemary,' he insisted brightly, clearly, to my eyes, going to extract information Rosemary hadn't shared with the Burns family.

I spread my hands helplessly. 'Carrie, is there anything I can do to help? I wish I could offer you our spare room for a nap before you have to go to work—'

She laughed, not unkindly. 'Nap? Don't tell the boss but there's a nice quiet corner I can usually get a bit of shut-eye in. I'm not one to ignore an emergency bell, though, not like some I could name. I reckon it's easier to get the old dear a bedpan than have to change stinking sheets later. And better

for them, of course,' she added quickly, 'though most of them
are so doolally they don't even know they're in a bed, let alone
a wet one.'

'What about you two?' I asked the kids. 'Do you want to
camp here like you did before or would you like me to come
down and sleep at your place – if that's OK by you, Carrie?'

'Babysit us, like?' Sian shot at me.

'Be with you to pass on any news,' I said evenly.

'News? Overnight? No, the filth are nine till five now,'
Mazza said. He remembered, belatedly perhaps, that I was an
ally. 'No, you're all right, Jodie, thanks all the same.' Which
I took to mean they'd rather manage without me.

'You'll call me if there are any problems, any at all,' I said.
It was more a statement than a question. 'Now, what about
food? Everyone knows I can't cook cakes for love nor money,
but you should try my curries.'

Sian made a wonderful retching noise; I was ready to be
offended, but suddenly I knew that she'd treated me as a mate
– and what greater honour was there than that? 'Thanks for
the vote of confidence,' I laughed. 'How about Chinese? I'm
a dab-hand with stir-fries.' And I had those lovely new pans
to try out.

'I think you've been reading John's Gospel about feeding the
five thousand,' Theo said as he washed the wok. 'Loaves and
fishes, sweetheart.'

'I've got that far. But why John's version?'

He started on the sauté pan, which had done sterling service
as a substitute second wok. 'Because that's the only account
of the miracle that includes someone donating food out of the
goodness of their heart.'

I wrinkled my nose. 'But wasn't it a little boy who did
that?'

'The point is that it wasn't one of the disciples, who were
supposed to do good. The boy was what our American friends
might call just an ordinary guy.'

'I don't think a parson's wife quite qualifies as an ordinary
guy,' I demurred. 'Anyway, I like cooking Chinese. And getting
the kids to prepare the vegetables took their minds off things.

I thought Rosemary did a good job too, getting Dave to tell us his better police stories.' We'd all ended up with tears of laughter. 'She's wasted on him.'

'A lot of people would say that about you and me,' he said quietly. 'A millionaire giving up everything—'

I put my finger to his lips. 'Ah, but I didn't, did I? And thank goodness I didn't, or how would I have paid all those no doubt eye-watering legal and forensic bills? There are times,' I said, stowing the new wok in the cupboard, 'when Monopoly money is quite useful. And I've got an idea lurking at the back of my head that means we might just need some more.' What I should have said, of course, was that even if I'd given up everything to marry him I'd have counted myself a winner. I'm sure Merry would have – probably did.

But he didn't seem to have noticed. He was too busy giving a final polish to the sauté pan. 'More saucepans as good as these?' he asked hopefully.

'Those too,' I agreed peaceably, tucking my arm in his and leading him off to bed.

SEVENTEEN

After coming up to the rectory for a short run with me – tacitly we agreed to avoid the long run along the ridge, and not just because it was cold and wet – Mazza mooched off to see which of his mates he could rouse at the unearthly hour of eleven, pointing out that if he couldn't get them out of bed the prospect of a job wasn't likely to. 'Unless that mate of yours would give me a bonus for everyone getting to work on time,' he said with a grin.

Reminding him by example that he ought to warm down with a good stretch, I joked, 'You could always suggest it.'

He grinned, still jogging on the spot. 'Look, I'll see you, right?' And off he ran.

Dave was ensconced in the living room, of course, his injured leg propped up. With no Mazza to challenge, how would he amuse himself? But my cousin could still surprise me. Eschewing the delights of daytime TV, he was engrossed in a good thick book, *Crime and Punishment*, no less.

'When I got slung on the scrap heap,' he declared, patting the spine as if it was a friendly dog, 'I told myself I'd read at least one good book a month. You know, a real classic. To make up for what I missed when I was young. Theo, who seems to have a better sense of humour than I gave him credit for, found me this.' Back went the reading glasses: I was dismissed. At least I could guarantee that I could shower in peace – even if the water soon ran cold. I longed for my apartment's unlimited supplies. Theo had worked hard to clear his appointments so we could travel up this afternoon and have our London time tomorrow. But we wouldn't be going tomorrow, would we? Neither of us would want to leave people who might need us if the news was what the pit of my stomach told me it would be – that the body was Burble's.

My hair still wet, I ran downstairs. 'Dave, I won't have to identify the remains, will I?'

He heaved himself to his feet and gave me a cousinly bear-hug, which was just what I needed, apart from one of his crutches slithering from his arm and crashing down my shin. 'Good news, bad news? Well, you might as well have the bad. According to Rosie's contact, there's not a lot of him to identify.'

'Him?' I repeated sharply.

'The pelvic bones. The usual give-away. As for the flesh and other tissue, the weather's been warm, and—'

'Scavengers?'

'I'm afraid so.' I felt his ribs expand as he took a deep breath. 'Again according to Rosie's source, there was wire nearby. The lad may have fallen and – with luck – broken his neck.'

We both knew what the alternative to a swift merciful death might be.

'But we won't know anything yet. The post-mortem's not scheduled till Thursday. Cuts, Jodie, cuts! And no, you'll have to wait for the official post-mortem before you can commission a private one. So you and Theo might just as well shove off and enjoy a day's breather – get your strength up for when the results come out.'

I shook my head firmly.

But then came an onslaught: 'Have you looked in the mirror recently, my girl? I know we've only really seen each other at posh events, and I must say you've scrubbed up very well for those, but like I said, you've really let yourself go.'

'How dare—' I began furiously.

He ploughed on. By now, I admit, I was listening. 'Go and make yourself look like the woman Theo fell in love with. And before you say that it won't be much fun for him sitting around while you're being returned to a fit and proper state, can you imagine anything better for him than sitting on your balcony with the sun on his face and a book in his hands? You may say you don't need a break, Jodie, but Theo must be near to burn out. The hours that poor bugger works! And for peanuts, too, I don't doubt. When did he last have a holiday?'

'Our honeymoon.' Those two weeks in South Africa seemed a lifetime ago.

'And since then he's on duty six days of the seven. Good schedule for a heart attack that – and no doubt wherever he goes he's pressed to eat cake or a biscuit to go with the vile tea and coffee. You need to watch him, Jodie. That's what Rosemary says, anyway,' he admitted. 'She'll keep an eye on me while you're off – and there's Mazza, of course.'

My regular London hairdresser promised that if I could get to her salon before five, she'd stay behind to deal with me; one of her colleagues could work on my hands while the hair colour was taking. Theo briefly havered about illicitly missing two hours of parish time, but agreed that he could actually work on the train and would go ahead to open up the flat while I got pampered. I arrived at the salon with four minutes to spare.

Theo was clearly pleased with the results. But then, our sex life was always immeasurably better away from Lesser Hogben.

While he slept in the following morning – though I hated to admit it, Dave had probably been right about his exhaustion – I had a disconcerting visit from Ravi, my favourite of the concierge/security team. Today he was channelling not Jeeves but a PI.

'I suspect we foiled a tired old scam the other day, Doctor Harcourt,' he said quietly. 'Someone dressed as a workman – overalls, cap, bag of tools, and so on – said you'd asked him to check your dishwasher. Or not,' he added, 'given that all the maintenance is under contract. The funny thing is that I'm sure I've seen him before. When he asked if you lived here.'

'Really? You look as suspicious as I feel Ravi. Thank you.'

'We thought you might like this.' He flourished a DVD. 'We downloaded the footage from all the CCTV cameras. Should there ever be any trouble, I'm sure the police facial recognition system would find them good enough to work on.'

He declined a tip, as I knew he would. It was strictly against regulations to accept one, after all. But we both knew that he was always welcome to watch the cricket from my balcony, whether I was there or not. A couple of times I'd been able to wangle him into a hospitality box; he and I had probably been the only ones watching the game, rather than drinking far too much far too early. Thank goodness my networking days were over.

I discovered he'd got an audition later in the week and was just wishing him a broken leg when he disappeared in response to a crackle from his radio.

I weighed the DVD in my hand. Did I need to worry about this? On the whole I thought I probably did. Firstly, my address was hardly public knowledge, not like Theo's, for instance. Could it be that in my past I'd annoyed someone sufficiently for them to seek me out after all this time? Or was the visit connected with my recent activities in Kent?

They had paid me a visit: I must pay a visit myself. It would be quiet and unobtrusive, and I certainly wasn't going to dress up as a workman. Reaching for the phone I fixed an evening meeting with an old contact of mine at my favourite restaurant, a tiny place, absolutely discreet, within walking distance of the apartment. When he heard whom I'd invited, Theo laid an ecclesiastical egg; he wasn't a vain man, but he'd pretty well come as he was, and though there were some of his clothes in the wardrobe, they were thick winter affairs, and today was unseasonably warm. It took me longer to persuade him into the shop than for the suit to be tried on and bought.

'Early birthday present,' I said, flashing the plastic. 'And you look very good in it. Do you want to go in mufti or in a clerical shirt? And there are a couple of things I need too . . .'
While I bought them I worked out exactly how to explain what I was up to. Perhaps it was better for him to wait till I told my dinner guest: good manners would prevent him from expostulating.

They did.

Naturally I'd organized menus without prices. Naturally the champagne was grand cru. Naturally the wines chosen to accompany the exquisite food were as good as my old friend the sommelier had promised. Naturally the proprietor waited on us himself, happy to talk about his children when I enquired, but equally happy to be the soul of silent service. All in all it was a delightful evening, and I achieved, over coffee and liqueurs, what I wanted.

'You can't really be serious,' Theo exploded when we'd waved my contact into his chauffeur-driven car. 'Arrive back in the village by helicopter! What sort of message does that send?'

'A pretty mixed one. I can always tweet that I won a flight in a competition. It does happen. I know it's not the truth, but telling everyone in the village I wanted to fly over what I believe is a highly suspicious building site isn't a good idea either, is it?'

'I really do not like it,' he declared, already walking faster than I could manage in my heels.

'In that case,' I informed him, standing stock still so he had to turn back to me, 'you don't need to come. You can use the return train ticket.'

His face fell comically. I caught him fingering his WWJD plastic wristband. What indeed would Jesus have done if he'd been offered such a treat with such a good ulterior motive? I'm sure I wasn't the only one to be offering up a silent prayer. Mine included one for the future of our marriage; I'd never challenged our relationship like that before.

'Or you could tell something nearer the truth,' he said at last, 'that someone offered you a flight and it would have been rude to turn it down.'

'As a matter of fact,' I said, 'someone else offered me something too . . .' He had to know about that footage sooner or later, and worrying about potential intruders would be better than remorse over luxury travel.

My contact had also suggested a professional photographer, pointing out that a casual sweep or two across the site was entirely reasonable, but persistent overflying was not and would draw attention to ourselves. I could snap away all I liked from one side with the new camera I'd had to buy – the one Burble had used was still in Rosemary's lab. She'd said she'd not found anything suspicious on it, and had offered to return it. But I couldn't have faced using it, and perhaps it would be

used in evidence, so I told her it was probably safer in her
lab than lurking in a corner of our loft. In any case, the snap-
per's gizmo would have made it look like a Stone Age Box
Brownie.

Our pilot risked a couple of circles up above the site, but
when workmen started to look up, as he'd promised, he did
a few stunts, as if we really were just fun passengers. How
would Theo cope? I simply wanted to die; I always did when
the bottom dropped out of my world. But Theo was roaring
with joyous laughter that he'd no doubt feel guilty about later,
in Lesser Hogben at least.

Perhaps landing on the village green wasn't the most tactful
thing I'd ever done, especially as Mrs Mountford happened to
be crossing it at the time. Though George and Alison Cox
seemed to enjoy the spectacle. We got back at eight fifty-nine
precisely.

While Theo dealt with a phone call almost certainly from
Mrs M, I pottered off to dispatch all the photographs, professional and my own, to Rosemary, who had a colleague who
was happy, for a considerable fee, to look at all the pictures.
However, since he was busy in court today, we'd have to wait
for the evening for him to examine them.

It was an edgy day. The first thing was to view the DVD,
with Dave, of course.

'You're dead sure you don't recognize this guy?'

'I'm not sure, in the circumstances, that that's the best way
of putting it,' Theo said.

'Right, first up burn a couple of copies. Send one to your
solicitor, one to my flat, another to – I don't know . . . How
about your bishop, Theo? And the original to a guy I used to
work with who'll bring it to the eyes of the best person – who
may not be the one in charge of the current investigation. For
God's sake, watch your backs, won't you?'

Theo looked him in the eye. 'How safe is this place? Fort
Knox doesn't begin to describe Jodie's London pad, but here
. . .' He spread his hands helplessly.

'*Here*, indeed. Not even modern double glazing to deter a
passing scrote. On the plus side the place is usually occupied;
on the minus . . .' He shrugged. 'If I wanted to inflict damage

here I'd resort to the time-honoured trick of petrol through the letter box and a lighted match. So I'd screw that up for a start, Theo. And get a few fire extinguishers on standby. I'm serious.'

'You're sure you're not being paranoid?'

'Just because you're paranoid, Theo, it doesn't mean they're not out to get you. Look, you do your bit, and I'll make a few calls. When all's said and done, I'm owed a few favours.'

'I've still got work to do,' Theo protested. 'I'm a priest.'

'And by the nature of your job,' Dave said, ignoring Theo's twitch of the head at the word *job*, 'very vulnerable. But I don't think it's you they want to – shall we say, talk to?'

'Is that supposed to make me feel better? That they're threatening Jodie?'

Dave held up a hand. 'You're jumping the gun there. No one's threatened anyone – yet. We're just going to take some sensible precautions. And I'd get CCTV installed right now. Not necessarily obvious stuff – nice and discreet. OK, Jodie? Try these people.' He jotted on our phone pad. 'Grace Brothers. As in the TV sitcom. No, I know that doesn't sound like any security firm you've ever heard of: that's the whole point, isn't it? They'll make it look as if they're just repairing your gutters – something that needs doing in any case, if you ask me. Everything the cameras pick up will come through to a monitor here, but more important, a monitor on their premises, where it'll automatically be stored. They won't come cheap but they'll come today.' He brought up a number on his mobile, which he handed to me.

'Thanks, Dave. It's only Monopoly money, after all, sweetheart,' I said, kissing Theo as I left to make the call.

I also did as I was told and emailed copies of the footage on the security disc to half a dozen people, including some of my own contacts who might just recognize the so-called workman. My in-box contained a few items to be included on the village website. Mazza, busily covering our letter box with another of his stray pieces of scrap metal, assured me that Sian was now spending hours catching up on her weeks of overdue homework, so I added them myself, and tidied up a few loose ends. The sun was shining warmly now, so what I ought to do was go into the garden again, though I was reluctant, to be frank, to mess up my hands and hair. And change, of course, from London to Lesser Hogben gear.

I was just psyching myself up to do my Cinders at midnight act when the front door bell rang. Our guest was possibly taken aback by my appearance, but, being Ted Vesey, he soon regained his aplomb and more or less invited himself in.

'I'm afraid, Ted, that you've missed Theo. He left some forty minutes ago.' In a rather belated response to that summons from La Mountford, who was presumably chewing his ears off even now about the chopper.

'In fact, dear lady, it was you I wanted to speak to.'

So where should I put him? He was not a kitchen table man, any more than I was a Theo's study woman. Dave, of course, was ensconced in the living room. I could always dispatch him to his room – where better to prop up an injured limb than the bed? – but felt an obscure desire for a witness. And Dave did a remarkable thing that made me suspect he must have been as good a policeman as he said he was. He made himself invisible, all six foot five of him. He shook hands with Ted, but then returned to his book, and disappeared from our consciousness.

'How can I help you, Ted?' I graciously gestured at a seat with the least view of Dave, drawing my own chair closer, clearly giving him my complete attention.

'I hear that you're able to access a charitable foundation, Jodie,' he said, with a frank smile that immediately put me on my guard. What was he up to?

'Indeed I am. Its exclusive aim is to support the development of young people lacking a formal education. So it helps fund apprenticeships, sometimes pays course fees and occasionally offers a degree of maintenance.'

'Its parameters are set in stone?' he asked delicately.

'You know what the Charity Commissioners are like: the trust daren't deviate so much as a semicolon from its terms of reference.'

'And it's *allowed* to support people with a criminal background?'

Could I guess what he was up to? 'Absolutely,' I declared with my sunniest smile. 'I wouldn't go so far as to say it prefers ne'er-do-wells, but its target is specifically the socially disadvantaged. Why, Ted, are you concerned that it might exceed its brief if it encourages young Malcolm Burns and his like?' Gotcha!

'The thought had occurred to me that there might be more worthy recipients. But it seems the fund was almost designed to help him and his ilk.' You could see the effort he put in to keeping his face bland.

'It was. And I'm proud to be a trustee of such a noble fund.' You could almost hear *Nimrod* playing in the background. 'Now, tell me, how are our church funds doing?' I'd drawn unwelcome discussions to an end before. And clearly it was a question I was entitled to ask. I was just glad to have got it in before he mentioned the chopper ride. 'You see,' I continued, without waiting for a response, 'I have a moral dilemma. You will be well aware that I have access to other monies.'

He gave a delicate cough. 'I am not unaware, though you hardly bruit it abroad.'

Was that a euphemism for going round dressed like a bag-lady? 'Would it benefit me if I did broadcast it? Or, more to the point, benefit Theo?' Then I waited. It might have been a rhetorical question, but it would be interesting to see if he answered it.

'It might benefit the church!'

'It might equally harm Theo's credibility. But I can hardly let St Dunstan's fall down about our ears. Your and George's ears, actually, because while you're both signed up for three years, rectors move on, don't they? Or are moved on – I've never quite grasped how it works. So do I swan in, a latter-day Lady Bountiful, or do I sit back and do nothing? What would you do?' It was a reasonable question, given the apparent affluence he enjoyed. 'I've already agreed to do a sponsored run, and made a match-funding offer, haven't I? It's usually in the ratio of one to one, but that presupposes the other participants in the bargain have the resources to raise a reasonable amount. How much would you say the sponsored teddy bear jump will raise, for instance?'

He snorted. 'Tens rather than hundreds. Certainly not the thousands we need.'

'The shop will bring in a tiny rental, I suppose, and share some of the day-to-day running costs. But I see a vast chasm between what we can raise and what the quinquennial report said we need. Come on, there must be something better than teddies – I'm so sorry!' I covered my face in embarrassment.

He gave a short laugh. 'Don't think I haven't heard that before. I was braced for it all the way through the PCC meeting that discussed the matter, as it happens. I thought about a sponsored abseil down the tower—'

'I'd certainly put up at least a thousand pounds if you did it!' Though I gave a social laugh, I was entirely serious.

'Not me personally,' he said tetchily.

'I don't see why not. You. Theo. George we might have to excuse because of his heart condition. Me. I can think of one or two others, too.'

'Ida Mountford, for instance? I can just see her in a hard hat and harness.' His laugh sounded genuine. Then his eyes narrowed. 'Why not just donate, Jodie? Think about rich men and heaven and camels and the eye of a needle.'

'If you just wanted to ask me to do that, you could have done it with far more tact, Ted. Now, what exactly did you come for? I'm sure your time's as valuable as mine, so I assume you'll forgive my blunt speaking. Ah! Please excuse me: Theo's not keen on my letting the phone ring on to answerphone, in case there's someone in urgent need. Dave, why don't you apply your skills to the coffee-machine? I particularly recommend the mocha. And I'm sure you know where the biscuits are. Perhaps Ted will carry the tray for you.'

The caller was the woman whose husband had left her on her own with the disabled child. Apparently he'd come back, tail between his legs, and she wanted to thank Theo for his prayers. I talked to her a bit about the nature of the child's medical issues and the difficulties they had dealing with the authorities. At last, I said, forthrightly, 'If I were you I'd contact my councillor and also my MP – they're good at stirring things up on behalf of their constituents.' I was exceeding my brief, wasn't I? 'But look, I'm not an expert. I'm not Theo. I just put my mouth into gear before my head. I'll get Theo to phone you – I'm sure he'd like to hear your good news in person. I'm sorry? I can hardly hear you . . .'

'One of those damned great JCBs outside the house. Oh, and it's woken Jason, just after I'd got him off . . .'

By the time I returned, Dave had moved to the opposite end of the sofa; he and Ted were affably discussing the changes made to Kent's St Lawrence ground. I joined in for a few minutes, but soon Ted was looking at his watch – a top of the range Tag Heuer no less – and getting to his feet. We exchanged bland farewells on the step, curtailed when a lorry bearing ladders and lengths of plastic guttering pulled up.

'I'm sick of getting dripped on,' I said by way of an explanation, 'and I didn't think I'd need a faculty for basic maintenance.'

'As one who's been dripped on many times, I'm quite sure you don't,' he said with a charming smile.

'So what the hell was that all about?' I asked Dave before he could pick up his Tolstoy again. 'I thought at first Ted was thinking about blackmail, but I can't think what he might have on me.'

'You always were the lily-white girl, weren't you? Perhaps it's something you're not embarrassed about but he thinks you might be. Which shows how little he knows you, I'd say. Of course there might be stuff you wouldn't want Theo to know about.'

'Which shows how little you know me. And him,' I said with a grin.

'Was he asking for money? No. Like you said, he'd have licked your arse a bit more if that was the case.'

'Did he say anything of note to you?'

'He thought Kent's prospects were better than I did. One thing – he looked at his watch a couple of times. Not in that finger-drumming way people use when they're sick of waiting – as he might have been for you. Now, Jode – don't book me into the funny farm – he couldn't have been establishing some sort of alibi, could he?'

'To prove he's not robbing a bank?'

'The big cheese in a gang is never there at the front end.'

'Like McCavity,' I suggested. 'And if you don't know *Old Possum's Book of Practical Cats* you could try it after *War and Peace.*' But he wasn't joking, was he? 'Actually, I've known no end of people who've wanted an unpleasant outcome at a meeting but didn't turn up to fire the bullets. They sent their apologies and someone else did the dirty work.'

'Excatly. And your Ted Vesey strikes me as that sort of man.'

EIGHTEEN

When TVInvicta led their lunchtime news with a story about a JCB scooping out the safe from an Isle of Thanet post office, Dave and I fell about with entirely inappropriate giggles, choking like school kids over our explanation to Theo, who all too clearly did not think that Ted was masterminding a distant bank raid.

'I just hope this won't lose support for our venture,' he said, already ten years older than when we landed this morning. 'It's one thing having the church fall down slowly for lack of maintenance, another to have it knocked down about our ears.'

'Don't start looking like Eeyore in search of his tail,' Dave said, trying to straighten his face. 'It all depends where they install the safe. Put it on the outer shell of the building where someone can just drive up to it and frankly you're asking for trouble. Install a few reinforced bollards, or in St Dunstan's case some Norman buttresses, and you should be OK. As for the church plate—'

'That's safe in Canterbury Cathedral treasury,' Theo said. 'So people can look but not touch. The plate we use now is EPNS – and I fancy the silver plating's wearing off.'

'It is. I tried polishing it when the regular cleaning rota seemed to have a hiccup. So what's in the safe in the nave floor?' I asked.

Theo blinked. 'What safe?'

'It's under the carpet that covers the De Villiers brasses. I should imagine that Ted and George have the keys, assuming Mrs Mountford let them slip from her hot little hands. Come on, I'll show you. A bit of fresh air won't do you any harm,' I said pointedly as he looked at his watch. 'Dave'll hold the fort.'

'No! You can't leave the house! What if . . .? All this security and you want to show yourself in public?' Theo added more coherently.

'I'm not going to be a prisoner.' I found I couldn't add, *in my own home.* Because it wasn't, was it? Not yet.

Before we could leave, however, a call came through for me. From Dilly Pound, of all people.

'That story about JCBs and post offices reminded me of our conversation the other day, Jodie. I just wanted to say I did make enquiries, but I've heard nothing yet.'

'We might have the worst sort of news,' I said gently, remembering her reaction to the thought of dying alone. 'A body was found not far from here. On the Downs. It's not yet been ID'd, but I'm terribly, terribly afraid . . .'

'Oh my God. I'm so sorry.' She sounded it. 'Oh, Jodie, keep me up to speed, won't you?'

The sun, though not as hot as yesterday's in London, was pleasantly warm. Dave adjourned to the garden, leg propped up on a decaying bench that just about took his weight. Although he had *War and Peace* on his lap, I had an idea he was hoping to engage in conversation with some of the workmen as he waved us off on our walk.

I thought it would do Theo's heart good if I set a spanking pace and took us the long way round. It might be safer too, come to think of it. Theo heard what he thought was a sky lark. There were no cuckoos – too early in the year, he explained – but the hedges were alive with avian building activity.

'*Oh, to be in England, Now that April's here!* Not that it is quite April, but the clocks go forward on Saturday, which always makes me feel full of the joys,' I said.

'And makes me terribly likely to be late for eight o'clock Communion,' he said. 'I'll have to rely on you to find a way to wake me up.'

And yet I had a sense that both Theo and I were being as cheerful as we could so that neither knew how badly the other was suffering. When he flagged a little, I chivvied him: 'Don't forget, you should just be able to speak, so you might as well tell me the feedback from our adventure this morning.'

'Not sure . . . if it's possible . . . to laugh . . . at this speed.'

I slowed obligingly. 'It's not often you get to laugh down here, darling, so here's your chance.'

He didn't pick up on the reference to *down here*. 'Most people – especially people like Violet and Alison – were delighted. Thought it was the best thing to happen to the village for ten years. Elaine wasn't so sure, I don't think, but she said nice things about improving your image and so on.'

'La Mountford?'

'She was so upset she had to take some of her pills.'

'Serves her right for dragging you out so early. I just wish I could ask you what for.'

'If you did I could tell you: it wasn't really pastoral business at all.'

'OK: what for?'

'To moan about the disaffected youths hanging round the village. I referred her to the police, or to the county council, who were, as I told her, the ones who closed the youth club. But she seemed to think that a youth club was a waste of public money anyway.'

'Not exactly a meeting of minds.'

He groaned. 'She's such a demanding woman. Sometimes it's hard not to tell her so to her face.'

'Being good's hard work, isn't it?' I remarked flippantly.

His forbearing half-sigh made me wish I hadn't. He changed the subject. 'What did Ted Vesey have to say about the helicopter? I was afraid it would blow all his beautiful windows in.'

I slapped my head in irritation. 'Of course! That was what was wrong with his morning visit: he didn't mention the chopper.'

'Perhaps he'd been away for the night too.'

'I'm sure you're right.' But I wasn't.

'I'm so ashamed,' Theo began, kneeling to roll back the carpet, 'that even after you mentioned them I've never been to see the brasses. And as for the safe, I haven't a clue where the key might be. Or rather the combination,' he said, sitting back on his haunches and inspecting what looked to be a remarkably solid mass of metal sunk flush with the stone paving that helped make the church so cool today – or so cold most of the time.

'I suppose if the churchwardens know, then there's no need for anyone else to,' I said. 'You could always ask one of them. Why not give George a bell now?'

'Because he, like Ted, does such an enormous amount in behind the scenes admin, I wouldn't want to disturb him.'

'Well,' I persisted, cocking an ear, 'why not go and interrupt him in one of his behind the scenes jobs? I'm sure he wouldn't mind if you interrupted his strimming.'

Nor did he. He took the precaution of grabbing a kneeler before he joined Theo and me on our knees as if we were praying that the safe might open itself. It didn't.

'I don't like being in the dark,' George said, reaching for his mobile, 'so I'll give Ted a call. If he doesn't know the combination, I'm sure Ida Mountford will. She makes it her business to know everything else, so I can't imagine she'd forget a secret like this. Otherwise it must be written down in one of those dusty tomes in the vestry no one ever gets round to reading. Leave it to me, Theo. I'll get back to you.' He smiled as we hauled him to his feet. 'Thanks, Jodie. Oh, the joints aren't what they used to be. They'll welcome a little break from the graves.'

Since neither the safe nor its possible contents were really any of our business, Theo responded to a phone summons to a distant part of the benefice with the promise he'd be there within the hour. So it was another brisk walk home, but the more direct route, so he could pick up the car.

Waving him off, I reflected that perhaps mowing the lawn was a job I could accomplish without ruining my hands. I stared at the battered-looking machine in puzzlement, eventually summoning Dave to hobble round to see what was vexing me.

'I can't see a cable point. Or an on-off mechanism,' I wailed.

He patted me kindly on the shoulder. 'You wouldn't, Jodie, would you? It's like your dad's remember – push and pull. Golly, he was so proud of the stripes on his lawn, wasn't he? Remember when I got it out again after he and my dad had nipped out for a snifter down the pub and I mowed the lawn the other way?'

'And it came out chequered like a chessboard? You got the hiding of your life, didn't you!'

'And no Social Services coming after Dad either. Times have changed a bit since then, Jode, and not necessarily for the better. Look, this thing's so old Noah probably chucked it out of the Ark. Heaven knows when it was last serviced.'

'Serviced? Like cars?'

'The blades sharpened and reset, and the whole lot oiled. You could try it on the grass,' he added doubtfully, 'but it won't do that back of yours any good.'

'My back's fine,' I objected.

'Used to be. Until you started to grow a permanent hunch. Look at yourself in a mirror, sideways on. It must be affecting your running times. Anyway, I give you ten minutes max with this mower. You'll be at a garden centre in thirty flat.'

After twenty minutes' gruelling effort, the lawn looked worse rather than better. The garden centre beckoned. But not before one of the workmen, coming to tell me their job was done, also told me that safety cameras or no safety cameras, he wouldn't want to sleep in the rectory at night. 'Not with the wiring in this state,' he added. 'Insulation rotten, fuse board years out of date. You want to get it sorted, sooner rather than later, too. Before it burns down round your ears.'

Another faculty? Or dare I get someone in on my own authority? I propped a note on Theo's desk.

A nice new shiny electric mower in the back of the Audi, I was tootling back through the village when I saw Alison Cox walking hard.

'Can I offer you a lift?'

She got in, arguing. 'George is up at the church and I can't get him on his mobile. He probably can't hear with that damned strimmer of his, but all the same.'

'All the same,' I agreed, ignoring the speed limit.

The strimmer lay abandoned against the hideous Victorian tomb. Hadn't he left it there when he came to look at the safe? I ran into the church. George had keeled over where we'd last seen him. But it wasn't the heart attack I'd always feared for him that made me dial nine-nine-nine; it was the raw head wound. Someone had knocked him out. In a man that age, the blow might well have killed him. It hadn't – yet.

Seeing her husband like that might well have killed Alison, too. But she took charge, pointing out even as we got him into the recovery position that she was a trained first-aider and had seen far worse than this during her stint in the prison service. It wasn't until the paramedics loaded him into an ambulance and the first police vehicles were arriving that she allowed her voice to quaver, but by then I was bundling her into the Audi. 'I'm taking her to A&E, Officer,' I declared to my old adversary, the sergeant, who clearly couldn't quite place me with the new hairdo and the flour-free trousers, 'and then I'll be back to make a statement. Doctor Harcourt, remember. The rectory.'

George Cox was still alive when Alison and I arrived at Ashford's William Harvey hospital. Clearly she wasn't going to leave him, so I promised to collect the list of things she hoped that he'd need. Insisted he would need. I wouldn't argue, though I thought a few prayers from Theo might be in order, as I told him when I phoned.

Poor George wouldn't be needing a shaving kit or his reading glasses and Kindle for a few hours, so I headed not to their cottage but to St Dunstan's. Despite Dave's bitterness, despite my anger at their treatment of the Burns family, I still felt a frisson of gratitude at the sight of blue and white tape and a couple of white-suited women looking calm and efficient.

The hostile sergeant, whose name I at last discovered was Carl Masters, passed me grudgingly to a young constable called Lily Glover, a name that seemed to suit her high-coloured prettiness.

'When I left George, he was about to make a couple of phone calls,' I told her. 'The first was to be to a man called Ted Vesey, with whom he shared churchwardens' duties. Incidentally, Mr Vesey's got a key to the church and will no doubt lock up if you ask him to.' I pointed out his cottage across the green. 'If Ted didn't have the information George needed, he'd have made a second call to Mrs Ida Mountford, their predecessor in the role.'

Lily smiled ironically. 'One woman does the job, she leaves, it takes two men. Typical.' She settled more comfortably on a table tomb, swinging her legs like a kid skiving off school. Deciding not to correct her impression of Mrs Mountford, I joined her. The sun felt good on our heads, calming and reassuring after all the drama. 'So why should he phone them?'

'To ask for the combination to the safe he was kneeling by when I found him. The floor safe. In fact, of course – I'm sorry, I'm not thinking straight – he may have got the information from the first call and not had to bother with the second. There was no sign of the mobile when I found him. I assumed he'd made his calls and pocketed it before he was attacked.'

'Big assumption,' she countered, clearly not one to be told her job by amateurs. 'More likely a visitor to the church saw him by the safe and tried to coerce him into opening it.' Her eyes rounded at the prospect. Then she tried a more banal theory. 'Or perhaps they saw him using the phone and chanced their arm. Lots of opportunist mobile phone thefts.'

'George's mobile was so old it would have reduced a thief to tears of pity. Its rightful place was in a museum.'

'Even so, there are a lot of disaffected youngsters round here. Hey, there's one by your car right now!'

Dropping her notepad, she started down the patch. Even though I'm no sprinter, I overtook her comfortably.

'Hi, Jodie, you been bending your plastic again? Bosch, eh? Burble will— would . . . He would have . . .' Mouth working, he turned away.

I hugged him. Hard. Poor, poor kid. No doubt his gut told him, as mine did, that the corpse on the mortuary table today was his mate's. At last, wiping his snotty nose on the sleeve of his hoodie until I produced a paper tissue, he said, 'I just thought – you know – maybe lighting a candle or something. Theo being the vicar and that.'

'A candle would be a great idea,' I said, though I suspected they did more for the living who lit them than for the dead, 'but as you can see the church is closed just now. I found George Cox laid out cold inside.' And I knew the instant the words left my mouth I shouldn't have been saying them.

'Isn't that Malcolm Burns?' Sergeant Masters demanded,

elbowing Glover to one side. 'You again. And no fancy lawyer this time. What do you know about this, then?' He pointed back towards the church with all the understatement of Laurence Olivier in *Hamlet*.

'Only what Jodie told me,' Mazza said innocently. 'I was just admiring her new mower, like.'

Masters turned to jab him in the chest. 'Get a good price for that, would you?'

'Jodie's a good friend . . . of my mum's,' he said, thinking on his feet for once. 'And she's been good to me and my kid sister. I'd cut off my right hand sooner than harm her. As for George, he's a decent guy. Tried to teach me how to bowl once.' To my delight he limited his expletives.

'Got his phone, have you? Come on, George's phone!' He made *give me* gestures.

Meek as a lamb, but clearly seething, Mazza turned out his pockets without even being asked. Along with a battered pack of condoms, some fags and a lighter, his mobile gleamed in the sun.

'Ah!' Masters was ready to pounce but found my arm in the way.

'Show them the pictures you took for the website, Mazza,' I said quietly, putting my hand on his wrist. 'That'll speak louder than any protests that you've had it a long time and that it's certainly not George's.'

In fact the first he showed them was me going base over apex over Ted's dog's lead.

'Whoever's that?' demanded Lily. 'Whoever it is doesn't like you much, does he?'

'That,' I said, wishing I didn't have to, 'is the churchwarden George said he was going to call when I left him earlier. Ted Vesey.'

NINETEEN

On impulse, having packed and delivered bags for both George and Alison Cox to the hospital, I stopped by St Dunstan's again. I wanted to talk to God on his own territory about poor unconscious George. The church door stood open, guarded by a community support officer. I'd hardly opened my mouth to ask if I might go inside when Theo drove up, greeting me with a weary smile as he walked up the gravel path. The PCSO crossed himself and genuflected as Theo approached him. It was easy to persuade him that Theo's idea of getting his own key and locking up was a good one.

I asked if I might put the strimmer in the vestry for safe-keeping. PCSO Blue Band thought it better if he did, if only he knew where the vestry might be.

Supper was a spread of excellent curries, all cooked by Rosemary. I suspect she'd fed us so royally because she knew none of us would have much to say: we were, after all, waiting for a call from the forensic photographer, not to mention the results of the post-mortem.

She and I did our best with an animated discussion about the best source of spice. Theo looked as if he was sucking lemons and Dave pulled steadily on the lager intended to accompany, not replace, the meal. There was a great deal left over. There was a great deal of evening left over, too – more than I could have believed. Perhaps there'd be something on TV, or maybe everyone liked card-games.

When the house phone rang it might have been a funeral bell tolling, but as it dawned on us all that anyone calling Rosemary or Dave would use their mobiles, everyone sat back in relief. Except me. Rectory receptionist, of course. The kitchen fell silent. Maybe it was best to take the call on the phone in the hall.

Alison! My stomach somersaulted. 'George?'

'Is still unconscious but improving, they assure me. I just thought you'd want to know. And I wanted to thank you for all you did today – well above and beyond the call of duty. Now, all being well I will take up your kind offer to collect me tomorrow morning. Good night and God bless you, my dear.'

To my shame, I didn't even remember having offered her a lift, but I was embarrassed to admit that to myself, let alone anyone else.

When I got back to the kitchen, Rosemary was just closing her phone.

The faces told me it wasn't good news. Theo pulled out a chair for me. I sat.

'We were all expecting this,' Rosemary said quietly. 'DNA comparison confirms it was Burble. He died, in layman's terms, of a broken neck. It looks as if he tripped and fell.'

'But he was young,' I yelled. 'He'd bounce. He'd fall and get his flesh torn. He'd not just break his neck.' And any moment I'd have to find Mazza and break the news. Or get Theo to do it. That was what clergymen did, wasn't it? Except . . .

Dave raised a hand. 'You missed a couple of words there, Jodie. Rosie said *it looks as if*. He wouldn't be the first person to have his neck broken and then his body arranged artistic-ally to make the death look natural. Of course, natural it might be if he had gone hard over one of those tripwires, in which case any cop worth his salt would be looking to prosecute whoever put the wires there. I would have, but then,' he admitted with a bitter smile, 'I might be biased.' He patted his injured leg.

'Do you think any unbiased cop will want to pursue the tripwire possibility?' I asked. 'Prosecution for manslaughter is better than nothing. But there's something else you haven't told me yet, isn't there, Rosemary?' I braced myself.

She nodded. 'The pathologist found something unexpected when he was examined. Highly unexpected. It's been damaged, but the tech girls and boys are wizards, and should be able to pull something off it.'

My mouth was dry. 'It's the memory card from my camera, isn't it?'

'Yes. From where the pathologist found it, it was clear Burble didn't want it to be found if the person I presume was his assailant searched him.'

'Whoever's in charge of the case had better have my camera as well. Just in case.'

'I'll take it over first thing tomorrow – don't worry, it's in my lab safe.'

Dave said, 'I'll call Don Simpson and get him to collect it. He knows some of the background, although it's still not his case. Pity his old boss had to retire – you'd have liked her, Jodie.' He fished in his pocket for his mobile. So did I, to call Mazza. Voicemail. No, I couldn't leave a message. Not about Burble. That had to be face-to-face.

Dave, on the other hand, did manage a conversation – short and to the point. 'Great. Tonight it is,' was how it ended. Then Dave turned to us to outline what I thought was a simply crazy plan. He wanted us all to leave the house together, using all three cars. Why anyone should want to put tracking devices on any of our cars was beyond me, as was his decision that we should take weird and wonderful routes to deter any physical tails. We'd fetch up at a pub where this Don Simpson character would be waiting, and Rosemary would hand over the camera she'd retrieved from her lab.'

'This is all a bit *Boys' Own*!' Theo objected. 'We're not snotty schoolboys having a Big Adventure.'

'Think what happened to Burble. That wasn't *Boys' Own*.'

'I've got a parish to run.'

'Change your answerphone message and leave your mobile number.'

Theo flushed. The answerphone was so old I'd swear he'd lost the instructions. 'My place is here.' He didn't look at me.

I said quietly, 'I think they're after me, not Theo.'

Wrong. Now Theo would be crushed between two lots of guilt, the Scylla of leaving his flock temporarily undefended, and the Charybdis of risking his wife, and knowing that whatever he'd chosen it might be the wrong one. In London, he'd have made a swift decision; here he still dithered. 'This is ridiculous – Rosemary, why don't you just hand over your lab keys to this Don character and let him get on with it?'

'And compromise all those forensic samples in my care? Only named persons get into my holy of holies, Theo, and because of the legal implications police officers are not among them.' She picked up her keys and handed Dave his crutches. 'What time did you agree to meet Don Simpson?'

'Nine thirty.'

'Let's hit the road, then.' She looked at me, not Theo.

'The Goose that Laid,' Dave said, scribbling on the phone pad. 'This is the postcode for the pub Don's selected. Don would really like to talk to you, Jodie, and you ought to talk to someone with enough clout to act.'

I dug in the drawer where Merry had always kept the car keys. 'OK. Mazza's been a target once – next time it could be far more serious.'

At last I'd pressed the right button. You could almost see a light switched on; certainly Theo's shoulders lifted and he managed a grim smile: 'What are we waiting for?'

I waited till he'd picked his route, then I went my way.

Cynical as I'd been about the mere thought of a tracking device on my car, I soon acquired a tail. At first I just assumed it was Joe Public out for an evening with his girl. But there was something about the way he speeded up when I did and slowed when I braked that worried me. So what were my options?

It was weird: they appeared in my head like a set of bullet points at a presentation:

- Find a police station and ask for protection – were any open in this area at this time of night?
- Find a filling station – though down here they were like hen's teeth unless you were near a supermarket.
- Drive up to a house with lights on and ask for help – assuming the house was occupied, and not using lights as a burglar protection; and who'd want a loony rector's wife asking for shelter?
- Something else.

Given the speed at which I was now travelling, none of the options seemed good. In fact, I was so flagrantly ignoring limits that the police might well come to me before I found them. But my story would take a lot of believing – far easier to give me a ticket and send me on my way. But if I joined the motorway at least I'd have the eyes of CCTV operators, especially if I was driving erratically – which, since I wanted the cameras on me, I did my best to do. I failed. Too much traffic: I didn't want to harm innocent people. Come to think of it, I didn't even want to harm me. So I made sure I flashed my lights vigorously every time I neared a camera. That ought to interest someone. I came off at an intersection, went round the island twice, and to my great pleasure found my tail whizzing off ahead. Sorry about the bad lane driving, everyone. Thence to this Don Simpson's pub – The Goose that Laid. Why not just call it The Golden Egg, for goodness' sake? The satnav insisted I took a narrow twisting lane. I'd have loved to slow right down, but still felt as if someone was breathing down my neck, although my mirror said otherwise. Once or twice I drove the satnav to hysteria by making unauthorized deviations: the poor thing nearly got hoarse telling me to U-turn as soon as possible. But at last, more exhilarated than I cared to admit, I pulled up as near to the pub door as I could and almost tumbled into the bar.

Anyone could have told at ten paces that Don Simpson was the cop in the group in the corner furthest from the fruit machine. BBC central casting might have supplied him, all bulky six feet of him. I bought a J2O and headed their way, looking around as if I had all the time in the world. The Goose was actually quite charming – a better patronized version of the Pickled Walnut – with a quiet game of darts in one corner and some lads playing pool in a yellow-painted annexe off the snug – the golden egg half, no doubt.

'You took your time,' Dave observed.

'So I did. Bit of a problem on the motorway. But better late than never.' I held his gaze, willing him to shut up. I really did not want to talk about my *Girls' Own* journey until I'd prepared a sanitized version for Theo's consumption. But, as if simply checking my phone, I made a note of the make and number of my pursuer's vehicle and would make sure this Don character had them before the evening was over. I assumed my camera was already in his hands – or more literally in the sports bag by his knees.

Don and I shook hands, both of us clearly evaluating the other. I saw a lot of common sense. Tenacity by the ton. Not much in the way of a sense of humour, maybe. But definitely the sort of man you wanted on your side. I didn't think my tentative approval was reciprocated unreservedly. Somewhere deep in Don was a residual belief that woman had certain roles, and I wasn't sure that making a pile was one of them.

Rosemary said quietly, 'I'm afraid my mate's still not looked at your photos, Jodie.'

'What?' It would have been crass to point out that I'd paid him a very great deal of money for the swiftest service.

'Sick child. He sends his apologies. He'll be on to them as soon as maybe.'

It was a good job I'd kept my mouth shut then. I fished in my bag, producing my new camera. 'Not analyzed, or anything, Don, I'm afraid, and I still haven't sorted out the dross from the decent pics, but you can have a look – take the memory card if you wish.'

Looking at me fiercely from under Dennis Healey eyebrows, Don took the camera and reviewed the photos then and there. 'Good snaps,' he grunted, as if we were talking about holiday pictures. He added, with a grudging smile, which finally widened, 'My retirement's not long away; I wouldn't mind a bit of kit like yours for my farewell gift.'

Kit. That was the word Burble had used.

I was about to tell him that as soon as Burble's killers had been dealt with he could have the camera he'd used as a thank you gift. But he couldn't. Sian must have that. If she could handle the emotion, that is.

'What do the photos tell you?' Theo asked.

'That there's a lot of work there that probably didn't get planning permission. Now don't flare up again, Jodie. That's Planning's problem, in the first place. They can demand access and can inspect what's been done. If it's something they can't approve, then everything can be pulled down and restitution made, particularly in the matter of ancient trees. I like it when things can happen without us getting involved.'

'I'll raise a glass to that,' Dave said, suiting the deed to the word. 'Softly, softly. And just as effective. Especially as it wouldn't appear to have any connection with you, Jodie.'

'Except it does, Dave. Apart from all the people who know

about the helicopter flight, at least one person in the village knows I was interested in the site.'

Theo sighed, 'Not Ted Vesey.'

'Two people, then. Ted Vesey met me after I'd been running one day. He asked very particularly what my route might be. I was trying to avoid the amorous intentions of that nasty little dog of his, so I gave him a pretty vague reply. But he's no fool. If I say up hill and down dale, he's going to know which part of the Downs I was heading for.'

Don nodded. He didn't jot in a notepad, as I'd possibly expected, but was using a phone to record the conversation. 'And the other person?'

I shook my head. 'I can't believe I'm saying this. A lovely woman, who teaches me to bake and is kind and imaginative and single-handedly trying to save our village pub.'

'Elaine Grant? You're joking!' Theo buried his face in his hands.

'Elaine's the nearest thing I've got for a friend in the village, Don. I asked her what was going on. She came back with a whole lot of stuff about dairy farming. She talked all about planning permission and making sure the slurry didn't enter the water supply and— No, she's my friend . . .'

'And . . .?' Don prompted me.

'She said she'd got it all off the Internet. But I'd already checked myself and found nothing.'

'And this is the woman who's forgotten more about computers than any of us here will learn in a lifetime,' Dave pointed out.

Don nodded. 'You couldn't have missed something?'

'Easily. Yes, easily. Other things to think about. I've only been in the village a couple of months, Don, I'm still feeling my way.'

His glance was surprisingly sympathetic. 'You give up a big, responsible job and come and live in a one-horse village – it must be hard. My old boss took months to adjust. You need a hobby.'

'I've actually got a new job – being the rector's wife,' I said, wishing I could reach to squeeze Theo's hand.

'Being second in command's not the same as you were doing, though, is it? Any other enemies?'

'Enemies?'

'In a manner of speaking, Jodie,' Don said, as if I was beginning to try his patience.

As one of the bar staff reached for our dirty glasses, rather prematurely, I thought, and decidedly clumsily, Don's phone sang a really naff little tune. One glance and, grabbing the sports bag, he was on his way. Almost. As he got up, he put his hand on my shoulder. 'We'll talk tomorrow, Jodie – my office or your house? I'll come to you,' he decided for me. 'Tennish.'

I got up to follow him, as if heading for the loo. By the bar, I said, 'I know you're in a rush, but I was tailed here. Here are the details.' I brought them up on my phone. 'Three series Beamer, about four years old. Driver white, baseball cap – couldn't pick up the logo. But your motorway cameras will.' I eased him outside. 'My car will show up on a lot of motorway cameras. Each time I passed one I flashed my lights. He'll be not very far behind me. As a tail he was useless, of course, because he followed too closely. Unless of course he wanted me to see him – a visual threat.'

'You sound remarkably knowledgeable.' It didn't sound like a compliment.

'I went out with one of Dave's mates for a few months,' I said. 'And every time we watched a police movie or something like *The Bill* he'd talk me through the mistakes they made.'

'OK, Jodie. I'll be on to this. And if you give me a couple of minutes, I'll organize some unobtrusive company on the way back.' He patted my shoulder and headed for his car.

I used the loo – might as well – and returned, hoping against hope that my extra conversation had gone unnoticed. It might well have done; Dave and Rosie were on their feet, announcing that they were heading back to her place. Theo hadn't quite finished his beer, so I sat down to enjoy a moment of quiet with him. And possibly tell him about our tail, and the need to wait for a tactful police escort.

But then I got a text. Mazza. Could I call him, like, now?

I could – and did. 'Theo, there's a problem at the rectory – Mazza's in a fix. I'm on my way. See you there!'

TWENTY

Unaware of anyone following me, legitimate or otherwise, I drove as briskly as I dared. Trust Dave to bunk off just when Mazza and I might need him. But I wasn't going to waste time calling him, even with Bluetooth. I needed all my powers of concentration.

When I got back to the rectory, the whole area was pulsing with blue lights, as a couple of police people carriers (was that what they called them? Probably something more portentous) joined a couple of police cars stationary in the road rather than parked against the kerb. No doubt it was the drivers of those who were arguing with five or six teenage lads sitting on the rectory wall. They weren't lounging threateningly, swigging from beer cans. They were remarkably upright and disciplined, like so many skittles, come to think of it. Throwing the car – neatly – on to the drive, I headed for the one in the middle – Mazza.

I reached him at the same time as a couple of what looked like combat troops. 'Hi, Mazza! Sorry to keep you hanging around,' I greeted him loudly. The occasion also called for a very public hug. Then I turned, a hand still on Mazza's shoulder. 'And good evening, officers. I'm Doctor Harcourt. I gather there's some problem?' How many times had I spoken to inadequately prepared junior managers like that? It was good to see the tone of voice still worked.

There was an exchange of glances. 'You can see for yourself.' The lead officer, my old friend Sergeant Masters, might have gestured with an accusing hand, but there was more bluster than conviction in his voice.

I looked, very ostentatiously. 'I see one of my running partners, who helped set up the village website. I see a neat stack of empty coke tins. I see a number of Mazza's mates sitting on the rectory wall. I don't see alcohol. I can smell tobacco – stupid kids – but not pot. No needles. No other way to ingest drugs. So the problem is . . .?'

'Unlawful assembly for a start.'

'Really? Aren't they just sitting waiting for me? Mazza helped put together the village website. Now he and I are trying to assemble a team for a community project linking the Women's Institute and the village pub. I promised to brief them.' I was out on a limb, here: who in their right mind would want to talk to a bunch of lads long past their bedtime – mine, not theirs? 'I'd have been here very much earlier, but I was in a meeting with Detective Superintendent Don Simpson. You can confirm it if you like. I just applaud their patience.'

'All the same, we had a call. They said the vicarage was under threat. And I can see why.'

'Of course you can, and I can see why my neighbours might have been alarmed. Would you happen to know who made the complaint so I can go and apologize in person?'

'I believe it was someone attached to the church,' he said, 'but you understand I can't give away confidential information. Anyway, if they're all your visitors, you'd better get them inside.' His eyes gleamed: he'd thrown down the gauntlet. Never would I invite half a dozen ill-favoured youths into my home.

At this point Theo's Focus arrived, parking alongside mine. 'Hi, darling,' I greeted him. 'I told you I should have left earlier. Mazza and his mates have been waiting for me all this time.'

'Best let them in,' he declared, flourishing the front door key. 'How are you doing, Mazza? Best bring that pile of empties with you and we can put them in the recycling bin.' For a man who didn't want a Big Adventure he was thinking on his feet remarkably well.

The officers looked nonplussed, as well they might, as the lads trickled in behind Theo.

'You don't need to caution them or anything, do you?' I asked with a regrettably winsome smile. I flicked a discreet but meaningful glance at my watch.

'What about them getting home?'

Somehow the question didn't sound paternal, but I treated it as if it was. 'The rector or I will run them back after our meeting.'

'That'd be a very good notion, Doctor. Don't want them nicking any bikes, do we?' At that point he clearly decided that honours were even, and that he had other things to do than fill in a load of paperwork.

I had something to do before I tackled the mob of kids. Poking my head round the living room door, I caught Mazza's eye. 'A word?' I mouthed.

It was clear from his face that he was expecting what I had to tell him as he joined me in the quiet of Theo's study. 'It's Burble, ain't it? Shit! Fucking shit!' He hit the top of Theo's desk again and again with his fists. 'The bastards. I'll kill the bastards . . .'

'Better still,' I said, grabbing his fists and turning them so I could hold them as hands, 'we help the police bring the killers to justice. And I know that was what Burble would have wanted. Because he saved a vital piece of evidence. The camera's memory card.'

'What? Swallowed it? Bloody hell!'

In fact I'd gathered that that wasn't the orifice he'd inserted it into, but there was no need to reveal that. 'So you know this is being taken seriously at last, I can tell you I was bending the ear of a top cop when you called. An old mate of Dave's. Things'll happen now, Mazza. Now, are you up to joining your mates? What were you doing, anyway, all of you?' I set us in motion, so Theo, who was wrestling with some sort of conversation with the other kids, would hear the explanation too.

You could almost hear how hard he had to swallow. 'You know you got me to block up your letter box? And you said something about getting security cameras and stuff? Well, I reckoned you'd been let down – couldn't see any cameras anywhere – so we thought we'd keep an eye on your house, like. And then that bastard with the snappy little ferret of a dog comes cruising past in his poncey car – and back again – and next thing the filth turn up and tell us to disperse.' He looked for support to the others. He didn't know that we'd be able to check it all on the recorder linked to the miniature CCTV cameras. 'But they didn't say it nicely, so we just sat. And then the rest of them turned up mob-handed and you arrived and that's it.'

'So you were protecting us?' Theo asked quietly.

'Best we could. No one's going to try anything with a load of us there.'

'I'm truly grateful,' Theo said. 'To all of you. I can't tell you how much this means to me and Jodie. It's been a bad day, what with one thing and another. Now, Jodie and I need to tell you something I guess Jodie's already told Mazza. We've heard that the body that was found on the Downs is Burble's. Jodie and I will always be here to talk to you, best of all to listen. I'm sure you and the rest of his mates will think of a fitting memorial to him.'

I wasn't sure he'd got quite the right tone, but the lads nodded slowly. One put up a nicotine-stained finger, as if back in the classroom. 'Burble didn't go to church. Does that mean he'll go to hell?'

'If he was going he'll have gone when he died; he won't be hanging round for the post-mortem to decide who he is,' retorted one of his mates.

There was a sharp intake of breath, then a barely suppressed titter. Perhaps the response helped Theo. I hoped so. I couldn't have argued with the logic.

'Burble had a tricky life, didn't he?' Theo asked gently. 'I think he tried to do good when he could. God is loving and forgiving, you know.'

'Like that magistrate who gave him community service and didn't send him down,' a third lad suggested.

That was meat and drink to Theo. 'If an ordinary human being could be understanding and compassionate, don't you think God could be too? I think God has taken him home at last. But I want to say a prayer. If you'd like to close your eyes and make it your prayer too, I'd like that, and I believe God would too . . .'

We got up early to check the CCTV. Everything appeared to have occurred just as Mazza said, except that several cars besides Ted Vesey's had driven past: Mrs Mountford's, Elaine's, the silent Jackie Simmons', for starters. Following the instructions, line by careful line, Theo saved the material, just in case. In case the security firm lost it? But I wouldn't be sarcastic. Since

Don Simpson wanted to see me, Theo offered to go and pick up Alison Cox and was just letting himself out of the back door to go to his car when someone battered the front door.

I opened it as far as the newly installed chain – another bit of Mazza's handiwork – would allow. At first, all I could see was a totally ordinary Vauxhall at the end of the drive; then a man, who'd perhaps been inspecting our daffodil pots, stepped forwards.

'Mrs Welsh? DC Pool. Superintendent Simpson's compliments, and would you care to join him at HQ instead?'

'Of course, I'll just get my bag. You'll excuse me if I just close the door? I can't release the chain unless I do.'

Or not. Grabbing the bag, I seized Theo's hand and dragged him out of the back door. 'Get in the car as usual,' I said, throwing myself in the rear foot well. 'Just drive in your dog-collar way. Wave to the guy at the front door as if offering him a blessing. And once you're out of his range, floor the accelerator. Just do it, Theo!'

He did. On my stomach, I dialled 999. It was hard to be clear and coherent, but I managed to convince the calm and efficient woman I was put through to that I was escaping an abduction attempt and needed to see Superintendent Simpson.

'Just tell me what on earth you think you're doing,' Theo snapped the moment the call was over. 'I mean, last night was bad enough, but this is plain crazy.'

'Someone comes to your door claiming to be a police officer and he doesn't show any ID: would you believe him?'

'I wouldn't scarper like a kid in the playground.'

'If he claimed to be a policeman and you recognized him from Ravi the security guy's photos as a so-called workman trying to get unauthorized entry into your apartment?'

'You didn't tell me—'

'Didn't want to worry you. Thought it was just a coincidence. Is he tailing us? Silver Vauxhall?'

'Could be.'

'Where are we?'

'Just joining the motorway.'

'Outgun him, then. At least he's not ransacking the house. I hope I shut the back door.'

Theo gave a bark of laughter. 'That's what my mother always used to say. Though not always in circumstances quite like these. He's getting closer, by the way. No, he's dropping way back. Letting a police car overtake.'

'I'm glad there's one part of him that's law-abiding.'

TWENTY-ONE

'What I can never understand,' Don Simpson said, with a heavy approximation of a laugh, 'is how you ladies always manage to grab your bags, which then turn out to have everything except the kitchen sink in them. Sorry. Not supposed to call you a lady, am I? My old boss would have fried my liver for that.'

Theo, more used to social inanities than I, or at least more tolerant of them, smiled politely, and complimented Don on his coffee, which came from a machine second cousin to ours lurking on a bookshelf behind his desk. He added as he finished it, 'Jodie, Don, will you excuse me? My church-warden's ill in hospital. I really ought to find out how he is – there's a chance I might be needed.' He patted his pocket. No phone.

'That's why we ladies have bags welded to us,' I said drily, passing him mine.

Extracting information from the hospital seemed marginally less difficult than extracting wisdom teeth. While he cajoled and waited, I filled in Don, who looked even more serious and checked his computer. But at last Theo got some sort of answer. Why hadn't the dear man put the call on conference? He must have known I was desperate to hear.

At last he ended the call. 'George is no better. I'd best shoot over – I can pray with Alison even if they won't let me see George.'

I knew he didn't really enjoy public displays of emotion, but I reached for him and held him as long as I dared; to my relief, he hugged me back.

'We'll get you over there and we'll do the honours when you want to come back. Meanwhile, I'll check Dave's theory that you've got a tracking device on your car. Both cars.' Don put his head round his office door and yelled for someone to organize a lift for Theo. 'He's a victim of violence, after all,' he added as he turned back towards us. 'You know what, I'll see if the budget will run to having a police guard put on him, just in case.' The men shook hands, Don clapping Theo's upper arm in a man-to-man gesture that surprised me.

The tone changed the moment Theo left the room.

'So, Jodie, is something from your past life catching up with you?' Don demanded, leaning back in his chair as if he was the sheriff in an old black and white movie. He didn't quite put his feet on his desk and puff cigar smoke in my face, but there was a distinct sense that he could have done, if provoked.

'I was always at the geeky end of business,' I said. 'I've seen colleagues in HR sack a thousand people without turning a hair or having any notion of the concomitant suffering. Youngsters with a career to build; people your age with a wealth of experience . . .' I drew my hand across my throat. 'I've never done that. I've never outsourced to India or wherever so jobs have stayed here in the UK. I've taken big bucks, Don, embarrassingly big bucks, but I've never flaunted the money. Even Theo – apart from the sums involved – can't find anything with which to trouble his conscience.' I tapped my phone. 'I'm sending you my CV. You'll find a list of all my charitable interests in there.' Another tap. 'These are all my investments. Everything. In confidence, of course. But you'll see why I don't flash my cash in the village: I think I'd get more enemies than friends.'

'Like when you had that chopper fly into the village?' he observed ironically.

'That was for a purpose: to get photos of the development.'

He gave a dry laugh. 'I suppose it's saved us the expense. I take it your helicopter friend could afford it?'

'He could afford to pay for the professional photographer too. But I'm paying for the forensic work.'

'And you're not going to say who this mysterious friend is? OK. Is this splashing your dosh around because you've got so much you don't know what to do with it or because you're dead nosy?'

My smile was cool. 'Does it have to be one or the other? I think young Burble was killed because he'd taken photos someone didn't want to be seen. He didn't hide that memory card for fun, did he? Have your techie people managed to get the photos off it yet?'

'They're working on it. Was it you who alerted Burble to the building work? Are you plugging away at this just because you feel guilty he died?'

'On the contrary, I was plugging away before Burble even got wind of anything. Apart from in a chopper, you can only see the building work from the top of the ridge where I regularly run. I saw them cut down trees – a lot of old ones. Then diggers and earth-movers appeared. What worried me – and don't we worry illogically? – was that the workers weren't wearing hard hats and that the deep excavations might be damaging archaeological remains. I used to work on skyscrapers in the City and watch them boring deep, deep down for foundations for bigger, better skyscrapers. Or not.'

He nodded. 'Carry on.'

'Then as Dave's probably told you, Mazza – Malcolm Burns – one of the lads from the village started running with me.'

He nodded with what seemed to be amused approval. 'I know about Mazza, and about his house-guarding tricks. The officers involved weren't best pleased, Jodie.'

'I don't see why not: I saved them a lot of paperwork.'

'And this Mazza knew Burble. And introduced you?'

'It was the other way round. Burble was hanging round one day when I was dragging the green bin out to the front. He offered to help. Him a pierced and tattooed yob! We started to talk. It seemed he needed some quick cash. I challenged him to earn it. He helped in the garden. I'd like to say he did it regularly, but to be honest it was only when he needed money.'

'Why did he need money?'

My eyes widened of their own accord: why did anyone need money? But I'd try to respond seriously. 'You know about his mother, Sharon Hammond? A druggy? She died of an overdose after he'd disappeared.' It was rather too clear that he didn't, but he made a note. 'Well, I should imagine, with hindsight, that he needed to eat. He did have a tenuous family connection

with Violet, who runs the village shop. She's not a fan of him
or his family, especially his dad. I asked Violet if she knew
anything about him, but she said she didn't.'

'But she may know other family members who do.' He
jotted again. 'I'm surprised you haven't already been badgering
her to give you the information.'

'Funnily enough . . .' I gave a rueful laugh. 'She told me
that to the best of her knowledge no one in the village would
have given him the time of day. Si Hammond, I think he is.
So I got one or two of my drink and drug counselling mates
on to it. They work right at the bottom of the poor lost heap,
so there was just a chance . . . I've had no word back, so I
assume a nil return.'

'Happens like that sometimes, as I'm sure you know. So
the only way you know this Burble is through his gardening.'

'Dave'll tell you that that's rather a posh word for what he
did – when he wasn't foraging for wild food, mushrooms and
samphire and such. I'm sure his mates are busy telling your
colleagues all about that. Or does the sight of a police officer
turn them into Trappist monks?'

'Monks with attitude!' He looked at his watch. 'In any case,
it's still a bit early in the day to talk to kids that age. And, as
my grandfather used to say, half the lies they tell aren't the truth.'

'They were telling the truth about their activities last night.
Our security cameras filmed them, of course, and a few cars
passing by. Here are the details of the security firm – Dave
put us on to them. Shall I call them for you? I may need your
email address.' I reached for my mobile again. 'Excellent. The
footage is automatically saved anyway, but they're copying it
to you now.'

Don's nod was ambiguous. I don't think he'd changed his
mind about bossy women but they certainly saved him and
his colleagues legwork. 'OK. Back to you again, Jodie. Who
in the village have you annoyed? Those enemies I spoke about
last night.' He checked his notes. 'Vesey and Grant.'

'Who aren't really enemies, I'm sure.' He pulled a face.
'Actually, there is one person some way from the village whom
I may have annoyed. I decided to go and have a look at the
building site from a different angle. Don't look like that! I

just drove up to the front gates, as anyone misled by their satnav might do. It was very clear indeed that Double Gate Enterprises and Elysian Fields didn't want chance callers. More CCTV than you could shake a stick at – I'm used to it in London, but out here?'

'You stuck to public roads?'

'You bet I did.'

'Did anyone know you'd had a look?'

'Apart from whoever looked at what their cameras were showing? Only Dave. I dare say my running, particularly with Mazza, drew their attention too.'

'These not-enemies, Jodie. Tell me about them. Come on. I can always ask Dave, remember.'

'OK. Ted Vesey. I'd never met him before I came to the village.' I gave him a sketchy biography, all the more vague because, of course, that was the image Ted favoured. 'Certainly on one occasion he deliberately tripped me up. Mazza got a photo of the incident; we showed it to one of your colleagues yesterday, when George Cox was assaulted in the church. Vesey may be the one who summoned your colleagues last night, incidentally.'

His frown deepened. But he spoke mildly enough: 'There's a hell of a lot going on in one small place, isn't there? Now, how does this Vesey get on with this George Cox character?'

'Fellow churchwardens,' I said. On the other hand, what about the whole truth? 'But I don't think they sang from the same hymn sheet – oh, shit!' I covered my face.

Don, on the other hand, roared with laughter. But he quickly became serious again. 'Did they dislike each other? I see they did. You may be a good businesswoman, Jodie, but you're not much of an actress. You might as well tell me – if you don't, someone else in the village will.'

'True. They may have to. I really know nothing about them or their history. Ted is suave and sophisticated.'

'And it's clear you don't like him.'

'Would you if he tripped you up like that? I'd done nothing, I promise you, knowingly to annoy him. He was simply hostile from the start. I'm an incomer, Don, and that pretty much sums it up.'

He nodded with what looked like genuine sympathy. 'My wife is too. We've lived in the same village for nigh on twenty years. She has a go at everything: PTA, neighbourhood watch, parish council, parish mag. And someone only the other day said to her, "In a few years you'll almost be one of us." It was the "almost" that floored her.'

'I can imagine. Funnily I sense that Ted's an incomer too. But he does a very good job of obfuscating his past. George Cox, on the other hand, may appear your quintessential countryman but in fact is a former head teacher. He's a lovely man. I like his wife very much too. She once ran a prison.'

His eyebrows shot up. 'Did she now?' He jotted vigorously. He was about to ask me something else when his desk phone rang. He raised an apologetic hand. 'Yes, sir. I'm actually with a witness – very well, sir.' He turned to me. 'I'm sorry. I should delegate. Just be here to deal with policy and budget. A facilitator. I spend half my life in bonkers policy meetings fighting the next budget cut. The only way I can stay sane is to do a bit of decent, honest work from time to time. But now I'm already late for a meeting. Do you want to continue this later or shall I get one of my colleagues to take over?'

'How long's later?'

'Long enough for you to have a coffee and check your emails. OK? I'll get someone to take you along to a waiting room. It might be a bit of an eye-opener. Actually, if you could make a few notes about the other issues I should know about it'd speed things up, wouldn't it? Here, use this iPad, no one else ever does.'

The waiting room could have served just as well as one in an inner-city GP's or dentist's practice, with plastic chairs and a heap of plastic toys in one corner. The posters tended to be less about hidden health diseases like Chlamydia, than about hidden crime like picking pockets. The viciously uncomfortable plastic stacking chairs didn't stack but were firmly attached to the floor. I settled in one furthest from the toys, hoping to be on my own as long as possible; with nothing to cushion the sound it could get very noisy indeed. One sip of the paper-cup coffee a young constable brought convinced me I ought to wait for Don's next offer of hospitality.

To the iPad, then.

I had to prompt Don to offer me coffee, but it was worth the wait. He also produced some biscuits, consuming three or four to my one. We studied the screen together.

'*Elaine Grant*,' he read aloud. 'Anything you need to add to what you've written here? She seems a decent enough woman, but I'll get her checked out. *Bicycle theft*,' he continued. '*DNA tested by Rosemary – no results yet. Why try to frame Mazza?* I'll get one of the team to call Doctor McVicar,' he said, writing a note to himself.

'I've already emailed her,' I admitted. 'She'll be in touch with you.'

'Helicopter flights, private photographers and forensic analysis, private DNA collection – you don't leave much to us, do you? Oh, and you paid for some very fancy lawyers for that Mazza and his mother.'

'Is it a problem? I can see the lawyer business might irritate you, but in the other cases I've saved you a great deal of money.'

He responded to my beatific smile with a predictable glower. 'And I'll bet you'll find that it's tax deductible.'

'Not if it's nothing to do with my work, Don,' I replied sweetly. A bit of mutual respect never came amiss.

'According to Sergeant Masters, the bikes weren't worth nicking in the first place,' he mused. 'There is a gang – we think they're from Albania or somewhere – hoovering up all sorts of garden equipment and the kind of expensive bikes commuters chain up hopefully outside stations. Perhaps these are their rejects, and framing someone else seemed like a good idea at the time. It's an interesting point you've made, though: why choose this Mazza of yours to frame? Because he's your mate, I suspect.'

As if I agreed, he heaved himself to his feet and, gathering the mugs, walked across to his coffee-machine. 'Same as before?' He didn't wait for a reply.

Plonking the full mugs on the desk, he settled heavily back

in his chair. 'OK, who's responsible? It's got to be someone from your past. It's time you were frank with me, Jodie.'

'I still think it's my present. It's whoever's involved with the big development.'

'Come on, with your contacts—'

'Not to mention my computer skills. You know what, I've only got one pair of hands. I had a poke round, sure, but it's a time-consuming business, and honestly it'd take a forensic accountant to find who really owns what and where. I'm sure your colleagues will do better. Actually,' I added with a grin, 'they could do what I couldn't do. *You* could do what I couldn't do. You could walk up to those big front gates and ask.'

He got to his feet: the interview was over. 'So I could,' he agreed, 'so I could.'

It was a pity I had to spoil his exit line. 'One thing we've not touched on, Don: the next heading of my notes. *How did our friend know you were due to meet me at my place this morning?* Someone who knew you by name, and could realistically suggest you'd prefer to meet me here.'

He stared, clearly wondering for a moment if I was alleging he might be complicit. But then his eyes narrowed in recollection. 'We were sitting at the table, right, and someone came and grabbed all the empties. Very efficient I thought at the time. Then you followed me to the bar and we spoke a bit longer.'

'Then we stepped outside.'

'Right. So we did. Out of earshot of anyone. You gave me your tail's details. Still on my to-do list, I'm afraid, for all I was here before seven. Traffic should have come back to me last night, probably did, but we've got a major case – maybe I should say *another* major case – on our hands and I've been tied up with that.'

'I always found delegation hard, Don. Still do. But sometimes it's the only way to survive. So you should dispatch a nice young constable to talk to the Goose's bar staff and delegate someone to check my car over to see if it's not just got a tracking device glued to it but also a little voice-activated recorder?'

He threw his head back and laughed. 'Tell you what, you can do my job and I can do yours – the Lady Bountiful bit,

anyway. Or better still, you could be the next Police
Commissioner round here. You wouldn't half put the fear of
God into our boss! Now, your car's still at the rectory because
you – er – hitched a lift with Theo. Right? So I'll get a couple
of officers to give you a lift back to Lesser Hogben. Unmarked
car. All casual – a couple of folk you happen to know. Then
one of them can drive your car back here to give it the check
over you recommend. And I'll go over the rest of your notes,
ma'am: *Church connection? Contents of safe? Ida Mountford?*
Unless,' he added with a sigh, 'you want to look into these
yourself?'

TWENTY-TWO

The two officers, a sharp-faced young woman called Jo, and Tony, a man old enough to be her father, and I, had a lovely silly time working out a reason – should one be needed – for their giving me a lift. It took more effort to work out a cover story, should one be needed, of course, than to get back to the rectory. Why should I hand over my new toy to Jo? She was the first to say that in real life she wouldn't be able to afford the insurance. We decided that Tony was another of my cousins, and that Jo was – why not? – his daughter. Tony would drive away the Audi, Jo would leave in the unmarked police Mondeo, having checked the rectory to see that all was well. We had to go round the back, of course, since I'd kept the chain on the front door. Yes, I had remembered to close the back door. The Yale didn't seem to have been tampered with. But since I'd not had time to deadlock it, or set the alarm, of course, I was glad of the moral support.

'I'll go in first, Jodie, if you don't mind,' Jo said without emphasis, but in a voice not expecting argument.

I nodded. My mouth was horribly dry, and my pulse decidedly fast. So far in the whole crazy day I'd not admitted, even to myself, that I was scared. Now my body did it for me, even though Jo assured me there was no sign of any tampering. We checked the CCTV footage together, just to reassure me.

'I'll download the CCTV images of the guy who came to the door. And if you give me your phone number I can send you some images of a guy who tried to get access to my London flat.' While she brewed tea I uploaded the images and sent them on.

'Yes: same man, I'd say. I'll see what the Super has to say, but I'm sure the tech team will use their facial recognition stuff and prove it. And better still, who it is. Someone as enterprising as this guy must be on record. I'd best be getting back. But what about you? Half an hour's shut-eye wouldn't do you any harm.' She peered hard at me, making me feel at least ninety-three.

'That kid they did the autopsy on yesterday, Burble – I ought to go and offer my condolences to one of his relatives. A very distant relative, so I don't think she needs the full-blown rector's visit,' I added drily.

'How are you getting there?'

I stuck out my legs and pointed to the turned up bits at the end.

'Is that wise?'

'In the absence of a car. If I stay here, I'm a sitting duck. If I'm out and about, at least I can waddle away as fast as my legs will carry me. Or run. I do marathons,' I added, just to convince her I wasn't too decrepit to be left to my own devices.

Suddenly she was my new best friend. For five minutes we had a proper conversation, though it might not have appeared so to anyone not interested in runners' accoutrements. Since I'd been deprived of anything like it since I'd left my regular running mates in London, I found it delightful. When she really had to go back to work, we strolled out like aunt and niece – perfect. But then, staring at the anonymous but still vulnerable car, I froze: 'Let me just check out CCTV – we don't want this to have been doctored, do we?'

She pulled a face. But then, with a let's-humour-auntie shrug, she nodded. We trailed back in together to review the footage. Unfortunately she'd parked just at the edge of the cameras' range. At this time of day there was very little activity from drivers or pedestrians, and ours wasn't the sort of village where cows or sheep made a regular rural appearance. One cyclist – helmet and goggles but not Lycra – headed out of the village, but appeared to change his mind and head back, though this time on foot. This was enough to put Jo on red alert, even though I pointed to what I was sure was a flat tyre second time round.

'Haven't got a biggish mirror, have you?' she asked.

'Bigger than my make-up one?'

'Please. And a torch.'

The mirror in the downstairs loo was nearest. Oh dear. Ashamed that I'd left such a pathetic specimen hanging anywhere in public for more than a day, I carried it out, its white plastic frame yellowing and slightly warped. The torch, from Merry's Useful Items drawer, was one you had to shake to activate the battery. It took its time to wake up, but eventually produced a glimmer. Squatting by each wheel-arch in turn, she checked with as much care as my dental hygienist looking for tartar.

'Nothing.' It was hard to tell whether she was relieved or disappointed. At any rate, she got in and drove off without incident, leaving me clutching the offending mirror and now defunct torch.

I toddled down to the shop, to pay the duty condolence call I was sure Merry would have paid. Putting a few things in my basket while Violet was serving someone else – I needed something to descale the kettle, come to think of it, before it gave up the ghost – I tried to work out the best words. Think tact and diplomacy, Jodie.

No point. 'You've had some news, haven't you, about that body? Thought so, with that Friday face of yours. Young Burble? Well, you know what they say, *Live by the sword, die by the sword.* I suppose he was so full of drugs he didn't know where he was going or what he was doing.' She didn't look as distressed as I felt.

'I don't know all the circumstances,' I said truthfully. 'But I'm sorry he died alone. So young, too.'

'Well, I'd normally agree, and add, *What a waste.* But no, he was a scrounger and a druggy and a part-time thief – dress it up as foraging, or whatever he called it, but it's still stealing, isn't it?'

'For all that, I still think his father ought to know. Assuming he's alive, of course.'

'Bad genes, that's what his dad gave him, and nothing else. The kid was doomed before he was born, if you ask me.'

I could have argued about forgiveness and redemption, and that yes, the lad really had been trying to turn his life, if not around, then on to a slightly different course. Think how he cherished that camera of mine. I swallowed a sob.

'Six pounds seventy, please. Thanks.'

I was so busy stowing my change as I crossed the little

lay-by of a car park that I almost walked into Ida Mountford – not a good move. Naturally I stepped back with fulsome apologies, but she recoiled as if she'd been sullied by the brief contact. To hell with all this!

'Mrs Mountford,' I began quietly, 'I really wish you'd tell me what I've done to annoy—'

This time she didn't step back: she pushed forward, almost shouldering me out of her way. I staggered, hardly keeping my feet. But now she wasn't there. She was reeling, collapsing on to the roughly paved area. At first I thought she was having a heart attack – her tablets had always formed part of Theo's narrative – but then I sensed, rather than saw, a car driving quickly away. Grey? Silver? I was too busy dialling 999 and getting ready to do first aid to check.

There was no sign of any external injury: she might have hit her head on something as she fell, but there wasn't so much as a bruise. But her pulse was definitely wavering. Failing. The emergency call centre told me to start CPR. So here I was giving the kiss of life to someone who'd rather go under a car than even speak to me.

Calm, efficient – the young paramedic who turned up on a motorbike was everything I didn't feel. At least before I'd been doing something and hadn't had to think or react. Now I was redundant, I found myself becoming a victim too. Or a heroine. Opinion among the little knot of onlookers attracted by the commotion, and more particularly by the flashing blue light, seemed divided.

A Police Community Support Officer had materialized; the one who'd genuflected to Theo, as it happened. He might have had a thought bubble over his head, wondering where on earth he'd seen me. Once I'd told him my name and address – still no magic light bulb moment in his head – I sat heavily on the shop's front step and let the conversations whirl round me. I reckoned if I kept quiet I might learn more than if I asked questions. Most people agreed that a car was involved, probably grey or silver. No one thought it was anything more than a bit of careless driving, until one person thought it headed straight for Mrs Mountford, an opinion flatly contradicted by someone else who thought I'd been the target. There was a lot of argument about my conversation with Mrs Mountford: the consensus was that she was a bossy old cow (couldn't have put it better myself), until someone pointed out you shouldn't speak ill of the dead – or in this case, possibly dying. When blues and twos announced an ambulance, which rather suggested she was still alive, the crowd parted like the Red Sea for Moses and, once deprived of any spectacle, most people drifted away. One remained, however.

'Mazza!'

He squatted beside me. 'You OK, Jodie?' Assured that I was, he got up in one easy movement I found I couldn't emulate, so I stuck out a hand. He looked embarrassed but obliged. 'There. Fancy a cuppa at me mum's?'

I did. Very much. As much for the gossip it would create as anything else. We started walking. 'You OK after last night?' I asked.

He nodded. 'You?'

'Spent ages with the police this morning. Actually, there's something I need to tell one of them.'

'About that guy trying to run you over?'

For a second the village street tipped and rocked. 'You're sure it was me, not Mrs Mountford?'

'Swear on Burble's grave. When he gets one. Or will he be cremated? Someone's got to sort it, Jodie.'

'Which do you think he'd have preferred?'

'Never asked. Not something you talk about.' *At our age* hung unspoken in the air.

'You ought to talk about organ donation though, you and your mates.' *Nothing of Burble's left to donate* hung there too. 'Theo and I will take care of the funeral service, but we'd want your input – music and so on. And deciding what to do . . . with . . . Burble. You and any other of his mates – it's up to you.' I added, 'A green burial, maybe?'

'You know,' he said slowly, 'I think he'd have liked that. Any news of old George Cox, by the way?'

'None good. His wife's with him. Theo's with them both. Good morning, Ted,' I called. 'Have you heard the news about George?'

With obvious misgivings, as if Mazza might give his little dog mange, Ted sidled towards us.

'Not just Mr Cox, either,' Mazza put in helpfully. 'Mrs Mountford got run over earlier. Mrs W here saved her life.' All these correct titles! He was taking the prospect of a job with Elaine very seriously. 'One churchwarden, one ex-churchwarden: you might want to keep an eye open yourself, Mr Vesey.' I might have put it more tactfully, but it was certainly a good point to make.

'Are you serious? About Ida Mountford?' Ted's face seemed stiff.

'Hit and run, they say. Mrs W had to give her the kiss of life.'

'Indeed! And did she survive, dear lady?'

My kiss or the accident? But I didn't think I should be flippant, not when Mazza was working so hard on politeness. 'She was alive when the ambulance took her away, at least. Mazza and I were just going to St Dunstan's, weren't we, Mazza?'

He nodded, as if it wasn't a complete surprise that I'd changed my mind about the cuppa. 'Ah. To light a few candles. You'd be the best one, Mr W not being around, to say some prayers, wouldn't you, Mr Vesey?'

To do him justice, Ted neither winced nor protested. Ignoring a few shreds of police tape, he unlocked the great oak door – it suddenly dawned on me how many deaths, natural and unnatural, they must have witnessed, and all the tears and consolations too – and switched on a few lights. The carpet was still rolled back from the safe.

Mazza wandered over to light his candles. I pointed to the safe. 'I was here when poor George said he'd phone you to get the combination. Did he ever reach you? Or did his assailant catch him first?' Even as I spoke I realized that Theo and I ought to have seen the attacker if George had been attacked immediately. Why had no one asked us that? And why hadn't we thought of it ourselves? Since we hadn't seen anyone, was it a reasonable conclusion that he'd failed to reach Ted and was trying someone else? Ida, of course. Perhaps Mazza had been right in his speculations. Perhaps someone was simply

after the wardens, not me at all. Nor Burble, of course, or
Mazza himself, I reminded myself with angry irony. Maybe
it was this morning's shocks that were making me stupid.

'I'm afraid I missed his call. He left a message on my
landline. Perhaps he didn't know my mobile number.'

'What's in the safe that would be worth killing a decent
man for?' I asked. It had been on my list for Don Simpson,
after all.

'Some plate. A good silver chalice and a large paten that
we only use at Christmas and Easter – you've probably seen
them. Nothing else, as far as I know.'

'Shall we check? If you're worried about security I'll turn
my back.'

A raised eyebrow and jerk of the shoulder indicated it was
Mazza's presence that worried him. But, on his knees, the boy
seemed totally absorbed with the candles: rapt in their golden
light, he might have been posing for a portrait by Joseph
Wright.

As quietly as I could, I drifted towards him. Why did he
have his phone in his hand? He raised a finger to his lips, then
touched the side of his nose. He was using the front of the
phone as a mirror.

TWENTY-THREE

I reached for my phone too. It was far too far away to see the combination, of course, but we could both see Ted heave open the heavy safe door – heard him grunt with the effort – and reach something out. Something small enough to be pocketed. Mazza turned quietly to use the phone in photo mode. I covered any noise stubbing my toe on a pew. Then Vesey called me – respectfully, as you'd expect of a church-warden. I joined him, stumbling slightly to draw attention away from Mazza so he could snap away all he wanted. As I bent by the safe, half of me expected a blow on the head, like George. No, that was stupid of me: no one would risk that in front of a witness.

With great reverence, Ted lifted a green baize cloth: there, underneath, was the silver he'd spoken of. 'All present and correct, as far as I can see. But worth stealing. I hope poor George didn't lay down his life to protect it – it's properly insured.'

'Thank you for showing me,' I said. 'But you really should contact Detective Superintendent Don Simpson. He's investi-gating the assault.'

'Someone as senior as that in charge of a simple assault case? My goodness.'

'Theo was summoned to George's bedside earlier,' I said, bending the truth slightly. 'It may be that by now Simpson's in charge of a murder case. Possibly two cases, given the frail state of Ida's health. Possibly three, if young Burble was killed, as the evidence is beginning to suggest,' I added, way out on a limb. 'Do you think the church is somehow a focus for someone's interest?' Another question on my list for Don, of course. 'It'd be a great shame if we all died trying to save it.'

'Let me just shut this,' he said, bearing the weight of the safe door once again and, hunching over the dial lest anyone wanted to spy, he reset the combination.

Behind him, Mazza made a little pushing gesture to . . . trip? Mazza nodded. I stumbled. Ted leapt to my rescue. The church was quiet again.

As we left, Ted was about to lock the door behind us, but I suggested that just for today it should be left open for people to pray for George. After some hesitation, he agreed. The blue and white tape gave a farewell flutter.

As soon as Ted was out of earshot, I turned to Mazza. 'What did you lift?'

'The envelope he got out of the safe. Back into the church, Jodie. I want to photograph it before he gets back. Officially he's dropped it, see? And I can run after him waving it under his nose.'

Slightly bent where Ted had folded it to stuff it into his pocket, it was standard A4, brown, completely blank on the outside, and lightly sealed. It would have been the work of seconds to slide a finger in and prise it open without tearing the paper. But we didn't have seconds. He held it up to the minimal light, shook it and then smelt it.

We clutched each other: was that the sound of footsteps? Was Ted coming back?

'Just the outside, then,' he sighed. 'There. OK? No, you get a snap too.' He grabbed the envelope and sped off. I returned to the kneeler by the candles. But I only had a second or two to pray; Mazza must have intercepted Ted very close to the church.

'Mrs – er – Jodie. This helpful young man here has reminded me we never did offer up that prayer together.'

'There seems to be something the matter with your front door,' Elaine called out as I approached the rectory, rather more slowly than usual. I'd never admitted to being anything like middle-aged, but now I ached with tiredness – or with lying face down in a car or being nearly knocked over. Take your pick. 'Oh, Jodie, there's something the matter with you too, isn't there? I was going to invite myself in for a coffee, but it seems to me I should be inviting you for a stiff gin and some lunch. Come on – hop in.' She opened her Range Rover door enticingly. The smell of new leather wafted towards me.

I'd have to ask her about it: I didn't think she had so much as a basic Smart car.

'I'd love to,' I said, accepting her hug gratefully. 'But I must just touch base first. Theo would never forgive me if I didn't check the answerphone.' I let us in, silencing the increasing hysteria of the alarm.

'That's new, isn't it?' she asked, pointing at the keypad that looked just like everyone else's. The CCTV images and recordings were safely hidden inside it.

'Yes. With all the goings on in the village, I felt so nervous being on my own so much of the time.' At least it was partially true. But I hated lying to a friend who made biscuits.

Her eyes narrowed. 'Don't you have to get a faculty for absolutely everything?'

'We will for the next job,' I replied cheerfully. 'Which is rewiring. The guys fixing the alarm said it was years out of date. Quite dangerous.'

'I heard you'd had your guttering done, too. I suppose that might class as an emergency. But a burglar alarm . . .' She pursed her lips.

'What you said about Merry last time,' I began, filling the coffee-machine reservoir, 'about her scrimping and saving. Well, there are some things I don't think you should cut corners on. One is security. People know I've got more money than poor Merry and might want to help themselves. And Theo's seen what happens to people's minds when they get burgled, even if nothing is taken. So we just did it.'

I should be checking the messages that were making the answerphone flash, but they had to wait a bit longer. Coffee was most certainly in order, especially as Elaine wanted to talk, rather ghoulishly perhaps, about the various ills that had afflicted the village this spring – actually, though she was too polite to say it, since my arrival. By the end of her litany, she had quite persuaded herself I was right to install security, even if she still insisted I should have told the churchwardens.

'I did tell Ted about the gutters,' I said duplicitously. 'Since he'd been a victim to the drips once too often he was quite happy to approve them.'

'He's such a funny bugger it might be a good idea to tell

him about the alarm, too,' she said. 'Of course, George would have been easier to persuade, especially if he thought you'd got important stuff here – though I suppose it's all insured, isn't it? He'd nod anything through that didn't absolutely require a full PCC meeting to approve it.'

'What sort of important stuff would we have here?' I retorted. There was nothing physical that couldn't be replaced: even Theo backed up everything on his computer, and shared, as my own computer did, a Dropbox with the system in my apartment. And we both had memory sticks – belt and braces.

She spread her hands. 'Who knows?'

It was better to pursue another line. 'Hell's bells, I'd forgotten the PCC's approval. Oh dear. Tell me, Elaine, what happens – well, even if George recovers fully, he's not going to be up to his churchwarden's role for a while, is he?'

'If you ask me he hasn't been for a long time. Him and that damned strimmer. They'd have to find a temporary replacement, I suppose. Ida Mountford would have been the obvious choice.' Not to Theo, she wouldn't. 'But now she's hors de combat too . . . Who knows? It might be my duty to step forward. Except the WI–Pickled Walnut link-up is taking so much of my time.' She shot a look at her watch. 'Actually, I really must go. How's the biscuit-making going?'

'It's not. I'm almost afraid to use the cooker now, after what they said about the wiring and the fire risk.'

The phone rang. Elaine crammed the last crumb into her mouth with a *silly-me* moue and grabbed her bag. 'Answer it – it might be important. I'll let myself out!' she called, suiting the word to the deed.

The last person I expected to be phoning was Dilly Pound. 'Have you had lunch yet?' she asked without preamble. 'I know it's very late, but how about the Crab and Basket? It's only just off the motorway. Here's the post code. I reckon you could do it in twenty minutes.'

'I could if I had a car. It's off the road at the moment.'

'Shit. We really need to talk. Supper this evening – assuming you could get a cab or something? Same place. I'll book a table for seven thirty. Bring Theo if you want.'

So I'd have to sit and watch her trying not to make eyes at

him. Or maybe she'd bring the man to whom she was attached by so many heavy rings.

How on earth had poor Merry felt to have women throwing themselves at his feet, as presumably they had all their married life? After all, some people thought a dog-collar made gorgeous men like him even more attractive. Elaine might well have been one of them: if she could find grumpy old Dave worth flirting with, how much more desirable might she have found Theo? And yet she was generous enough to befriend me. Theo had never mentioned any link between them, but then, he'd got discretion in his DNA.

There was just time for a sandwich before I worked my way through the messages – eight of them – waiting on the answerphone. After all, if anything was truly important, to me as opposed to Theo, they'd surely have used my mobile. Mouth full of cheese and salad, I texted Theo: news, please. Another text to Don Simpson, asking him to phone when he had a free moment or a free minion: I had information for him and needed one of our cars back. I also sent him a photo of the envelope Ted Vesey had 'dropped'. Had there been anything suspicious about it? Had Mazza's young nose detected anything I hadn't?

Armed with a mug of tea, I turned my attention to the landline phone. All the messages were to do with parish or benefice business. I wrote them all down carefully, with time and action taken – which in every case was a return call to say that Theo was with a sick parishioner. That was enough information for now.

Before I could wash up, the ghost of Merry still forbidding so much as a dirty mug on the table, Dave called. He seemed inclined to chat, but was on the receiving end of a doleful list of woes. On the other hand, he was a good listener, managing sympathy and anger but also more than common interest in the narrative. 'You've told Don all this? A text's good because he might be in a meeting, but on the other hand, he may not realize how significant all this is. And you certainly need one of your cars.'

'OK, I'll hire one.' A bit of anonymity never went amiss, did it?

There was still no communication from Theo, and no reply

to repeated texts and messages. Heavens, he wasn't still with George and Alison, was he? Things must be very serious. So why didn't I get that hire car to come to me? Then I'd set off to the hospital myself.

I was just about to leave when Theo rolled up. 'You caught the bus? But country buses only come when they feel like it. Why not take a taxi? Oh, Theo!'

'I suppose next you'll say I should have done what you've done.' He pointed at the anonymous silver Vauxhall sitting on the drive, the delivery driver waiting with less and less patience for his ride back to the depot. 'My darling, I know you mean well, but your extravagance will make you the cynosure of the parish.'

My eyebrows flickered of their own accord. 'It probably has already. You must make sure I don't have a flashy funeral. Oh, yes, someone tried to run me down this morning—'

His expression changed almost comically from anger at my sarcasm to something bordering on terror. 'Dear God! You're sure? I mean, last time you thought it might just be accidental . . . Oh, sweetheart . . .'

'I'm OK. You can see I'm OK.' I waved my hands in front of his eyes. 'Look, I have to get this guy back to his office. Please, just hop in the car with me so we can talk.' He seemed to be wavering, as if Merry was pointing an accusing finger bidding him to return to his study. 'By the way, I've changed the answerphone message to add in your mobile and mine.'

He goggled. 'How did you do that?'

'I'll explain in the car.' I grabbed the memory sticks I'd herded up, stowed them in my bag and headed out to the hire car.

TWENTY-FOUR

As a matter of fact, talk about answerphones was ideal, given the extra pair of ears in the car. Theo's dead phone battery took us another mile. When we'd dropped the driver, whose name, to my shame, I never knew, and turned for home, I asked about George at exactly the same moment as Theo asked about my near-accident.

'George first.'

'A slight but perceptible improvement. Alison will stay at the hospital. I promised to get more clothes to her – goodness knows how or when, while the car's . . . Unless I'm allowed to drive this? No, surely we'll be getting ours back soon.'

He didn't need to know how much the extra insurance was for a second driver – a crazy amount, which had outraged even me, with my cavalier attitude to money. 'Of course you can drive. I've not heard back from the police about ours. Or about this morning's accident. Or not accident. Whoever the driver aimed for, he or she hit Ida Mountford. She was carted off to hospital – heart, I suspect, rather than any injury.'

He clapped a hand over his mouth. 'God forgive me, you know what I nearly said?'

'Same as I thought, I should imagine – it's nice to know she's got one. I'd really like to talk to Don Simpson again. Particularly as I sent him a photo of something Ted Vesey removed from the floor safe. No, not silver, though there was plenty of that. A plain envelope. Mazza and I tried to work out what was in it, but failed.' I explained, implying that Mazza had simply found the envelope. From the long sideways look I got, Theo suspected more. 'I also had a visit from Elaine, who took one look at my pale and dishevelled state and invited me to lunch. Eventually we settled for coffee, chez nous, but I rather lost my temper with her, I'm afraid. She was wittering on about the need to get a faculty for the gutter and for the alarm system; she seemed genuinely annoyed that I'd stepped out of line. And she's my friend! I just hope she doesn't see this car,' I added, taking his hand and squeezing it to show I might be conceding a point. 'Anyway, I told her we were worried about the wiring; after all, it's been there since – what's that expression you use? Since Noah sailed his boat up the Thames?'

'Typical Londoner, thinking he'd ever use your river. No, Noah sailed his ark up the cut, of course.'

'Cut meaning canal. Silly me. I never was very hot on the Old Testament and Noah's peregrinations. Anyway, when she replaces George as churchwarden—'

'Did I hear that right?'

'Well, George won't be able to resume his duties for some time – if ever. And I doubt you'd get many other volunteers. But she seemed very interested in protecting valuable items in the rectory. Have I missed something? Is there another floor safe in your study also stuffed with silver?'

'I wish. Do you really, truly like Elaine? I know you said she was your friend, but would you have chosen her as a friend in London?'

Before I could answer, my phone rang. Theo took the call. 'OK. No problem. We'll be with you in less than half an hour, I should think. Don Simpson,' he told me. 'Wants what he calls A Word. Do you think it's just his way to sound meaningful and portentous, or do you think he's got something serious to say?'

'Who knows?' I turned the car back towards Maidstone. 'I know someone who has. Dilly Pound. She wants us to eat with her tonight. Actually, she wanted to meet at lunchtime, but I hadn't thought of this then.' I patted the steering wheel.

'Police protection?' Theo echoed, half out of his chair in Don Simpson's office. 'How can I go into protection in my job?'

'I didn't say witness protection,' Don said pacifically. 'Do sit down, man. I'm not asking you to go and live in Scunthorpe as a retired postman. I just want you somewhere we can keep an eye on you, Jodie in particular. Before someone kills her, Theo. According to two witnesses, the car that knocked Mrs Mountford down was aiming at Jodie. It was only because the old lady barged into Jodie that she took the force of the impact, not Jodie. And I must say, it's not often that the intended victim saves the actual victim's life – especially not an old bat like our witnesses say this Mrs Mountford is. Have you somewhere safe to stay?'

He looked at me, rather than at Theo, so I replied, 'I'd have said my London flat, but you know about the so-called workman there – the guy who pretended to be one of your colleagues this morning. In any case, how could Theo leave the village? The weekend's his busiest time. My place is there with him. And maybe we'll somehow lure whoever it is out into the open. I could always drive over to Double Gate Farm or Elysian Fields just to provoke them,' I added limpidly. 'In the hire car, of course. With,' I raised a hand to silence their combined outraged protests, 'a little company in the form of a couple of your colleagues. It's clear they know my face; we just need to identify theirs.'

Don leant back, his chair creaking alarmingly. How on earth did he meet police fitness requirements? 'As it happens, thanks to your material, we've managed to identify your would-be visitor. Small-time crook, works for anyone as a hired hand. As soon as we can pick him up, we'll find out who's pulling his strings: he's never very discreet.'

'So long as he's still in England,' Theo put in. 'Kent must be the easiest place in the world to escape from: ferries; Eurostar; the Chunnel.'

'And airports and hot air balloons.' Clearly Don didn't like Theo's descent into gloom. 'Everything's covered by cameras these days, Theo – even your house, Dave tells me. Well, maybe Jodie's right – where on earth did you get that name from, by the way?' he asked tetchily.

I blinked but answered serenely, 'By blending Josephine and Diana. Neither a fashionable handle. So if we've got our cameras and you've got yours, are we safe to return to the rectory? Lots of police patrol cars driving by?'

'Professionals time the intervals between visits, don't they? Just don't go home yet. We'll see what turns up in the next few hours. I've got a lot of officers working their arses off – sorry, Theo – and modern technology can sometimes help

us cover ground surprisingly quickly. Meanwhile, watch your
backs. Jodie, don't even think of going out to stir things with
a big stick: understand?' He added with a heavy smile, 'Maybe
a few prayers wouldn't go amiss, Theo.' The interview was
obviously over, as far as he was concerned.

'God helps those who help themselves,' I said. 'Ted Vesey's
envelope: is someone going to ask him what was in it? Mazza
sniffed it; he seemed disappointed when my nose wasn't as
acute as his, so perhaps he thought he smelt drugs? And surely
there must be some connection between the contents of the
safe – including, perhaps, this envelope – and the attack on
George.'

'Just because you've never enjoyed a good relationship with
Ted doesn't mean he's a bad person.' Theo seemed to be trying
to convince himself as much as me. 'Please don't make the
sort of assumptions people make about Mazza or Burble, for
instance.'

'My colleagues and I never make assumptions,' Don
growled. 'But we follow leads, Theo, and clearly this has to
be one line of enquiry.' He stood, looking meaningfully at his
watch. 'A police team is like an ants' nest full of anonymous
men and women working their socks off to solve a case. I'm
just the ant you get to see. And you only get to see me because
of Dave, by the way, on account of we go way back. For better
or worse – sorry again, Theo – as I told Jodie this morning,
my job's mostly administrative these days. I worry about
budgets; I make sure people are in the right place at the right
time. There are loads of other ants toiling away, and now I've
got to go and see what they've been up to.'

George and Alison lived about a mile from the village centre.
We told ourselves that this was far enough from the rectory
for a quick dive into their cottage to pick up the things she'd
asked for, and for us to be safe. After all, no one knew about
the hire car, did they? Then we took the bag to the hospital.
She left George's side long enough to kiss us both and tell us
that there were now minute signs of improvement. In fact he'd
been moved from one-to-one care to a ward with three other
patients.

'Quite a promotion,' she managed to say, wiping away her tears and straightening her shoulders as she prepared to return to her vigil. Holding her hands, Theo prayed with her. I joined in the Amen, though he'd spoken so quietly and gently I could barely hear.

Back at the car, he sank into the passenger seat as if it was his favourite armchair. Not that he had one at the rectory; he never seemed to sit down long enough to choose one.

'It's strange, isn't it,' he began, barely stifling a yawn, 'that we live in one of the most beautiful parts of the country, but we never ever just take time to look at it. When did we last see the sea? Take a gentle stroll along a river? Have a quiet pub lunch in a village as picturesque as ours? We just bolt to London.'

'We don't have to. We could bolt to all sorts of places provided we stayed there for the time the bishop told you to take for R and R.' I squeezed his hand. 'I love the Smoke, and during the cricket season there are few better places than my balcony. But I'd love to get to know Kent too. I'll check out some bijou B and Bs. We might even get to see something of your Birmingham?'

'Too far for just thirty-six hours, I'm afraid. But I do miss it, even after all these years. It's like a physical ache sometimes. That lovely engineering brick by the cuts. The warm, kind people – travel next to someone on a bus and it's as if they're lifelong friends . . . Anyway, what's this about eating with Dilly Pound?' It would have been hard for him to sound less enthusiastic.

I was in the middle of telling him, when his mobile rang.

'Ida. Good to hear from you. Are you feeling any better? No, I'm afraid I can't come round this evening. My car's in dock. Just rest and we'll talk tomorrow.' He cut the call with as much emphasis as is possible when you can't throw a handset on to a cradle.

Without comment, I checked my watch. 'There's just time to nip into Canterbury if you want to pick up a nice new clerical shirt. And we could say hello to the Cathedral, too . . .'

Dilly Pound looked as immaculate as you'd expect of someone who spent her life in front of a camera. However, there was something about her eyes that worried me. Her smile too was decidedly brittle. She said something about her husband being unable to join us; I didn't feel she regretted his absence too much. But the ice-cubes in her gin and tonic rattled alarmingly when she raised the glass. Theo, who apparently hadn't eaten since he left the house this morning, was eager to order. I was equally keen to cut the niceties and hear what she had to say. Salmon on samphire seemed to be what we all wanted, though I felt my eyes welling unpleasantly at the connection with poor Burble. To my astonishment she noticed; I had to explain.

Her nod was disconcertingly understanding – it didn't feel as if it was just one of her professional skills. 'Then I'll get straight to the point. You know I said I'd keep an eye open for things that might help locate him? Well, sometimes when you look for one thing you find another. One of my friends who keeps an eye on the cameras covering the motorways and major roads for the local radio travel bulletins tells me she's seen a larger number of JCBs on low-loaders heading your way than she'd expect. And then I had a mate who was working on a nature programme – you know, all those wonderful aerial shots that go with sweeping gloopy music. I got him to fly low over your valley with TV-quality cameras rolling. The footage should be in police hands now.' As a group of men in business suits sat at the next table, she stopped short. She got up, heading for the ladies' loo. A twitch of her head summoned me too. Still without speaking, she adjourned to a cubicle. I followed suit. When we were washing our hands, she turned on the taps full blast; it seemed I was to do the same, though I'd thought that was a technique simply to drown out sound – and who'd be bugging this place anyway? Only then did she hand over a jiffy bag, as discreetly as if she were dealing drugs.

'Thank you,' I mouthed, rather than murmured. 'Shall I get my police contact to come here or will you come to see him with us?' Not that I was at all sure that Don could be summoned like that.

She looked at her watch. 'Neither. As soon as I've eaten I have to be on my way. But you'll find all the relevant footage on that DVD.' She led the way back to the table.

By now the men were well down their first pints, and their voices were loud enough to persuade her that it was safe to talk, even though we both had to strain forward to hear her.

'Now, your friend Burble. The police press office has told us all the facts they have, apparently, which isn't actually saying very much. What's happening about his funeral? Because – but I'd want this to be entirely confidential, right? – I'd be happy to cover some of the expenses. I gather there's no family.'

Theo might have been an exhausted man glad to have his hand wrapped round a half-pint glass, but he was transformed before our eyes into a caring priest. I'd seen it before, but always found it disconcerting and very moving. Dilly's eyes filled, as if his sympathy was directed purely at her.

'That's a wonderfully kind offer, Dilly. Jodie and I had intended to take care of that, but if you would like to help, please do. We've not had time to discuss it yet, to be honest, but I'd want to give him a fairly traditional funeral service – even his reprobate friends might find that a comfort if they chose the hymns and other music. As for his body—' He turned to me with an enquiring smile.

'Burble's friend Mazza and I were talking about a green burial.'

Dilly nodded. 'Of course. Just what a forager would have wanted. How would you feel about press coverage, Theo?'

He shook his head gently. 'Let's not get ahead of ourselves. The body's not yet been released. No one's been arrested in connection with his death, as far as I know, let alone charged. It seems police mills are even slower than the mills of God.'

'But they both grind exceeding small,' Dilly said, with some satisfaction. '*Every heart has its secret sorrows which the world knows not, and oftentimes we call a man cold, when he is only sad,*' she added disconcertingly. Perhaps she would have said more if our salmon hadn't arrived.

Though it looked delicious, we all left the samphire.

TWENTY-FIVE

Before we left the Crab and Basket's car park, just on the off-chance I phoned Don Simpson, telling him what Dilly had handed over. I had a strong impression that he was leaving the building, and why not, at eight fifteen at night? But he sounded interested enough, and invited us over. Meanwhile, he'd check on what had happened to our cars.

He greeted us with a smile that edged towards perfunctory, nonetheless reaching out a surprisingly slender hand for the DVD, which he slipped without comment into the player in the opposite corner of his office from the coffee-machine. Almost as an afterthought, but a welcome one, he switched on the machine too: 'Decaf at this time of night? Growing old's a bugger, isn't it?'

The footage from the motorway cameras showed more JCBs than I for one knew existed, though I admit my expertise was somewhat limited. Then there was a lot of complicated farm equipment that looked eye-wateringly expensive. Don watched with a deepening frown that said, clearly enough, that someone should have told him about this before. He jotted vigorously. 'And where might that JCB be heading? To your site, of course. To clear it, no doubt.'

'It's an SSSI,' I said quietly.

'Which means none of this should be happening anyway. Why haven't the Planning department got back to me?' he demanded rhetorically. 'Cuts, I suppose. Look at the size of those things. What can they need all those for – bloody hell!' Freezing the footage, Don smacked the side of his head theatrically, and reached for the phone. His short conversation ended with the suggestion that his interlocutor got his or her arse back in, presumably to the CID office.

He started the footage again. This was of a young woman I vaguely recognized as a reporter for TVInvicta, doorstepping – or rather gate-stepping – a middle-aged man wearing a suit so sharp he could have cut himself on it as he tried to drive his shiny new Range Rover out on to the road. The registration was clear. Don jotted.

She didn't get very far with her yelled questions about the developments on his land, which turned out, as the camera panned first to the departing vehicle and then to the beautiful sign on his gate, to be Elysian Fields. Don snorted with laughter. 'Do they buy truckloads of Ambrosia rice?'

'Is it still available? You know, the tinned rice pudding,' I added for Theo's benefit, because he didn't seem to have picked up Don's food of the gods quip. 'I was practically reared on it.'

'Why haven't I seen this before?' Don asked.

'Dilly assured me she forwarded everything to the police – but says she's heard nothing. Maybe she sent it to the wrong email address or something?'

'Well, we've got it now. Looks like the basis for a good piece of investigative journalism: these reporters can some-times ask questions we can't, you know. This wasn't one of your headings, Jodie!' He gave a crack of laughter.

'It should have been. This is my thesis, Don, for what it's worth. Elysian Fields and Double Gate – and don't forget that so far my enquiries haven't found out who actually owns either organization—'

'I can find who owns the Range Rover for starters,' Don said, tapping his computer and jotting. His eyebrows bobbed up and down over the furrows of his forehead. 'Sorry. Carry on.'

'I think Elysian Fields and Double Gate are a front for something. Right? And I keep seeing on the news pieces about post office raids, carried out by JCBs that are then loaded on to convincing-looking low-loaders and driven away. Possibly, just possibly, to the building sight we flew over in that chopper.'

'So this could be a multi-storey car park for earth movers?' Theo suggested, disbelief dripping from his voice.

'It's supposed to be a cow shed, according to a friend of mine,' I said, wishing I didn't have to. 'Have you had a chance to check out the photos yet?'

'They're in my case to look at when I get home,' Don admitted. 'But let's see the rest of this, shall we?' He pressed the zapper.

'Ah, you won't need to do any homework,' I said with a

comradely grin. 'That's the moving version of our stills. Dilly said it was part of a nature programme.'

'At least we're spared a soundtrack,' Don said dourly. 'Have you noticed how the music gets especially emotional and dramatic when a lion or whatever kills some poor defensive antelope and starts tearing it— Hey up!' He froze the footage. 'You're right, Theo,' he said, as generously as if he'd not noticed Theo's sarcasm. 'It does look like a multi-storey. And that looks like a container to me. Down there: can you see?'

'Not a cattle truck,' Theo, back on our side, put in helpfully. 'What's that – in the opposite corner? All those – they look like giant chocolate rolls.'

'Turf,' I said. 'Rolls of turf. You can just see the green fringes peeping out at the edges. Some lawn!'

Theo pointed. 'Can you get back to the frames showing the top of the construction? Look, there are heaps of what looks like soil over there. This sounds crazy, but it's by no means a new idea. If you want to hide something from the air then it's a very good idea to make it look like the surrounding countryside. Nuclear silos; aircraft hangers – that sort of thing. Suppose that's what they're doing.'

'Weapons of war?' It was Don's turn to snort in derision.

'More likely proceeds of crime and stolen property,' I said. 'There's more farm equipment there than even a big conglomerate can use, surely. We've got people trafficking from Eastern Europe to the west; is there parallel heavy plant and equipment trafficking in the opposite direction?'

'Bloody right there is. At one point manufacturers made it easy for thieves: each one of the same batch of tractors or combine harvesters had the same key, would you believe? Things are better now: most sensible farmers fit tracker devices which sound an alarm when someone moves a vehicle out of a yard. So if you want to steal them you must get them into a container as quickly as possible to shut off the signal. And I suppose, though I'm not expert in such matters, a place like that would provide cover for your containers. It might even prevent the signals being transmitted while they're prepared for export. Yes?' he called tetchily in response to a quiet knock.

One of the tiniest police officers I'd ever seen put her head round the door and slid into the room. She was so petite I only realized she was an officer when Simpson grudgingly, even disparagingly, I thought, introduced her as DI French.

'She's in charge of the unit dealing with agricultural theft. And you've been doing all her work for her.' He ejected the DVD and flipped it to her. 'Say thank you kindly.'

I winked at her and she responded with an almost invisible smile; we both knew whose side I was on.

'So which of you would be investigating Burble's death, assuming it's in this context?' I asked. 'Money's only money, but this was someone's life. And, to be selfish for a moment, in what context are the attacks on me to be dealt with?'

DI French looked horribly blank.

'You go and invite Range Rover man to come and have a conversation with us, French, will you? I'll sort out a search warrant. Best go mob-handed, and have some armed back-up. No heroics, French, from anyone. If you're protecting that much money,' he continued, pointing at the DVD, 'you don't fight fair. And we're running out of good officers. Keep a team on to it all night and tomorrow, if needs be. You won't get them all in one fell swoop. Oh, and get the ports and airports alerted. The gang may not be taking flights to Eastern Europe, but that's where they'll be headed when we start picking up the big cheeses.'

She left. Theo rose to leave too. 'Our cars?'

'How did you get here?'

I smacked the side of my head. 'Hire car. Oh, bloody hell. Sorry. It's exactly the same colour and model as the one that was driven at me. Why on earth didn't I ask the rental people who else they'd loaned one to?'

'Perhaps because it wasn't your job to poke your nose in? And they wouldn't have told you. Shouldn't have, anyway. Which rental company?' He pressed a button on the phone. Someone was going to get on to it. Now. His smile had a valedictory quality about it.

'Ted Vesey's envelope?' I prompted him, not moving.

'Tomorrow. I promise you. Time to go home.' He nodded in Theo's direction. He was fast asleep.

TWENTY-SIX

A s I drove back into the village I had an awful sense of déjà vu. The area round the rectory was full of blue flashing lights. My first thought was that Mazza had installed himself once again as a private security guard and that the police were having another bite at what they thought was a tempting cherry. Then I realized that some of the blue lights were much higher off the ground, and that there was a reddish background. Red as in bonfires. There was no denying the smell of smoke. It was time to wake Theo. Though I suspected it was too late for prayer.

The ubiquitous Sergeant Masters greeted me with an ironic smile tempered by what seemed genuine if reluctant sympathy. 'At least we've got the mongrel that started it,' he said. 'Your cycle-collecting friend. A passer-by caught him red-handed on camera. How about that?'

'Mazza? No! He wouldn't do that! He's a friend. He's a good kid.'

'He's an arrested kid now. Bang to rights.'

'No! Please, I must talk to him!' I was tempted to fight off Theo's restraining arm, but subsided; there was no point in hitting the man's pompous, self-righteous chest.

'No can do, Doctor. Oh, and before you make a song and dance about it, his mother's with him. OK?' In other words, end of discussion.

'Not quite. His sister. She's a minor. Who's looking after her?'

'A friend, I think. If you really insist, I suppose I could check. And I'll get Social Services on to it.'

I wasn't going to be in any position to look after her myself, was I? 'Thank you.'

He nodded, as if accepting his due. 'Now, best you have a word with the lead fire officer about the house.' He turned away, even his shoulder officious.

Theo fished in my bag and grabbed my phone. 'I'm calling

Don. I don't care if he's got his slippers on and his feet up on the sofa. He needs to know.'

Meanwhile a young man who introduced himself as the watch manager had come over. 'Jason Heath,' he said, shaking hands. 'In simple terms, the fire started in the kitchen. We're not sure yet if it was an electrical fault or if accelerant was involved.'

'So it could have been arson?' Theo asked sadly, returning my phone.

'It could. And I understand that there are witnesses to say that an individual was seen breaking into the premises and was subsequently apprehended.' He gestured in the direction of Sergeant Masters.

'Is it possible to get into the house? To get some clothes at the very least.'

He shook his head sadly in response to what he clearly thought was a silly question. 'We're still damping down, sir. Is there somewhere you could stay? Friends in the village?' He didn't wait for an answer but headed back to his colleagues.

Had he waited he'd have received a reluctant negative. Though half the village seemed to be watching the entertainment, there was no sign of either of the people who might have been expected to have some sort of duty of care towards Theo at least: Ted Vesey and Elaine Grant. All I wanted to do was bolt to my dear, clean apartment. In the heat, the smoke, the dust, I could have sat down and cried. The thought that Mazza might somehow be involved made it worse. No time for crying. I dug in my bag. My turn to use my phone.

'What are you doing?' Theo asked quietly.

'Calling the solicitor who represented Mazza last time he was framed.'

He produced his own phone, tilting it so I could see the image. 'Sergeant Masters forwarded it to me. It does indeed look as if Mazza was involved, Jodie. I'm so sorry.' He held me while I stared. Mazza was indeed about to throw something, though it was hard to tell what. Whatever it was, in a case as serious as possible arson, the police and fire service would be meticulous in locating his missile. 'Come on, let's sell one of your Monopoly houses and find a hotel for the night.'

'That's the best idea I've heard all evening,' Don Simpson declared; to say he'd made me jump would be a masterpiece of understatement. 'But I want us to talk first thing. This is looking personal, Jodie. Arson and attempted murder.'

'I'm not sure it is.' Goodness knows where that came from. 'No cars, no lights on, no indication anyone's at home.' I waited for one of them to agree. When neither spoke, I shook my head, almost apologetically. 'Perhaps I shall think more clearly in the morning. Hang on, Don – that photo Sergeant Masters sent us of Mazza throwing something. Who sent it to him?'

'Even asleep on your feet, can you imagine I can tell you that?'

'It's just that there's something missing from the image. If I wanted to take a picture of someone torching a place, I'd make sure I got the bottle of petrol or whatever in frame. All I could see was his upper arm, not the lower part and the hand.'

'That's good enough for me,' Masters said, with the same ability as his boss to materialize unannounced.

But not for me. We got in the hire car, me motioning Theo into the driving seat. I had a call to make. If only, and my brain seemed as heavy as my drooping eyes, I could remember the name of the security firm that had installed our magic invisible cameras. Other security firms advertised their names on square red alarm boxes, but ours was far too discreet. I'd just have to switch off the conscious part of my brain and wait for the name to pop up.

We checked into the Maidstone Mondiale, a modern building so imposing that in other circumstances I'm afraid Theo would have driven straight past in search of a hotel with far fewer stars. Not this time, thank goodness. The night staff rallied round with wonderful kindness, providing us with everything they could, from luxury bathrobes to basic toothpaste.

At last, perching on the bed and sipping hot chocolate, Theo said in a far from convincing voice, 'We have a lot to be grateful for – or at least we shall realize in the morning that we have.'

'We have a huge amount to be grateful for,' I said quite sharply. 'Each other – alive and well. The best solicitor money can hire for Mazza. Social Services on to Sian. Hey, a text I missed earlier – no, it's just that this guy keeps late hours. Do you recall my having a pointed conversation with the local drug-dealer? Philip, known as Pill? No? Anyway, this is from that friend of mine in Nottingham who's found a job and accommodation for him. Thank God for that.' Though as he'd predicted, there'd no doubt be others to fill the drug distribution vacancy in the area.

'Amen.'

He so rarely said that, church apart, of course, that I stared. 'Grace!'

'A bit late for that,' he said through his second biscuit.

'Not with twenty-four-seven coverage,' I declared, reaching for my phone.

Even Theo didn't argue about the need for new clothes, so we descended on the centre of Maidstone to bend some plastic. What we'd worn last night went into bin liners, since neither of us had the faintest clue if the police would want it as some sort of evidence. So when we presented ourselves once again at Don Simpson's office we were as smart as we could make ourselves. Don's eyes narrowed. 'At least you're not creeping in like victims. We've released young Mazza, before you ask. Dave dropped by to take him and his mother home. You're right. He's not a bad kid. That footage your security people sent through – well, you might want to see it.'

He brewed coffee and, as before, operated his DVD player. 'At first, as you can see, his actions look decidedly suspect. What's a lad doing prowling round the back of the rectory? Why does he run back, armed with a brick he's prised from your front wall? What's he going to do with it? Well, I know you think we function at a snail's pace, Jodie, and I can see you must get frustrated having been used to people tugging their forelocks and asking how high when you tell them to jump, but sometimes we get it right – as your security people have done. Because there's a bit of footage I've not shown you: a lad frantically using his mobile. He says he was dialling nine-nine-nine. He was. His call was logged. He said he was afraid you might be asleep in the rectory and was going to break in – hence the brick.'

Theo's smile threatened to break his face. 'Thank God for that.' He didn't say that lightly.

'So who's the malicious bastard who sent you the footage of him ready to throw the brick? Did he actually break the window, by the way?'

'He scarpered when he was challenged. And why not? He knew the emergency services were on their way. He says he wished he'd stayed put, but he could see the fire was so intense he'd not get in through the kitchen.'

'And the photographer?'

'Is that friend of yours. She said she didn't dare challenge the young man but she wanted evidence. And she scarpered too. In the opposite direction, of course.'

'Elaine? So why wasn't she in the crowd watching the show?' asked Theo, taking my hand.

'She was afraid she might get lynched for grassing up a youngster known to the mob of rubberneckers. She said that she felt totally betrayed: she was about to entrust some very important work to this Mazza and now she finds he's a common criminal.' He did a remarkable imitation of Elaine's clipped enunciation. 'We've no evidence that she set the fire, either,' he added regretfully. 'But our friends in the fire service will be invaluable there. Plus, if they find any accelerant, they can tell us what sort it is – even the make, if it's petrol – and decent everyday police work will find out where it was sold and to whom.'

'But why, if the kitchen was alight, should she think that Mazza was holding a petrol bomb or whatever? Wouldn't the light – the glare – from the fire illuminate everything?'

He nodded, as if I were some rookie constable who'd had a bright idea. One he'd already had himself, of course. 'I think there may be further conversations with her,' he said quietly. His phone rang. 'Ah. A meeting I tried to forget.'

'We'll go and visit my very sick parishioner,' Theo declared. 'Just tell us what time you want us back here.'

Don spoke directly to Theo. 'I want your word that you

won't take any foolish risks. This is our case. Your input's been invaluable, but you have to leave it to us now. And you, Jodie, do I have your word too? You're the tricky one,' he added dourly, ushering us out.

Predictably, the only spaces left in the hospital car park were miles from the entrance. It was a lovely sweet spring morning, with life-affirming birds finding even the puny car park saplings a good place to sing from.

Paradoxically it was a vehicle tucked away on the furthest corner of the car park that drew my attention as, hand in hand, we started walking to the entrance.

'Isn't that Elaine's new beast?' I asked, pointing at the silver-grey Range Rover. 'Keep going. Don't stop to look. But I think something's up. I'm going to pretend I've forgotten something – silly me! So wait here looking impatient.' I jogged back to the car and fiddled in the glove box. All the time I was trying to see inside the Range Rover. I even got a quick photo and sent it to Don. Why on earth hadn't I asked him if he'd organized a guard for George? He'd got so much on his plate I wouldn't be surprised if he'd forgotten. I jogged back to Theo, heaving my shoulders in a huge shrug that said, I hoped, to an onlooker, that it was his problem and he had to look for the mythical missing object. 'Elaine's in the driving seat, with someone at the back holding a knife to her throat. The passenger seat is empty. Theo, I've got a terrible fear. I've sent a pic direct to Don, but dial nine nine nine and tell them to alert hospital security too. ICU, of course! Pretend you're cross with me and stalk back to the car.' Slinging my bag across my body, I jogged off. Once out of sight I ran. I hared. You're not supposed to run in hospitals, are you, but I zipped along those corridors and hurtled up the stairs. At long last my behaviour attracted attention, but the security guard wanted to stop me, not help. So I shook him off and took the stairs two at a time.

I was stopped good and proper in ICU. 'Doctor Harcourt,' I snapped, as if irritated I'd lost my ID. 'For George Cox.'

A burly lad in scrubs stepped in front of me; sidestepping him, I grabbed his wrist, dragging him along. 'Someone's planning to kill George. They're holding his partner as a hostage. I need your muscle. And beep for back-up!'

He didn't argue.

At the door to the ward, we froze. Ted Vesey was leaning tenderly over George, as if talking to a dear friend. His hand, holding something small, moved slightly but perceptibly. Scrubs Lad was on him with a roar, knocking him backwards on to the floor. Delicately I removed the syringe from Ted's grasp, placing it on a cardboard kidney bowl a nurse held out as calmly as if all this was normal procedure.

I knelt down beside Ted, still pinioned. 'Ted, what do you have to do to get Elaine released? I know she's got a knife at her throat. What do you have to do to make them remove it?'

Ted sobbed, started to gibber.

'I know it's not your fault. And you didn't manage to kill poor George, did you? Look, there are sick people in here: this young man and I are going to take you into the corridor, and then you are going to tell us all we need to know to save Elaine.' I was whippy strong and Scrubs Lad was rugby-player strong: together we dragged him out, the nice shiny lino assisting us as he slithered along the floor. Then we kindly helped him to his feet, and by the time security arrived he was sitting down quite comfortably. Had we used undue force in our citizens' arrest? It wouldn't be the first time a criminal tried to sue those who'd apprehended him for common assault. There'd be incriminating CCTV pictures, no doubt, and it might be time to use my clever lawyers for myself this time; I might have to lend them to Scrubs Lad too. On the other hand, Ted, relieved of his burden, looked up almost gratefully.

'Elaine,' I repeated. 'What do you have to do to make him release Elaine?'

He shook his head. 'I'm supposed to call in and say something. But even if I do, I think he'll kill her. And I think, when I get back to the car, he'll kill me too. He can't afford to have us alive, can he?'

Scrubs Lad – now I had time to check his name-tag I found he was Eddie Barnes – produced a mobile. 'Best use it anyway.'

'It's got to be my own phone. But what if he breaks his word and . . .'

'Just have to risk it. At least,' Eddie continued drily, 'it'll be in your favour when the case comes to court. You tried to save her. You can say that much.'

It was a good job he had the number on speed-dial: his hands were shaking too much for him to have hit the tiny digits with any accuracy. I have an idea he muttered, 'Goulash.' I couldn't be sure. Goulash? Why goulash? Why was Alison holding my hand and smoothing back my hair? Where had she sprung from? Why hadn't she been at George's bedside when Ted came a-visiting? A comfort break, maybe . . . And why was my brain bothering to tangle itself up with silly speculation when there were more urgent matters in hand? Such as contacting Theo to make sure he'd done nothing foolishly, fatally heroic. When he didn't pick up I wanted to sit beside Ted and sob. I didn't.

TWENTY-SEVEN

There was blood all over the inside of the Range Rover's windows. I could see that, but I couldn't see Elaine. In fact soon no one would see much. The police were already erecting a screen and some were wrestling with a tent which I guessed would fit over the entire vehicle. The place swarmed with people already in white suits and others struggling into them. I wasn't supposed to be anywhere near, of course, but I'd insisted on coming to find Theo. Eventually someone located him: he was behind someone's car on his knees, not praying but throwing up the hotel breakfast.

He waved me away.

For once I didn't argue.

An unmarked car screeched up, blue lights as authoritative as if they were announcing a more conventional police car. Don Simpson emerged, mobile in one hand, radio in the other. He sent a young constable over to me, a man as slight as Simon Barnes had been burly. In the whole frenetic scene the young man was a tiny oasis of sense: this was Jake, alongside whom I'd paced out my last Great North Run. This time we didn't fall into a crossing-the-finishing-line hug, but I fetched up in his arms anyway, as my legs concertinaed.

'Elaine?' I gasped. 'The woman in the Range Rover?'

'Safe. The blood's her assailant's, I believe. Let's get you out of here, shall we?'

'Not without Theo. My God!'

At least he was on his feet and walking towards me, but his face was blood-spattered and his shirt blood-soaked. Jake yelled as I ran towards him, 'It's the assailant's blood, Jodie. Theo got the woman out the moment the marksmen shot him. Quite the hero, though you won't hear the Super saying that.' Theo was tearing off his clothes. Who could blame him?

Jake conjured a paper suit from somewhere. While Theo tugged it on, he continued, 'OK, I'm supposed to be taking you back to Maidstone to take your statements. But a proper change of clothes takes priority in my book. You've no home to collect them from, have you?'

'We're still checked in at the Maidstone Mondiale,' I said. 'Room seven-oh-three. Everything's still in his and hers bags,' I added over my shoulder as I took the trembling, retching Theo in my arms.

We sat hand in hand in what Jake told us was a soft interview room, a claim backed up by the huge and vastly uncomfortable sofas, prints the visual equivalent of easy-listening, and the odd box of tissues. In one corner was a box of toys, the lid not quite closed. Several teddies and a rabbit regarded us benignly as we sank tea. On my own, I'd have helped myself to a bear and cried into its fur. A plate of biscuits lay untouched on a low coffee table: I suspected I'd never want a biscuit again.

'She's my friend. Elaine's my friend.' Perhaps I was insisting more to myself than to Jake. 'A friend who's been held at knifepoint. But she lied about Mazza, she burnt my house down.'

Theo squeezed my hand; he was now the calmer of the two, outwardly at least. 'There may be extenuating circumstances. Let's make our statements as Jake suggests and then I'm sure Don will explain everything.'

I wasn't, but there was no point in arguing. We had to be questioned separately, Jake explained apologetically. For now it would be just about our activities this morning, he added with an ironic grin. He handed Theo over to a man who looked old enough to have retired years ago; perhaps he had, and was now helping out. I ought to have cared but didn't.

Jake and I got to work. Maybe talking would be cathartic.

One thing I'd never have imagined would be on the agenda was having lunch with the rural dean. Don Simpson had popped his head round the interview room door to tell me he was still tied up but would ensure I was debriefed at about half-past four. Meanwhile, if I was up to it, I should nip off and have a bite of lunch – oh, and Theo's boss was waiting with Theo in reception.

If not the Boss, a boss. The area dean, Barney Anderson, whom I only knew slightly, smiled at me as if I was an old friend and enclosed me in a remarkably comforting hug. Chattering inconsequentially, he carted us off to lunch at a pub in Bearsted, a pretty village I'd never been to before. He was rather younger than Theo, with a full head of hair prematurely white. As he got older, and his still-boyish chubbiness turned to real and regrettable flesh, he'd look as if he'd stepped out of a Trollope novel. Meanwhile he had the sharp keenness of mind to offer practical help that we might have needed even more had it not been for my Monopoly money. A house. Furniture. Help with insurance. A flying curate – Theo would need a reduced schedule for a bit, and he'd certainly need support while the trial was on. It was entirely possible, he said gently, that we might choose not to return to the parish at all; the bishop would understand and help us to move wherever God called us. We declined his rather hesitant offer of a few nights in his own home, because of his triplets and because his Labrador had recently pupped.

The Mondiale would suit us nicely for a bit longer, we assured him. Tomorrow's services apart – and he insisted he wanted to take those he was on the rota for – Theo wouldn't countenance flitting off to St John's Wood as long as George and Alison might need him. Head bowed, he had to accept Barney's suggestion that it would be, to say the least, inappropriate to try to speak to Ted or Elaine until the police had charged them. Christian forgiveness was one thing; interfering with the processes of justice was another, particularly in connection with the death of Burble and the framing of Mazza. Having topped us up with more wine than we ever drank at lunchtime, Barney delivered us back to the Mondiale, where the police would contact us later.

'He used to be a barrister,' Theo said as we waved him off. 'His wife was a chemist, but was made redundant at a shake-up at Pfizer's. That's why she breeds dogs. It's a lovely family, but not restful.'

And rest was clearly what he needed. He collapsed into a Merlot-fuelled sleep the moment we were in our room, not even stirring when Dave phoned. How were things?

I gave him an edited version.

'I'll come straight over.'

'Stay where you are. I'm just about to keel over and have a snooze. I'll call you later.'

Don Simpson looked as if he needed a snooze too. But there was a grim satisfaction to his smile as he ushered us into his office again.

'We really are getting the star treatment today,' Theo said. 'We didn't expect to see you again till the trial, Don.'

'If I were fifteen years younger, you wouldn't. The thrusting young Turks deal with their cases and delegate the rest. Though I told you I'm just one ant among many, I like to see a job through, and Dave would never stop sneering if I didn't fill you in with all I know so far. And I have to take my hat off to you both: Theo for dragging Elaine clear, and you, Jodie – I didn't know about this earlier – for dragging that pompous old guy out of Intensive Care. Ought to be on YouTube, that ought.' He registered the expression on Theo's face. 'Hasn't she told you yet? Here, sit and watch it while I make my caffeine fix.' He turned his computer monitor so Theo could watch the whole incident – heavens, I was falling into police lingo now. I stood behind Theo to get a better view. We'd been remarkably foolhardy, with that syringe waving in front of our eyes. I thought it better to say nothing. So, it seemed, did Theo.

Don plonked coffee mugs on the table. Espresso for him – no doubt he'd be working late tonight – and gentle lattes for us.

He settled himself comfortably again.

'Ted and Elaine, Mazza and Burble,' I prompted him.

'And you. Don't forget they had a couple of attempts to shut you up too. Because I reckon it all started with your seeing stuff they didn't want seen – these people building illicitly in the valley. An Eastern European gang, fronted by a couple of nice British Mr Bigs – as it happens, actors who were resting, as they call it. As you deduced, they were building what the Americans might call a facility – in fact, an underground depot to house stolen combine harvesters and so on. The project was pretty well self-funding – yes, all those JCBs your TV contact picked up, Jodie, busily harvesting cash machines.' He paused to allow us to respond to his little joke.

'Why did everything seem to centre on my wife, though? She never harmed anyone.'

'I wouldn't go that far,' I admitted. 'But I never knowingly interfered with these people. I went running, that's all. Ah. Ted was very keen to find out my route, wasn't he? And then when I became friends with Burble, who was well known for roaming round the countryside foraging for food and might blab—'

'Worse than that, Jodie, I'm afraid. You gave Burble that camera. Clearly someone spotted him using it.'

I clicked my fingers. 'Mazza said something about his taking a whole series of photos of the same house until he was satisfied with the result. I never knew which house.'

'Would you be surprised if I told you it was Vesey's? Yes, the technical people have worked wonders with that memory card. The last photo was of Vesey emerging from his front door and shaking his fist. More important, Burble took at least thirty of the site. Someone spotted him – and obviously did more than shake his fist. Even though he knew he had to run away, he also knew the pictures he'd taken were important and made sure someone found them.'

'Even though he must have been afraid he was going to die?' My voice broke.

'Yes. A brave kid. I for one will want to pay my respects at his funeral, Theo.' He added, more quietly, 'He had a record as long as your arm, you know. He'd have been behind bars sooner rather than later. And yet he found it in him to be heroic.' He bowed his head as if before some mental cenotaph. 'As for young Mazza, once he became your running partner he became a danger too. Framing him for the bike crimes, which were a sideline of one of the junior members of the gang, was the obvious ruse to get him out of the way. Thanks to you it didn't. We've asked your friend Rosemary McVicar to check those bikes for Ted Vesey's DNA, because we think he was responsible for stowing them at Mazza's place.'

I shook my head. 'Ted would be an organizer; he'd not get his hands literally dirty, would he?'

'I'm sure you're right. He's a man to delegate.'

'Did he delegate the attack on poor George?' Theo asked. 'Because I can assure you that not many people even knew there was a safe in the church, let alone that someone was kneeling in the aisle trying to open it.'

'And he was certainly the one who removed an envelope from it,' I added. 'What was in it, by the way?'

He looked straight at me. 'We've still not found it. Or any trace of it. We've not had a chance to question him yet, and I doubt if we will for a bit. He's been kept in hospital for observation. He may have banged his head when you and Doctor Barnes floored him.'

Theo went white. 'You're not thinking of charging them with attempted manslaughter, are you? They saved George's life. If anyone's to blame it's you people for not having someone on guard.'

Don shook a regretful head.

'Don't tell me,' I snapped. 'Budget cuts. Staffing cuts.'

'Yes. We're supposed to be maintaining front line policing. No damage to public service. Actually, I'm surprised we're not conducting this discussion in Essex: we've now got a combined unit for dealing with serious crimes. It's only because we thought this one was manageable that you're sitting here with me.'

'Isn't that what people want? To be able to talk to a local man who knows the local problems?'

Don spread his hands eloquently.

I was aware that time was passing. 'Elaine. How did she get involved? She's a lovely, kind woman, the only friend I've got in the village. She's important in the parish, a pillar of the WI, almost single-handedly responsible for saving the pub. What's her Achilles heel?'

Don snorted. 'A heel of the other variety. A cad. A bounder. A very attractive man who met her online – God, don't these people realize the dangers they're exposing themselves to?'

Theo nodded sagely, the old hypocrite. But then he looked at me and smiled. 'I've never recovered,' he said, taking my hand. 'Even if I was supposed to be dating someone else. Long story, Don. A pint or two one evening, eh? When we both have an evening we're not working, that is. But Elaine's man?'

'Wooed her. Won her. Took her off to faraway places. Introduced her to his friends. Then he cooled off. But he still had sufficient power over her for her to want to please him. Maybe she was a little afraid of him. Occasionally he'd ask her to do something – you know, make a phone call, take a photo, go and visit someone's house, stay with them to keep them away from other more interesting things. But she, more than Vesey, is a victim in all this, I'd say. Even if she did make a couple of feeble attempts to run you down, Jodie. A pro would have made sure. And she can't be very happy that one of her boyfriend's henchmen was under orders to slit her throat if Vesey didn't kill off George.'

I gripped my head to stop it spinning. 'This isn't making sense. Why does anyone on this earth want George dead? The poor man didn't even know the envelope was there, let alone what was in it.'

'What if George had opened the safe?' Theo asked. 'And found the envelope? And, since he knew nothing about it, popped it back in the safe only to ask Ted when he turned up. Maybe taunted him a bit. They loathed each other after all. Maybe Ted socked him but someone else turned up – you, for instance – before he could reopen the safe.'

Maybe it was the coffee, maybe it was the last kick from the Merlot, but I was getting sick of all the *if*s and *maybe*s. 'Talk to Elaine again,' I said curtly, as if I was the other side of the desk. 'And to Mazza. He handled the damned envelope more than I did. And kick Ted back into consciousness – we didn't hit him for goodness' sake, as the CCTV footage will show: I'll bet he's just playing for time.'

'Let me talk to you first,' Don said quietly. 'You've got an image of the envelope on your camera. Have a look at it. Go on. What can you see?'

'The longitudinal fold where Ted made it fit in a pocket. It's a bit puckered round the edges. The seal's not very secure – someone might have opened it and resealed it.'

'Why on earth didn't you challenge the bugger?' Don asked, as if I was on his team.

'No authority. He and George are in charge of the church,' Theo said.

'If someone had opened it before, that person might have been George,' I said. 'Don, you've only just taken on the case, but someone would know if there was anything untoward in his pockets, wouldn't they?'

'He was the victim, Jodie, so it's possible his clothes are still in a paper bag back at the hospital.' He reached for the phone.

The call didn't take long.

'Fake Euros. Thousands in high value notes. Some more of our Bulgarian friends' activities, no doubt. George only had a few in his pocket, shoved in anyhow, according to the staff who logged everything.' Don reached not for the coffee but for a bottle of whisky. He touched his nose; no doubt this was strictly against every police regulation, but we all sank it without turning a hair. 'So Ted is entrusted with them as samples, maybe – or even nicks them. He stows them where no one will think of looking, since no one even recollects the presence of a safe there until Jodie goes exploring. George realizes they're not part of the church silver and is ready to take some.'

'As evidence, if I know George,' Theo said, a challenge in his voice and in his eye.

'As evidence. We won't know the conversation that took place until George comes round or Ted is cleared by the medics for questioning.' He turned from us to his screen. 'Ah. Latest updates: we've had news from our French colleagues that they've picked up your would-be workman, and we've also found the glass collector at the Goose that Laid; someone slipped him some cash to report back our conversation – someone being the same guy. Busy little bee.' He leant back and counted on those slender fingers: 'The tiddlers in this are under arrest and are likely to be denied bail. The bigger fish were picked up for their involvement in agricultural machinery theft and robbing post offices. They certainly won't get bail. Incidentally, the fire service think accelerant started your blaze.

At first they thought it might have been an electrical fault, since they say the wiring's a disgrace, but they've found petrol. Asda, as it happens. More legwork for my team, but since we've got a fairly narrow range of suspects, that shouldn't take long, and with luck one of them can be persuaded to confess. I'd call that a good day's work. I'll have a mound of paperwork to complete but that can wait till Monday. Time to go home, I'd say.' He flushed brick red. 'I'm really sorry, you've not got a home to go to, have you? It must have been bad seeing it burn before your eyes.'

I could have said that the anonymous room at the Mondiale was more homely, that if I'd had a chance I'd have thrown petrol on the flames consuming the drab, constricting place, and that wherever Theo and I set up would become our real home. Kent, St John's Wood, Birmingham – wherever he was called. Even, heaven help me, Lesser Hogben.

But Theo was laughing quietly. 'Don't you think it's rather appropriate, Don, for a rector to have an illuminated address?'